SAINT'S REST

Also by Keith Miles

Murder in Perspective

SAINT'S REST

A MERLIN RICHARDS MYSTERY

Keith Miles

WALKER AND COMPANY
New York

Copyright © 1999 by Keith Miles

All rights reserved. No part of this book may be reproduced or transmitted in any form or by any means, electronic or mechanical, including photocopying, recording, or by any information storage and retrieval system, without permission in writing from the Publisher.

All the characters and events portrayed in this work are fictitious.

First published in the United States of America in 1999 by
Walker Publishing Company, Inc.

Published simultaneously in Canada by Fitzhenry and Whiteside

Library of Congress Cataloging-in-Publication Data
Miles, Keith.
Saint's rest: a Merlin Richards mystery/Keith Miles.
p. cm.
ISBN 0-8027-3332-8
I. Title.
PR6063.I3175S35   1999
813'.914—dc21   98-52922
CIP

Series design by Mauna Eichner

Printed in the United States of America
2 4 6 8 10 9 7 5 3 1

Oak Park's other name was "Saint's Rest." There were so many churches for so many good people to go to, I suppose. Nevertheless, the village looked like a pretty solid, respectable place. The people were good people, most of whom had taken asylum there to bring up their children in comparative peace, safe from the poison of the great city.

—Frank Lloyd Wright, *An Autobiography*

SAINT'S REST

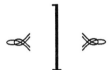

I've never seen a murder," he said. "I mean, I've been in Chicago for the best part of a year now and I've never actually seen anyone killed."

"Is that why you came here?" she asked.

Merlin Richards laughed. "No, of course not!"

"Then don't sound so disappointed."

"Sorry."

"What did you expect? Blood on every sidewalk?"

"No."

"A shooting on every street corner?"

"Not exactly."

"Then what?"

"Well—"

"Go on," she prompted. "Gang warfare on Michigan Avenue?"

"Sally, this is *Chicago*."

"So?"

"It has a reputation."

"An unfair reputation."

"Not according to that film."

"Don't believe what you see in the movies."

"It seemed pretty realistic to me."

"Wait till you've lived here as long as I have."

"Chicago has a huge crime wave, Sally."

"Show me a city that doesn't."

"You only have to read the papers or—"

"Or watch the movies," she teased, anticipating him. "Yeah, sure. This place is a jungle. You fight for survival. Walk a few more blocks and we're bound to witness at least two stabbings and a daring bank robbery. We might even get lucky and see a couple of cops being riddled with bullets from a tommy gun. That satisfy you?"

Merlin laughed again. He liked Sally Fiske. She spoke her mind. Her comments were sharp and her mockery always good-humored. He was so used to the reflex agreement and obliging smiles of his previous girlfriends that it was refreshing to meet someone who challenged his remarks. Also—and this impressed him—Sally was so relaxed in his company. It was difficult to believe that this was only their second date.

"Didn't you like the film?" he asked.

"I loved it."

"But you think it was far-fetched."

"Too much black paint and not enough white."

"Black paint?"

"Yes," she argued. "The movie only used dark colors. I'm an artist, remember. I like to use a full palette. Strike a balance between light and shade. *Little Caesar* was all shade and no light."

"But it was very exciting."

"Yeah. Edward G. Robinson was terrific."

"But not a typical resident of Chicago."

"No, Merlin. Believe it or not, most people here are good,

honest, law-abiding citizens. Even the crooks are not as bad as they're made out to be. They're kind to their mothers and never kill anyone on a Sunday. Not until they've been to Communion, anyway. And before you ask me," she added, turning to him, "in all the time I've lived here, *I've* never seen a murder either."

He grinned. "I won't hold it against you."

"So what did you think of the movie?"

"Amazing!"

"Bet you never saw anything like that back in wherever-it-is."

"Merthyr Tydfil," he said. "And you're right, Sally. Never even saw a talking picture there. All we ever had were silents, flickering away in the local fleapit while Mrs. Prosser beat the daylights out of the piano."

"Mrs. Prosser?"

"The old lady who was the accompanist at the cinema. She didn't so much play the piano as pound it into submission. She was a sort of cross between Paderewski and Jack Sharkey. Music with muscle. Real character, Mrs. Prosser. Poor dab! When the talkies hit Wales, people like her will be out of a job."

"Happens to us all!" she sighed.

He shivered involuntarily. "Let's talk about something else."

"Over a cup of coffee."

"Coffee?"

"I have to work this evening."

"Oh, yes. I forgot."

"Coffee is all I have time for, Merl."

"Where shall we go?"

"I know just the place."

They were part of a large crowd that surged out of the cinema and made its way along Lincoln Avenue. Discussion all around them was loud and fevered. *Little Caesar* had left its patrons feeling exhilarated. Snatches of dialogue were being recalled, favorite scenes remembered. To impress their wives or girlfriends, amateur impersonators were already trying to mimic Rico. One guy even reenacted his death at the end of the film and went down in a heap on the sidewalk. Sally nudged Merlin.

"Now you *have* seen a murder in Chicago."

She led him down a side street, then checked for traffic before crossing it diagonally. They were soon letting themselves into a small restaurant. Merlin was glad when they were shown to a table. Seated opposite her, he was able to look at Sally properly for the first time, and she did repay study. Short blond hair framed a pale, oval face given definition by generous lips, a delightful snub nose, and the biggest pair of blue eyes he had ever seen. It was a clear, open face, untouched by the distortions that come from concealment and deception. The cinema had bestowed a token intimacy on them, and they held hands during the latter stages of the movie, but that did not compare with the pleasure of appraising Sally Fiske afresh.

Merlin was an architect. He preferred a front elevation.

They ordered coffee and pastries, then subjected the movie to closer analysis. Both had enjoyed it, but for very different reasons. It seemed only seconds before the waitress returned with their order. Merlin sat up in surprise. He caught sight of the clock on the wall. Time was racing by at a cruel speed.

"Do you really have to work this evening?" he said.

"Afraid so."

"Can't you give it a miss?"

"They need me."

"So do I."

She smiled. "The hotel pays me more than you do."

"You don't belong there, Sally."

"How else do I earn the rent?"

"You're a creative artist. A questing spirit. What you need is the freedom in which to experiment and develop."

"What I need is more commissions, Merlin," she said bluntly. "Then I could afford to buy some of that lovely freedom and follow my vocation. Until then, I have to work as a hotel clerk or whatever else brings in the bucks. Besides," she said, her smile broadening. "I like the hotel. The job has its compensations."

"Is that all I am?" he protested. "A compensation?"

"A very nice one."

"Thank you!"

"How else would we have met?"

"In an art gallery, probably. Yes, that would have been much more appropriate. Bumping into each other in the shadow of an old master. Welsh architect meets commercial artist from Illinois. Kindred spirits. Instead of which," he recalled with a sigh, "I charged into your lobby in a state of panic because I was late for an appointment with a potential client, and you were the faceless member of the hotel staff who told me where to find him."

She bridled. "Faceless?"

"Anonymous."

"Jeez!"

"What I mean is, I took you for what you seemed to be."

"A faceless, anonymous freak!"

"No, Sally. Truth is, I didn't give you a second glance. You were just one more attractive girl behind a reception desk. Part of the hotel furniture. Handsome but functional. It never occurred to me that you made a living illustrating books."

"I don't, Merlin."

"You did. For a while."

"Those days are gone."

"They'll come back one day."

She raised a skeptical eyebrow. "Will they?"

"Of course!"

"I admire your optimism."

"It's not optimism, Sally. It's self-belief. Don't forget that I'm in the same boat as you. Struggling to find employment worthy of my talent. Work dried up on me as well. Completely. It was only by sheer coincidence that I managed to land a position here."

"You told me. After trudging around Chicago until you wore out your last pair of shoes, you had a stroke of good fortune."

"Two strokes. One was the job with Westlake and Davisson."

"What was the other one?"

"Sally Fiske."

"I thought I was only part of the hotel furniture."

"Not anymore!"

"Handsome but functional."

"That's what I'm hoping," he said with polite lechery.

"Drink your coffee. It'll calm you down."

"Never give up," he urged. "Never surrender your ambition. Who knows? A whole flurry of commissions might be waiting for you just around the corner. Believe in yourself, and you'll get there in the end."

"If only it was that easy."

"Things are bound to improve soon."

"Yeah. Less suicides among stockbrokers."

"You call that an *improvement*?"

They shared a laugh, but it only covered their uneasiness. Sally's own career was on hold, and she knew that Merlin's prospects were far from rosy. His show of optimism was tempered by a deep insecurity. He had a job but no indication of how long it might last. Work for architects was increasingly scarce. Westlake and Davisson might soon be one more extinct Chicago practice. Sally hoped this would not happen. She was very fond of Merlin. He was an interesting mix of shyness and confidence. He treated her with respect. His big, round face was pleasant rather than handsome, and his crooked nose had a fascination all its own. Merlin would win no prizes for smart dressing—his tie was loose, his suit crumpled, his hair unacquainted with brush and comb. She admired his take-me-as-I-am attitude, and she adored the Welsh lilt of his voice. There was something else she had learned. For a man with the build of a heavyweight boxer, he had the most incredibly soft and sensitive hands.

"What time do you have to be there?" he asked.

"Pretty soon."

"Do you always work on a Saturday night?"

"When the chance comes my way."

"But Saturday nights are for fun."

"Someone has to be on duty in reception."

"Why must it be you?"

"Because I can earn extra if I work late."

"When do you finish?"

"At midnight."

"Midnight!"

"The night porter takes over from me."

"Isn't it dangerous?"

"No, he's a sweet old guy when you get to know him."

"I wasn't talking about the night porter, Sally. I meant this city. Chicago. There're some weird people out there. I don't like the idea of you having to go home alone that late."

"You get used to it."

"Do you take a cab?"

"Not if I can help it."

"But that would be the safest way."

"You don't know cabdrivers," she said wearily. "Some of them ought to be locked up. Besides, cabs cost money. They're a luxury." She saw his concern and reached out to squeeze his arm. "Don't worry about me. I'm a big girl. And I grew up in this city, remember. I'll be fine."

"I'll pick you up," he decided.

"At midnight?"

"I'll be in the lobby when you come off duty."

"Merl, that's crazy!"

"Why?"

"Staying up that late when there's no need."

"I want to see you get home safe."

"I always do."

"Tonight, you'll have an escort."

"But you'll have to wait for *hours*."

"Who cares?"

"You should be asleep in bed by midnight."

"I'm a night owl," he lied.

"What will you do between now and then?"

Merlin shrugged. "Stooge around. Kill time. I'll find something to keep me out of mischief. Might even go to the office. Yes, that's an idea," he said, warming to the notion. "I could put in some overtime. Finish those drawings I had to leave. That would impress Brad Davisson. Great! It's all settled. When I've walked you back to the hotel, I go straight to the office and get my head down."

"So you'll be working as well as me."

"That's right."

"I thought Saturday nights were for fun."

"Architecture *is* fun. And they've given me a key to the office now. It shows they trust me. I can let myself in and work all alone. It'll be bliss. I'm only four blocks from Randolph Street. I can walk to the hotel and arrive on the stroke of midnight." He rubbed his palms together. "It's all settled. The Merlin Richards Protection Agency is at your service."

"But I'm not sure that I want it," she said crisply.

"Oh."

"Yet."

There was a long pause. She could see the disappointment in his face and feel his embarrassment. He was clearly afraid that he had offended her. His shoulders hunched in apology. They had reached a boundary line in their relationship, and Sally was hesitating to cross it. She searched his eyes to find out what sort of a guy he really was. With an appeasing smile, Merlin sat back in his chair.

"Sorry."

"That's okay."

"I didn't mean to sound so . . . proprietary."

"Forget it."

"Trying to make your decisions for you. Stupid of me."

"No harm done."

"Do you forgive me?"

"Nothing to forgive."

"I only made the offer because I care, Sally."

"I know," she said. "But it was more like an order than an offer. Do this, be there, listen to me. I appreciate your concern, but I really can find my way safely around this city. Even after midnight."

"I thought you might value some company."

"That's a different matter, Merl."

"And it would have put my mind at rest."

"Go back to your apartment. Have an early night."

"No," he said firmly. "I've got a surge of energy. I feel like getting back to the drafting table. When the muse calls, you have to pick up a pencil and go. If you have to work tonight, then so will I. Good way to build character."

"Maybe I should stop by and pick *you* up at midnight."

There was a laugh in her voice that revived his hopes. He put his arms on the table and leaned across to her. Their faces were close.

"It was lovely to see you again, Sally."

"Thanks for asking me."

"Pleasure. At least we managed a few hours together this time. All we had on our first date was a hasty lunch."

"I had to get back to work that afternoon as well."

"How many hours do those slave drivers keep you at it?"

"Too many."

"Exploitation."

"A job is a job, Merl," she said levelly. "In any case, you put in even longer hours than me. Didn't you say that you sometimes have to work seven days a week?"

"When the pressure's on."

"There you go, then."

"It's temperamental."

"Come again."

"I get caught up in a project," he admitted, "and find it difficult to let go. It takes over my life. Becomes an obsession. I think of nothing else until it comes to an end."

"Then what?"

"I move on to the next commission."

"And lose yourself in that?"

"Completely."

"So there's a definite pattern here," she said quietly. "Your work gives you a real buzz. You go from one high spot to another. I'm just wondering where I fit into this pattern."

"That's up to you, Sally."

"I'd hate to be just one more stop on your personal subway."

"You're not!" he insisted.

"How do I know that?"

"I thought you'd have worked it out by now."

There was another long pause, then she noticed the clock on the wall. It made her nibble a piece of her pastry and wash it down with the last of her coffee. She picked up her purse.

"I have to go."

"One more question."

"Well?"

"Supposing I happen to be passing the hotel at midnight?" he said. "Quite by accident. I might just stroll into the lobby to take a look around. If you feel that you'd like an escort home, all you have to do is ask. On the other hand, if you'd rather go out into the night alone, I won't try to stop or follow you. And no recriminations afterward. Is that fair?"

"Very fair."

"It's a deal, then."

Sally nodded and rose to her feet. Merlin gulped down the last of his coffee, then left some money with the check. They came out of the restaurant and headed toward Randolph Street. All that they talked about on their way to the hotel was the movie. It was a neutral zone. They could move about freely inside it. However, while they traded comments about *Little Caesar*, their minds were on something else.

As they passed a shop window, Sally saw them mirrored in the glass. They looked good together. She was relatively short but had a full figure that saved her from being dainty; looming over her, Merlin moved with the easy swagger of a sportsman. He kept himself in good physical condition. That was not true of all the guys she tended to attract. And Merlin was only a couple of years older than she was. That, too, was unusual. Sally was normally a target for those who were trembling on the edge of middle age and saw her as a last staging post. Merlin Richards was in his prime. He was rather special. She thought once more about the curious softness of his hands.

For his part, Merlin was relishing some of the moments they had shared during their brief time together. Sally had an air of independence about her that was quite breathtaking. She asked for no favors and expected no allowances to be made for her. Behind a hotel reception desk she was bright and efficient, but there was no sign of her natural vivacity or her wicked sense of humor when she was on duty. The real Sally Fiske emerged only when they were alone together. Merlin was touched when she brought some examples of her work to show him over lunch. Her illustrations were superb. She had serious talent. Merlin winced when he reflected on how that talent was lying fallow.

They were still arguing about the movie when they reached the hotel. Merlin was about to follow her up the steps to the revolving door, but she came to a halt and turned to face him. Sally took a quick inventory of her feelings before speaking.

"Thanks again," she said.

"Lovely to see you."

"Sorry we couldn't lay on a real murder for you."

"Only a question of time," he said with a grin. "I'll probably see half a dozen on my way to the office."

"At least."

"Right, I'll let you go now, Sally. But I'll be back at midnight."

"Merl—"

"You're under no obligation. You don't have to speak to me or even look at me. Ignore me altogether, if you like. Have the night porter throw me out. But I'll be there. You know—just in case."

"You're a gentleman."

"Does that mean you want me here at midnight?"

"No," she said, touching his cheek with her fingertips. "It means you won't complain when you learn the hideous truth about me."

"What hideous truth?"

"Brace yourself, Merl."

He swallowed hard. "You're not married, are you?"

"Heck, no!"

"Or living with someone else?"

"What do you take me for?"

"On the run from the law, then? Hiding out after a terrible crime?"

"Nothing like that."

"I've got it. You must keep strange pets. Snakes, maybe? Polar bears? Tame alligators?"

"Nope."

"So what is this hideous truth?"

"I'm a lousy cook."

"I don't follow."

"You will," she said.

She brushed her lips against his before going up the stairs and into the revolving door. Merlin was baffled. As the door came full circle, Sally stepped out with an explanation.

"Wait till you taste the breakfast I'll cook for you."

She disappeared into the hotel for good this time.

Merlin simmered with delight.

Bradley Davisson stared at the letter in his hand as if he was reading his own death warrant. He was a short, slim, wiry man in his fifties with a bald head that seemed too large for his body and a white mustache fringed with brown coffee stains. Seated behind his desk, he was facing the daily ordeal of going through the firm's correspondence. When the letter had deepened the furrows in his brow and sown a fresh crop of despair in his soul, he set it aside, reached for another Lucky Strike in the pack that lay before him, lit the cigarette with a match, and inhaled absentmindedly, then grabbed the next envelope, slitting it open with a paper knife like an assassin cutting the throat of a victim.

The letter was handwritten, and he peered at it through a veil of cigarette smoke. It made him flinch. Unable to finish it, he scrunched it up into a ball and tossed it into the wastepaper basket. Davisson looked with dismay at the rest of the unopened correspondence, fearing that it would contain more shocks and wondering why he was always given the privilege of learning the bad news first. It got his day off to a most depressing start. He was still pondering the injustice of it all when he heard the distinctive sounds of his partner's arrival.

The door of the outer office opened and shut. There was a loud exchange of greetings, followed by a braying laugh. Then heavy footsteps approached the inner sanctum. Davisson drew deep on his Lucky. The door opened, and Augustus Westlake filled almost every inch of space that it left behind it. He beamed paternally.

"Hi, Brad!"

"You're late," grumbled the other.

"Genius follows no timetable."

"There's lots to discuss. You promised to be here, Gus."

"I *am* here," said Westlake, striding into the middle of the room and flicking the door shut behind him. "Large as life and bright as sunshine."

Westlake lowered himself into the chair in front of his partner's desk. He was a big man with a permanent smile, which combined with the long nose to give the impression of an anchor tattooed on his face. Piggy eyes twinkled merrily. He was immaculately dressed in a light blue suit, with a spotted tie exploding out of the top pocket of his jacket. Westlake exuded such prosperity that Davisson used to wonder if he was siphoning off money from the practice account, but his suspicions were unfounded. Five years older than his partner, Westlake looked ten years younger and vastly healthier. His sandy hair showed no trace of gray. He spread his hands in a questioning gesture.

"What gives, Brad?"

"We got problems."

"Tell me something new."

"Serious problems, Gus. We've had another letter from that lawyer."

"Which lawyer?"

"The one acting for Heindorf."

"Oh—that pain in the ass!"

"He's threatening to sue us."

"Let him threaten."

"We can't afford any more litigation."

"We can if we win," said Westlake airily, "and we're bound to in this case. Heindorf hasn't got a leg to stand on. We fulfilled the terms of the contract. He got what he wanted and paid up."

"Now he says he didn't get what he wanted."

"Tough!"

"It looks bad for us."

"Things always look bad on a Monday morning. That's why you need me around, Brad. I'm a Friday-afternoon kind of guy. Always got that spring in my step, knowing the weekend is beckoning. Let me handle this lawyer. I'll tie him in knots and get Heindorf to back down."

"It's gone beyond that stage, Gus."

"All it needs is some sweet talk."

"You'll change your mind when you read the letter."

"Lawyers are jerks. They should be strangled at birth." He gave a reassuring chuckle. "Cheer up, Brad. You scare too easily. Learn to take this kind of hassle in your stride."

"The morning mail terrifies me."

"Then don't read it."

"Someone has to."

"So we find a new secretary."

"We can't afford a new secretary," said Davisson, stubbing out his cigarette in the ashtray on the desk. "That's why we had to let Joyce go. She was too expensive. I have to do my own typing now."

"That will soon change."

"It will if Heindorf sues us."

"Forget him," advised Westlake. "Forget all whining clients. Forget the bills. Forget the debts. Forget the people who owe us money. Forget the commissions we lost and the secretary we had to fire. Ease up, Brad. Give yourself a break. Forget the whole darn lot of it."

"I can't, Gus. It gets to me."

"Fight it off."

"It's no use. The anxiety cripples me when I'm here, then follows me home at night. Eleanor tells me that I talk in my sleep and twitch violently. No wonder I wake up feeling exhausted."

"Yet I sleep like a baby."

"You don't take things to heart the way I do."

"I got more sense."

Davisson reached under his desk to retrieve something from his wastepaper basket. He held up the ball of paper between his thumb and forefinger.

"Know what this is?" he asked.

"Tell me."

"It's a letter from Bill Marion."

"Dear old Bill?"

"A *begging* letter, Gus. Like so many other Chicago architects, Bill is on the scrap heap. His practice folded under him. Think of that. Bill Marion, who designed some of the finest buildings on State Street. Out in the cold. Imagine the effort it must have cost him to write this," he said, tossing the letter back into the wastepaper basket. "I couldn't bear to read it to the end. Jesus Christ! Bill Marion and I started out in this game together. He made partner while I was still a junior draftsman. Bill is twice the architect that I am, yet he's asking *me* for work. It's crazy."

"No, Brad. It's a sign of the times."

"Yeah. No matter how good you are, down you go."

"In some cases."

"In all cases. Bill is only the latest casualty. Look at Haygarth and Pike. Look at Stern, Venner and Crombie. Look at Adnam and Rogerson. Established practices that went up in smoke. Yes," he added, slapping the desk for emphasis. "And what about George Wybrand? Two years ago he was designing skyscrapers. Now he comes banging on our door, trying to sell architectural supplies. It's demeaning, Gus."

Westlake gave a dismissive shrug. "It's life."

"Don't you feel sorry for those guys?"

"Yes and no," said the other easily. "I feel sorry for anyone who loses his job and has to scratch around, but I'm not going to shed tears over rival architects who hit the dust. It's them or us, Brad. That's business."

"I don't see it that way."

"You should. Then your wife might get a decent night's sleep."

"You're a hard man sometimes."

"I'm a practical one. That's why we're still here, and guys like George Wybrand are selling pencil sharpeners and cartridge paper. Listen to their sob stories, and they'll drag you down with them. Think positive. Westlake and Davisson will pull through because this practice has got something that the others didn't have."

"What's that?"

"Me?"

"Yeah," said his partner wryly. "A coldhearted bastard without a vestige of human sympathy in him."

Westlake guffawed. "I like that! Remind me to have it carved on my tombstone. It's my definition of a good businessman. But I have an even greater virtue, Brad. I bring in work."

"Now and then."

"These things take time." He beamed happily. "Finished?"

"Finished what?"

"Your daily dose of misery."

"We're under fire from all directions, Gus."

"Then learn to duck. Let the bad news go whistling past harmlessly over your head. Concentrate on the good news."

"What good news?"

"I'll tell you when you're through wailing and gnashing your teeth."

Davisson reached out for another Lucky and lit up.

"Is this something to do with the Niedlander deal?" he said.

"No, but that's still in the offing."

"So what gives?"

Westlake kept him waiting for an answer. Rising to his feet, he crossed to the window and looked down at the traffic below. When he turned back to the desk, his smile was even more complacent.

"I had dinner on Lake Shore Drive last night," he boasted.

"Oh?"

"A very profitable dinner. With a potential client."

"Who is he?"

"It's more a case of, Who is *she?* Does the name Alicia Martinez mean anything to you?"

"No. Should it?"

"Beautiful lady. Small-time movie actress with ambitions out of all proportion to her talents. Since she couldn't make money, she decided to marry it." He saw the look of recognition in his partner's eye. "Is it all coming back to you now?"

"Hobart St. John!"

"Her husband."

"Their picture was on the front page of the *Tribune*."

"Old Hobart commands publicity."

"And he is interested in retaining us?" said Davisson with a mixture of surprise and excitement. "A commission from Hobart St. John?"

"He'll do anything to please Alicia."

"What kind of a deal is it?"

"A new house. In Oak Park."

"But he already has that mansion on Lake Shore Drive."

"Built for his last wife, Cornelia Rose. To her specifications. It's a wonderful place, but Alicia can't settle there. It holds too many memories of her predecessor. Alicia wants a house of her own. A big one."

"And we're really in with a chance?"

"It's more or less in the bag," said Westlake confidently. "But only because I belong to the same golf club as Hobart St. John. I partnered him in a foursome some months back, and I've been working on him ever since. It finally paid off. See what I mean, Brad?" He let out a whoop of joy. "Your coldhearted bastard of a partner can still do it!"

"This is terrific news—if it comes off."

"It will. I've got Alicia eating out of my hand."

"What kind of a house does she want?"

"The best kind—an expensive one."

"In what style?"

"That's between her and the architect. When we decide who to assign to the project, I'll take him out to meet her."

"You'll take on the commission yourself, surely?"

"No, Brad. I'm getting too old for that. My creative juices are drying up. I'm far more use to this practice reeling in clients. Besides," he said as he moved back to the desk, "we've got someone here who'd be ideal for this particular job."

"Who's that?"

"Merlin Richards."

Davisson was stunned. "Merlin? Are you serious?"

Westlake's smile was intact, but his voice hardened.

"Dead serious," he said.

IT WAS HER evening off, and they arranged to meet in Grant Park. When he finally got there, Merlin found her sitting on a bench, a sketch pad across her knee, engrossed in her work. He crept up behind her and studied the drawing over her shoulder. Sally Fiske's pencil moved swiftly as it shaded in the trunk of a tree. Merlin let out an approving whistle, and she sat up with a start.

"That's good," he said.

"You made me jump, Merl!" she complained.

"Sorry. You seemed so happy in your work."

"I was until you interrupted me."

"I can see the trees and bushes," he said, pointing to the drawing, "but I haven't noticed a lion prowling around Grant Park. Has he vanished into the undergrowth?"

"He was never there."

"Ah." He sat beside her.

"I imagined him."

"Artistic license."

"I was just playing around with ideas."

"For what?"

"A book that I may get to illustrate."

"Sally, that's great!" he said, embracing her. "Well done!"

"Don't get carried away. All that my agent said was that he was putting me up for it. There's no guarantee that I'll get it. Though his letter was encouraging, and that makes a change."

"What sort of book is it?"

"It's for kids. About wild animals."

"We should have met at the zoo."

"I didn't want to tempt providence," she said, closing her sketch pad and slipping the pencil back into her purse. "I've learned from experience not to believe I've landed a job until the contract is actually signed. But at least I'm on parade with a New York publisher again. So I've just been sitting here in the evening sun and enjoying the sheer pleasure of drawing once more. Letting my imagination roam."

"My imagination has been doing a bit of roaming as well!"

"Down, boy!" she said, giving him a playful nudge.

"I've missed you."

"Have you?"

"I keep thinking about Sunday morning."

"Why? Nobody ever cooked you spaghetti for breakfast before?"

"Not the way you did it!"

"You've led a sheltered life, Merl."

"So I'm discovering." He gave her an affectionate peck on the cheek. "But you're not the only one with a big opportunity on the horizon. Looks as if I might have one as well."

"That's wonderful!"

"Keep your fingers crossed for me."

"I will. What is the job?"

"Designing a house in Oak Park."

"Wow!"

"That's what I said, Sally. I mean, of all places—Oak Park. It's a dream come true. Frank Lloyd Wright lived and worked there for years. Some of his most famous buildings are in Oak Park. I remember the first time I went out there. It was overwhelming."

"Was it?"

"I just goggled in wonder."

"Nice neighborhood," she observed. "When I was a kid, I

used to visit an aunt who lives in Cicero. She took me to Oak Park a few times. I remember how peaceful it was. Almost rural. You'd never have thought you were so close to downtown Chicago."

"I'd give my right arm to get this commission!"

"Make it your left. You'll need the right to design with." She gave a lazy smile. "Though from what I recall, both hands are pretty magical. Never met anyone as ambidextrous as you."

"Comes from playing the harp."

"The what?"

"The Welsh harp. I was brought up on it. Used to practice every day when I was young. Keeps your hands strong and supple. You must hear me play sometime. It's the one thing I do really well."

She elbowed him. "Stop fishing for compliments."

"Sorry. That was a bit obvious."

"Tell me more about this commission."

"It's not definite yet."

"But it's a real possibility?"

"I think so," he said, trying to control his excitement. "Gus Westlake had a quiet word with me this afternoon. Told me to keep it to myself until it was set in stone."

"But you've just told me about it."

"I can trust you, Sally. And I have to share the thrill with someone, or I'll burst. In any case, what Gus really meant was that I mustn't tell either Reed or Victor."

"Who are they?"

"Two of my colleagues. Senior colleagues. Reed Cutler's been with the practice for over ten years, and Victor Goldblatt is their star architect."

"Not anymore. Merlin Richards has taken over."

"Victor won't like that."

"Is he the jealous type?"

"He's very competitive, Sally. I foresee trouble from him."

"What about this other guy?"

"Reed's been very friendly to me so far. He showed me the ropes when I first started there. I've been out to his house, met his wife and kids. No, I think Reed will take it on the chin—if the deal goes through, that is." He heaved a sigh. "Victor Goldblatt is different. He could get awkward. He's the sort of man who bears grudges." He gave a short laugh. "Mind you, if Victor was in the running for this job, *I'd* be the one bearing the grudge. I'd kill to build a house in Oak Park."

Sally was worried. "Is it that important to you?"

"Of course."

"Why?"

"You know how much I worship Frank Lloyd Wright."

"Oh, yeah!"

"Apart from anything else, he got me the job with Westlake and Davisson. Or, to be more exact, his name did. Gus Westlake once worked with him almost forty years ago. If I'd been one of Frank Lloyd Wright's boys, he said, I must be good."

"You are, Merlin."

"I learned so much from him."

"Now you've got a chance to prove it."

"Touch wood," he said, fingering the bench. "Right. What shall we do? Are you hungry?"

"I'm not sure."

"Shall we find somewhere to eat?"

"In a while."

"Rather stay here for a bit?"

"No," she said, "let's take a stroll."

"Why not?"

He helped her up, and they walked side by side along the

winding path. The warm weather had brought a lot of visitors to the park, and the birds were out in profusion. There was a sense of security that belied the fact that they were in what the newspapers had dubbed the crime capital of America. They felt supremely safe. Grant Park was a haven. They strolled for fifty yards or more before she broke the silence.

"Why did they choose you?" she wondered.

"They?"

"Gus Westlake and Brad Davisson."

"Oh, I don't think I've got Brad's blessing on this one."

"Why not?"

"He doesn't rate me as highly as Gus does."

"Would he have gone for one of the others?"

"Probably. But I was lucky enough to be Gus's choice. And in that practice, Gus Westlake usually calls the tune. He knows how to talk Brad round to his way of thinking."

"I see."

"Gus has put this whole thing together himself."

"So why did he want you on board?"

"I wish I knew, Sally."

"You must have some idea."

"Well, I've worked hard since I've been there. Sweated blood for them. Turned in some good stuff as well. On the other hand, so have Reed Cutler and Victor Goldblatt. Yet I seem to have pipped them at the post."

"Maybe you have more flair than they do."

"That comes into it."

"What else?"

"Search me. I'm just so pathetically grateful."

"Who is the client?"

"Gus did mention the name," he said, scratching his head. "Now, what was it? Somebody who lives on Lake Shore Drive."

"You *are* mixing with money!"

"Unusual name. Reminded me of Tasmania."

"Tasmania?"

"Yes," he said, ransacking his memory, then clicking his fingers. "Hobart. That was it. Hobart. Capital of Tasmania. The man was called Hobart something-or-other."

"Hobart St. John?"

"Yes. Have you heard of him?"

"Everyone in Chicago's heard of Hobart St. John."

"Who is he?"

"One of the biggest meatpackers in the business," she said coldly. "Mogul of the Union Stock Yards. Hobart St. John is a millionaire many times over. You'll be rubbing shoulders with a very powerful guy."

"You don't sound as if you like him that much."

"I don't approve of anyone owning *that* much money."

"What sort of person is he?"

"The kind that gets ahead, Merlin. All I know about him is what I read in the papers. Hobart St. John is always expanding his empire in some way or other. When he's not getting married again."

"Married?"

"Yes. He's had three or four wives. Seems to change them like automobiles. I think the latest was a movie actress."

"Gus said something about that. The house is really her idea."

"That figures."

"What do you mean?"

"Every woman wants a place of her own, something new and unsullied. Something on which she can stamp her own character. We're sensitive creatures, Merl. I know I'd hate to live in a house that my husband shared with his previous wife. If not two previous wives. Three, maybe."

"When you put it like that, it starts to fall into place."

"I could be wrong."

"Your instinct is usually sound."

"It's a bit more reliable than my spaghetti, anyway."

"That's certainly true!"

"Still leaves us with two big questions, though."

"Questions?"

"Yes, Merl. I've already asked the first. Why you?"

"Only time will tell."

"If you do clinch it—and I hope that you do—it's going to mean a helluva lot of work for you. Not to mention regular trips out to the site in Oak Park. This is a big break," she sighed, coming to a halt. "You'll be working around the clock."

"So?"

"That brings me to my second question."

"What's that?"

"Where will it leave us?"

"Exactly where we are now, Sally. As good friends."

"Good friends *see* each other, Merl."

"So will we."

"Not if this house becomes an obsession."

"It's still only a fantasy at this moment."

"But if it goes ahead—"

"If it goes ahead," he interrupted, taking her by the shoulders, "we'll both get the benefit. It will give me a great opportunity to establish myself, and I'll make the most of it. You can share in my good fortune. I'm not letting you go now, Sally," he said, hugging her on impulse. "Not after last weekend. You have my solemn promise. If I do land this commission, it won't make the slightest difference to us."

But they both knew that he was lying.

Alicia Martinez scrutinized her face in the mirror while the beautician hovered nervously in the background. A demanding client, Alicia was never happy until she had reduced her underlings to a state of cringing servility. In giving them the privilege of working for her, she believed she was bestowing a signal honor on them, and she made sure that they earned it. As the beautician arrived at the house, the hairdresser had been leaving in tears. Alicia was in top form. Running a sharp eye over every inch of her makeup, she was disappointed that she could find no fault.

"Well," she said at length, "I suppose it will have to do."

The beautician blanched. "Madam is not satisfied?"

"Not really."

"What is the problem?"

"*You* are the problem, Jessica."

"Me?"

"You never *listen*."

"I did exactly what you requested, madam."

"But not in the way that I instructed."

"I'm sorry," said the girl, obsequiously. "Can I start again?"

"We don't have time. That was my husband's car we heard arriving a moment ago. We're expecting visitors this afternoon. I hoped to be ready to receive them."

"You look wonderful to me," ventured the other.

"That will be all, Jessica."

"Yes, madam."

"Send your invoice in the usual way."

"I will."

"Today's session hardly justifies a tip. You do understand that?"

"Yes, madam."

"Good-bye, Jessica."

"Er, actually . . . my name is Ruth."

"Oh? What happened to Jessica?"

"She will not be coming anymore, madam."

Ruth nodded a farewell in the mirror, gathered up her things, and left the dressing room. She could see why Jessica had flatly refused to come to the house again. Ruth had been let off lightly, and yet she still felt thoroughly jangled. Evidently the hairdresser had borne the brunt of their client's disfavor, and yet, in the beautician's opinion, the girl had done an excellent job. Alicia Martinez's coiffure was superb.

Alone in her dressing room, Alicia came around to the same view. She stood up and pirouetted slowly so that she could see herself from every angle in the mirrors on each wall. She was a tall, slender, graceful woman with the narrow hips and full bosom that enabled her to decorate a movie screen so well. Long, dark hair and a Hispanic cast of feature had confined her to the role of a sultry maiden with a pouting beauty. Dangerously past thirty, she was still waiting for her full talent to be discovered. As she spun around, the mirrors silently applauded her.

The gravelly voice of her husband interrupted her reverie.

"Are you there, honey?" he called.

"Just a moment, darling."

"I managed to get away early."

"Good."

"They won't be here for an hour or more yet."

"I know."

"Can I come in?" he said impatiently.

"No, no," she chided. "I'll be out in a second."

After a final parade in front of the mirrors, she adjusted the sash on her silk robe, then practiced her wifely smile a few times. Alicia Martinez took a deep breath, drew herself up to her full height, and swept regally into the bedroom as the fourth Mrs. Hobart St. John. She struck a pose in front of her husband and switched on the smile.

Hobart St. John gazed at her in wonderment spiced with lust.

"You look gorgeous, honey!"

"Thank you."

"Good enough to eat."

Alicia simpered and allowed him a tiny peck on the cheek.

"Garbo would be invisible beside you," he said effusively.

"That's what they all believe."

"I'm so lucky to have such a beautiful wife!"

He moved in for another kiss, but she kept him at arm's length and gave him a teasing grin by way of consolation. Her husband marveled afresh. He was a stout man of medium height with the remains of a flashy handsomeness. There was such an air of certainty about him that it crackled like an electric discharge. On first acquaintance, nobody would have realized that he was exactly twice as old as Alicia. His hair was well-groomed and expertly dyed, his podgy face remarkably unlined. A gold tooth glinted when he gave an approving grin.

"Perfect!" he decided. "Just perfect!"

"How many wives have you said that to?"

"None. Apart from you."

"You're lying, Hobart."

"I know. But I do it so well." He gave a high-pitched cackle.

She drifted across to the window. "Shall we have them out in the garden?" she asked.

"Up to you, honey."

"Is there a wind today?"

"Light breeze. Nothing more."

"It could affect my hair. We'll stay indoors."

"Anything you say, hon."

The huge bedroom was luxurious to the point of excess, with a richly canopied four-poster, a crystal chandelier, gilt-framed mirrors, and costly paintings adorning its high walls, but only one item of expenditure interested the owner at that point. Hobart St. John feasted his eyes, massaged her lovingly from a distance. He gasped with delight.

"I married the most priceless piece of ass in Hollywood!"

"What's his name?" she said coolly.

"Who?"

"This architect." She swung around. "What's he called?"

"Gus Westlake. You've met him."

"The one who's going to design the house."

"Ah, him. Merlin Richards."

"What do you know about this Mr. Richards?"

"Only what Gus told me. Speaks very highly of him. Merlin used to work with Frank Lloyd Wright. He's young, keen, and full of bright ideas."

"Young and keen I like," she said, "but I can do without his bright ideas. I've got more than enough of those myself. What I want is an architect who can do what he's told."

"He will, Alicia."

"Does he understand that?"

"I made it clear to Gus Westlake."

"Good."

"And I'll spell it out again when they arrive." He checked his watch, then leered at her. "That won't be for at least an hour," he said, moving in on her. "We've got ample time."

"I've just had my hair done, Hobart."

"I'll be careful."

"And my makeup."

"We can get the girl back."

"Besides," she said, sniffing and taking a step backward, "you've been to the stockyard. I can smell it on you."

"No, you can't!"

"I can, Hobart. The stink is in your clothes."

He reached out for her. "I'll take them off."

"It's in your hair as well," she said, evading him. "Have a shower."

"Alicia!" he moaned.

"We have guests coming, sweetie."

"Not for ages."

"You don't want them to notice the stench."

"There *is* no stench!"

"I hate animals."

"Honey!"

"It's always the same when you've been to the stockyard."

"No, it isn't."

"Take that shower."

"Afterward."

"I insist."

"Alicia, for chrissake—I want you!"

"Don't be silly," she said, heading for the dressing room. "I must decide what to wear. That will take up all the time before they show up."

The most priceless piece of ass in Hollywood vanished.

AFTER ENDURING HOURS of silent hostility, Merlin Richards finally spoke out.

"Look," he said. "Why don't we call a truce?"

Bent over his drafting table, Victor Goldblatt ignored him.

"Victor," said Merlin, stepping toward him. "I'm talking to you."

"I'm busy," grunted the other.

"This is important."

"So is my work."

"It can wait."

Merlin suddenly took the pencil from Goldblatt's hand and forced him to stop. Goldblatt's eyes smoldered. He opened his palm.

"Give it back, Merlin."

"When we've sorted it out."

"There's nothing to sort out. Now, give me that pencil."

"Listen," said Merlin, adopting a conciliatory tone. "We're colleagues. I'd like to think that we're friends as well. We work alongside each other here in the office, and we've got along fine until now. I'd hate this to come between us, Victor. It wasn't my decision. Heaven knows why Gus and Brad chose me, but they did, and that's all there is to it."

"Oh, no, it isn't."

"I know how you must feel."

"You couldn't even begin to understand!" said Goldblatt,

snatching the pencil back from him. "Now back off, Merlin."

"It's not my fault."

"Matter of opinion."

"Gus is to blame. Take it up with him."

"I did."

"What did he say?"

"The usual crap. I'm wasted in this practice. They don't seem to have heard of words like loyalty and seniority. And they wouldn't recognize real talent if it leaped up and bit them on the dick."

He addressed himself to his drawing board again, using a T square to add a flat roof to the house extension he was designing. Victor Goldblatt was a tall, angular man in his thirties with bushy black hair and a beard that was already peppered with gray. He used a finger to push his spectacles back up to the bridge of his nose. Tense at the best of times, Goldblatt was now as taut as a piano wire.

Merlin was embarrassed. His good fortune had produced a lot of bad blood. He glanced across the room at Reed Cutler, a big, beefy man with expressive dimples in his cheeks and chin. Cutler replied with a sympathetic shrug, then semaphored an offer to speak to Goldblatt himself. Merlin shook his head, then turned back to his other colleague.

"What am I supposed to do, Victor?" he said softly.

"How about shutting the fuck up?"

"That's not the answer."

"Neither is all this soft-soap. So drop it. Okay?"

"I'm going to be working on this project only yards from you."

"Think I don't realize that?"

"It'll be hell for both of us if we don't settle this."

"It is settled. You got the glory—at my expense."

"Victor—"

"Don't ask me to kiss and make up, Merlin," said Goldblatt angrily. "This goes deeper than one commission that should have come to me. You've been Gus's bright-eyed boy ever since you joined the practice. Why? What have you got that Reed and I don't have ten times over?"

"Nothing," conceded Merlin.

"Exactly! From what I can see, your only qualification is that you once worked with Frank Lloyd Wright."

"Pretty good qualification, I'd say," observed Cutler.

"Wright is a has-been."

"Not in my book."

"Keep out of this, Reed."

"Then stop trashing Merlin. He's a fine architect."

"This is between him and me."

"I work here as well, remember."

"So do I," snarled Goldblatt. "I've been in this dump for ten years. Ten long, hard, miserable, unrelenting years. But it might as well have been ten minutes for all the good it's done me."

"Come off it, Vic," said Cutler pleasantly. "You're the cock of the walk. When the work comes in, you usually have first peck at it."

"And so I should!"

"This time, Merlin is in favor. Good luck to him, I say."

"Well, don't expect me to lead three cheers."

"I'd settle for a handshake," said Merlin.

"Be grateful I don't slug you!"

Goldblatt flung his pencil aside and turned to confront Merlin, realizing at once the folly of threatening someone who was patently so much stronger and more agile. Merlin had rolled up his shirtsleeves to reveal muscular forearms. His shoulders were broad. Goldblatt knew about his sporting prowess—another reason to despise him.

"We can't go on like this," said Merlin reasonably.

"Get out of my face!"

"It creates such an atmosphere."

"That's your problem."

"Merlin's offering you a peace pipe, Vic," said Cutler quietly.

"Well, he can stick it up his ass!"

Grabbing his coat, Goldblatt stormed out of the office and slammed the door behind him. Merlin would have gone after him, but Reed Cutler put a restraining hand on his arm.

"Give him time to cool down, Merl."

"What's got into him?"

"Professional envy."

"I had no idea he resented me so much."

"He doesn't," said the other with a sigh. "That was his insecurity talking. Victor has domestic problems. Comes to the office to escape them. He can strut a bit here, trade on his seniority. This has caught him on the raw. Long story, tell you sometime."

"I wish somebody would."

"Vic Goldblatt is an edgy guy. Always has been."

"Thanks for what you said, anyway, Reed. And thanks for taking the decision so well. I'm glad it hasn't poisoned relations between us."

"Hell, no! You win some, lose some."

"Victor doesn't see it that way."

"Forget him."

"I don't think he'll let me do that."

"We'll work on him together." Reed Cutler grinned, then looked him critically up and down. "Say, aren't you and Gus going out to Lake Shore Drive this afternoon?"

"Yes. Gus is taking me there."

"Then you'd better spiff yourself up or you won't get past the front door. This is no ordinary client you're calling on,

Merlin. You'll be shaking hands with millions of dollars. Not to mention getting close to Alicia Martinez." He gave an obscene chuckle. "Now, even I could start to get jealous about *her*."

GUS WESTLAKE SAT behind the steering wheel of his yellow-and-black Lincoln coaching brougham and eased it through the traffic. The vehicle complemented its owner—big, sleek, and conspicuous. Throughout the journey, he gave Merlin copious instructions about how to behave at this first meeting with the clients.

"There's much more to architecture than sitting at a drafting table," he counseled. "That's where you create the product. The real art is in selling it. You must learn to handle clients."

"That's what Mr. Wright always said," recalled Merlin.

"He was a past master at it. Unlike poor old Brad. Set him an architectural challenge, and he'll meet it head-on every time. Send him out to talk up work, and he gets tongue-tied. That's why he needs me."

"So I noticed."

"Here we are. Let's go get 'em!"

Westlake turned the nose of the car into a long curving drive, and Merlin got his first look at the mansion. It was a vast house, built of red stone, running to three stories, and combining a variety of styles. He liked the classical portico but had severe doubts about an outbreak of Gothic extravagance around the windows. There was an ornamental pond at the front of the house and a well-tended formal garden. When they got out of the car, Merlin noted that they were cleverly screened from the road by the trees and bushes.

A butler admitted the visitors and conducted them to the living room. Hobart and Alicia St. John were waiting for them, the one in the center of the room, the other perched carefully on the arm of a chair so that the light flooded in on her. When she rose to her feet, she was framed in the window and edged in sunshine. Merlin thought she looked like an angel. He wondered why her husband's hair was so wet.

Introductions were made, drinks poured, and seats taken. When the niceties were out of the way, their host turned a shrewd eye on Merlin.

"Gus tells me that you're Welsh," he said.

"That's right."

"What brought you to America?"

"Frank Lloyd Wright."

"He sent for you?"

"Not exactly," said Merlin, recalling the brief message on a postcard that had prompted him to leave the family architectural practice in Merthyr Tydfil. "But I ended up being taken on by him. In Arizona."

"I have a friend whose house was built by Frank Lloyd Wright."

"Here in Chicago?"

"Yes," said St. John. "He was thrilled with the design but reckoned that Wright went way over budget. That mustn't happen here."

"It won't," promised Westlake.

"I'll hold you to that, Gus. When we agree on a price, that's it."

"You have my guarantee."

Merlin was interested to see how different his employer was in the company of clients. Brash and braying at the office, he had toned himself down completely now. He was polite, attentive, and relaxed. Occasional bursts of flattery were reserved for Alicia, and she basked in them. For his part, Merlin was trying to resist the urge to look at her all the time. He had never been so close to such a calculated display of glamour before.

"How much has Gus told you?" asked St. John.

"Everything that he knows," said Merlin. "You have a two-acre site in Oak Park, and you want us to build a new house on it."

"House, garden, and swimming pool."

"I don't see any problem there, Mr. St. John."

"That depends."

"On what?"

"How well you and Alicia get on. She'll make the major decisions."

"That's fine," said Merlin, turning to smile at her. "Just tell me what sort of a design you had in mind, and we'll take it from there. When I've been out to inspect the site, I can prepare some preliminary drawings for you to study. Whatever you don't like, we can change."

"Sounds promising to me," she said.

"Ideally, I'd like to visit the site with you so that you can point out any special features you want me to take into account. Would that be possible, Mrs. St. John?"

"It's more than possible," said her husband. "It's arranged."

"Is it?"

"All four of us will drive out there this evening."

"Excellent," said Westlake. "So is this whiskey."

"Canadian," explained his host, raising his glass. "To Prohibition!"

Merlin joined in the toast, then sipped his own whiskey, but without any relish. A conflict of loyalties worried him. He was pleased at the idea of visiting the site but acutely conscious that he had arranged to pick up Sally Fiske from the hotel that evening. Gus Westlake had given him the firm impression that the visit to Lake Shore Drive was simply to effect introductions and establish the basics. It was scheduled to take an hour or two at most. Merlin had made no allowance for a ten-mile drive to a western suburb, yet he could hardly refuse the invitation.

Turning back to Alicia, he tried to move things along.

"What sort of a house did you have in mind, Mrs. St. John?"

"A special one," she said.

Westlake beamed. "Any house with you inside it is special."

"Thank you."

"But what style did you have in mind?" pressed Merlin.

"*My* style," she said firmly.

"Could you be a little more specific, please?"

"Show him, Alicia," suggested her husband.

"Shall I?"

"Go on. We'll join you in a moment."

"Very well." She stood up and smiled at Merlin. "Let's go into the library. I have some photographs to show you."

"Good."

Merlin rose to his feet, collected an encouraging wink from his employer, then followed Alicia out into the hall and clacked his way across its gleaming marble floor. She opened a heavy oak door and took him into the library, a large room with shelves along three walls and wing chairs in front of a marble fireplace. Noting the leather-bound editions that filled the shelves, Merlin wondered if Hobart St. John had ever read any of them. His host did not have the air of a literary man. Though cluttered with furniture, the place felt empty and unused, a library that was there purely for reasons of status and decoration.

Alicia took him across to a long table on which a series of books and albums had been set out. Now that she was alone with him, her manner changed slightly. She was less imperative, more confiding. She never let him forget that he was her employee, but an element of curiosity had crept in. He could feel her appraising him.

"Do you like Chicago?" she asked.

"I love it, Mrs. St. John."

"Why?"

"It's so full of life. I've never been anywhere that has so much raw energy swirling about in it. It's invigorating. Also, of course, it's the home of American architecture. For that reason alone, I had to come here."

"Well, I don't share your admiration."

"Oh?"

"It's a hateful city. I prefer California."

That was the cue for her to open the first book. She indicated the photograph of a sunlit mansion in Beverly Hills. Merlin thought it had an element of vulgarity about it that completely vitiated its finer points, but she clearly admired it. Her long fingers caressed the sepia image.

"Something like this," she said, then flicked to another page. "Or this, perhaps—Pola Negri's house. I'm not sure that I don't like that even more." She found a third photograph. "But this is the one I really used to covet. I've been inside it lots of times, so I can describe the layout in detail. Our house must be on these lines—only different."

"Individual," he said.

"Unique."

Merlin nodded obediently. It was obvious that his companion had no knowledge of architecture and no interest in its deeper mysteries. In place of genuine ideas, she simply had vague notions. Merlin was shown an endless succession of houses with a feature or an aspect that appealed to her. The nature of his assignment became clear. He was not there to create an entirely new design for her and her husband. What Alicia St. John really wanted was to transplant a home of movie-star opulence from California. To import Hollywood into Oak Park, Illinois.

The thought depressed Merlin, though it made his task easier in some ways. He just hoped that Frank Lloyd Wright would never see the finished result. Alicia continued to hurl suggestions, orders, and pictures at him before opening the first of the albums. Photographs of other houses were on display, but there was a difference. Alicia Martinez appeared in each one of them. She leaned against pillars, lazed beside swimming pools, reclined on patios, presided at dining tables, descended long staircases, even stretched out, albeit clothed, on king-size beds. Though she picked out architectural details each time, Merlin knew that she was really putting herself on display for him.

He was still wondering why when the gravelly voice boomed.

"How are you two getting along?" asked Hobart St. John.

"We're almost through, sweetie," said his wife.

"Some great photos there, Merlin, aren't there?"

"Yes, Mr. St. John," he said, nodding.

His host was standing in the doorway with Gus Westlake. Both held glasses of whiskey. Merlin had no idea how long they had been there or how much of the conversation they overheard. He was surprised when Alicia put her hand on his arm and squeezed it.

"Merlin agrees with all my suggestions," she said happily. "I knew right away that he was the architect for me."

"For *us*, honey," corrected her husband. "There is a small matter of finance here. Gus and I have just been discussing it. Since I'm putting up the dough, I insist on making one decision at least."

"What's that, Hobart?"

"The name of the house."

"Of course. I forgot to mention that to Merlin."

"Then I'll tell him. Know what they call Oak Park, Merlin?"

"Saint's Rest," he said.

"Exactly. What better name for the home of Mr. and Mrs. St. John?"

"Move the apostrophe," said Westlake, "and there you have it."

Hobart St. John's gold tooth came back into view again.

"I name this house—Saints' Rest!"

His cackle reverberated around the library like a fire alarm.

Sally Fiske spent most of the day looking forward to the evening meal she was having with Merlin Richards. The anticipation helped her through the tedium of her job and steeled her against the routine passes that occasional guests always seemed to make at her. When she first started at the hotel, the stream of offers had merely annoyed her, ranging as they did from the subtle to the downright insulting, but she soon learned to treat them with polite disdain. Something happened to guys when they were staying alone at a fancy hotel. They seemed to think that every pretty face was fair game.

Since the manager objected to his staff chatting with husbands or boyfriends on the premises, she arranged to meet Merlin in the street outside, and she was standing there at the appointed time. Merlin was habitually late, and she was not worried when he did not show up during the first twenty minutes. After half an hour, however, she began to rehearse a few stinging remarks, and she was muttering them under her breath fifteen minutes later, but still there was no sign of Merlin. Apart from being irritated, she also felt herself in a vulnerable position, exposed to the admiring and ribald comments of hotel patrons.

When she was propositioned and offered money by a drunken passerby, Sally could take no more. She went back into the hotel to see if Merlin had rung with a message, but the girl who had relieved her shook her head. That left his office as a possibility. She set off at a brisk pace and soon walked the four blocks to the building that Westlake and Davisson shared with a number of other firms. The janitor assured her that everyone had left, but she insisted on going up to the office in the elevator, knowing that Merlin's working hours were very elastic. It might just be that he was so absorbed in a project that he had not even noticed the time. It was a long shot, but worth trying. But the visit was in vain. After pounding hard on the door without reply, she finally accepted that he was not there and gave up.

Irritation now shaded into concern. He had never let her down before, and she began to wonder if something dreadful had happened to him. By the time she left the building, she had almost persuaded herself that he had been involved in an automobile accident and debated whether she should contact the police or ring the nearest hospital. It was difficult to believe that Merlin had either forgotten the date or deliberately left her in the lurch. Whatever his defects, he was a kind and thoughtful friend. There had to be a logical explanation for his absence.

It was only as she was drifting aimlessly along the street that she remembered the restaurant. Perhaps she had made a mistake. Perhaps she was supposed to meet him there. Merlin insisted on that particular restaurant because it had been the place where he took her for lunch on their first date and thus held a special significance for them. Her spirits picked up slightly, and she set off toward the restaurant, convincing herself on the way that it was she who was at fault and that Merlin would probably be waiting there and agonizing about her whereabouts.

Once again, however, there was no trace of him. But there was one hopeful sign. A table had been reserved in his name. Sally decided to sit there and wait for him. If he arrived late at the hotel and found she had left, he would surely realize that she had come on to the restaurant. The comments she rehearsed were now much more barbed. After toying with a glass of water for an age, she eventually agreed to order, prompted by a growing hunger and by the impatience of the staff, who needed the table for paying customers. The food was a welcome distraction, and she savored every mouthful. Even though she stretched the meal out as long as she could, Merlin did not appear or phone the restaurant with a message for her. Sally was hopelessly torn between anger and fear.

When she came out in the night, steady rain was starting to fall, compounding her misery. Sally either had to scurry three blocks to catch a streetcar or go home by taxicab. The latter option would be an expense, but it would save her from getting soaked. An approaching cab made the decision for her. She hailed it and got in. They headed south. The driver said very little on the journey, but she could see him flicking glances at her in the rearview mirror, so she had some warning of what was coming. When they reached her street and she got out of the cab, all that she had to give him was a ten-dollar bill.

He was a middle-aged Italian with a knowing smirk.

"I shouldn't be taking money off a pretty girl like you."

"Just give me my change," she said, offering the bill.

"You're my last fare. I'm done for the night."

"Take the money."

"Tell you what, lady. Invite me in for a coffee, and we call it quits."

"No chance, brother!"
"It's not much to ask."
"Stay in that cab, or I call the cops."
"I'm offering you a free ride!" he complained.
"Well, I'm not offering you one!"
"Come on! Give me a break!"
"Get lost!"
"I'm only trying to be friendly."
"Good night, mister!"
"Okay, okay, okay!" he shouted. "Please yourself!"

And before she could stop him, he grabbed the money from her, pressed his foot down hard on the gas pedal, and shot away. She had no time even to get the number on his license plate. Sally was distraught. Her whole evening had been a disaster. Deserted by Merlin, she had been forced to eat a meal she did not really want and take a cab that cost her ten dollars and aggravation from the driver. As she stood on the sidewalk in the rain, she was on the point of tears, but her torment was not yet over. She looked across at her apartment block and saw a figure hauling himself up from the ground in the darkness of the doorway. Her heart sank. There was one more ordeal to endure before she could reach the safety of her room.

She screwed up her courage and tried to sound authoritative."

"You can't sleep there!" she announced.

"Sally?" said a weary voice. "Is that you?"

She was shocked. "Merlin?"

"I must have nodded off," he decided, lumbering toward her out of the gloom. "The noise of that car woke me up. It fairly screeched away."

"That was my cab."

"You came home in a cab?"

"No," she said. "I roller-skated all the way to the South Side!"

"Where've you been?" he said.

"Where have *I* been?" She punched him hard. "You ask *me* that? I waited outside the hotel for ages, but you didn't show up."

"I did. Eventually."

"When?"

"After I'd been to the restaurant."

"You never went near the place, Merlin!"

"Yes, I did," he insisted. "We were so late getting back that I asked Gus to drop me off at the restaurant. I assumed that you'd go there when I didn't turn up at the hotel."

"That's exactly what I did do."

"You weren't there when I was, Sally. I looked through the window. The table I reserved was empty. I asked for the same one we had on our first date. The table by the potted plant and the—"

"I know which table it was!" she said vehemently. "I was stuck there for hours on end and finished up eating twice as much as I wanted to. I know that table far too well! It was the one with the empty chair right opposite me."

"How on earth did I miss you?"

"God knows!"

"Unless you arrived when I went off to the hotel."

Sally gaped. "You went to the hotel?"

"Of course. It was the only other place you could be. They told me you'd left quite some time ago."

"I did, Merlin. I went to your office."

"But I wasn't at my office."

"You knew that—I didn't."

Merlin tried to think it through. "When you were at my office, I was at the restaurant." He gave a short laugh. "When I got to the hotel, *you* were at the restaurant. We kept dodging each other. It's really funny when you think about it, isn't it?"

"Fucking hilarious!"

"Sally!" He reached out to console her.

"Don't touch me!" she warned.

"But it was one of those things. An unfortunate mistake."

"Very unfortunate!"

"At least we're together now."

"Where the hell were you?"

She paused long enough to get part of the answer. Merlin was swaying slightly, and there was enough light from the streetlamp for her to see the benign smile on his face. She caught a whiff of his breath."

"You've been drinking!"

"Let me explain."

"I can smell whiskey."

"I only had a glass or two."

"While I was standing outside that hotel, you were boozing!"

"That's not strictly true."

"Then where were you?"

"In Oak Park."

"Oak Park!" she hissed. "What about our date?"

"I hoped we could get back in time."

"Who's we?"

"Gus Westlake and our clients. Hobart St. John and his wife. You were right about him, Sally. He's rolling in it. That house on Lake Shore Drive is like a palace. Their swimming pool is bigger than my whole apartment. And, hey, you'll never guess. You know his wife, that film star, Alicia Martinez?"

"I don't think I want to hear this," she said through gritted teeth.

"But this will interest you."

"Don't bank on it."

"Alicia Martinez is not her real name at all. I thought she was Mexican or something, but not a bit of it. Gus told me that she began life as plain Alice Martin from some hick town in Wyoming."

"Never!" said Sally with mock surprise.

"She's an amazing lady."

"Why didn't you take *her* to the restaurant, then?"

"Sally!"

"Out of my way. I'm going to bed."

"But I want to tell you what happened."

"I already know, Merl. You saw clients. They came first."

"Somehow I just couldn't get away."

"Ever heard of an instrument called the telephone?"

"There was never one handy."

"You mean that you were too busy with Alicia Martinez."

"She did rather hog my ear, I must admit. I was forced to listen. Honestly, she's got some weird ideas about this house of theirs."

Sally exploded. "And you've got some weird ideas about what a date is. You ask a girl out, you don't leave her high and dry like that. You invite her to a meal, you don't sneak off and get drunk instead."

"I'm not drunk."

"Then why do I find you sleeping in my doorway?"

"I was tired. I waited there for hours."

"Join the club!"

"How was I to know you were at the restaurant?"

"Who cares?" she said in disgust. "I don't."

She pushed past him and found the key in her purse. As she fumbled for the lock, Merlin came up behind her and tried to shake himself fully awake, uncomfortably aware that he must have had far more whiskey than he realized. His head was quietly pounding, his mouth felt dry. Guilt surged through him. The ugly truth was that he had become so intrigued by the visit to Oak Park that he temporarily forgot his arrangement with Sally Fiske. He needed to make amends.

"It will all seem very different in the morning," he assured her.

"Go home, Merlin."

"What we both need is a nice cup of coffee."

"I don't believe I'm hearing this."

"I'll make it," he volunteered. "I know where you keep everything."

She opened the door and stepped inside, closing it swiftly until only a crack was left open. When he tried to follow her in, she thrust out a hand to push him forcibly away. Merlin took a step backward and blinked in disappointment.

"Aren't you going to invite me in, Sally?"

"No."

"Why not?"

"I'm out of spaghetti."

She pulled the door shut.

"ALL I'M SAYING is this, Victor. Don't create an atmosphere out there."

"You're the one who did that, Gus."

"I asked Merlin Richards to take on this commission, that's all."

"Yes," said Goldblatt sharply. "Even though you knew that I could have done the job far better."

"That wasn't the only consideration," said Westlake.

"No," added Brad Davisson. "This is no reflection on your

work, Vic. You must realize that. Gus and I have the highest respect for you."

"So why let the office junior leapfrog over me?" asked Goldblatt.

"Merlin is not the office junior," said Davisson.

Westlake took over. "He's a first-rate architect with a lot of experience. He designed houses, office blocks, factories, even a Methodist chapel back in Wales."

"Why didn't he stay there?" muttered Goldblatt.

"You know the answer to that one."

"Yeah, Gus. Frank Lloyd Wright. Merlin came to worship at his altar. I may have my limitations, but at least I've evolved my own ideas in this game. Merlin Richards hasn't. He's just a pygmy version of Wright."

"Now, that's not fair, Vic."

"Oh, we're talking fairness now, are we? Good!"

"Take it easy," advised Davisson. "No need to get riled up."

"We called you in here to straighten this out," said Westlake.

Goldblatt was fuming. "You called me in because Merlin came running to you to complain that I was being awkward. What else do you expect me to be? Overjoyed? This commission had my name written all over it, and I've been cheated out of it by our Welsh wonder boy. And we know exactly the kind of design he will come up with." His hands gestured wildly. "Goddammit! If you're going to build another Frank Lloyd Wright house in Oak Park, why not engage Wright himself to design it!"

Turning angrily on his heel, Goldblatt stalked across to the window and rested both hands on the sill. Davisson shook his head sadly, then shot an accusatory look at his partner. Westlake held up both palms to indicate that he would handle their disturbed employee. The three of them were in the office that was shared by the two partners but inhabited almost exclusively by only one of them. It had been years since Gus Westlake's drafting table had any working drawings on it. If there was any rancor in the outer office, it was Brad Davisson, still a practicing architect and shackled to the premises, who would have to deal with it. Gus Westlake would be out on a golf course somewhere or haunting his favorite speakeasies, tracking down potential clients and ensnaring them with a combination of charm and anecdote.

Westlake strolled across to Goldblatt and put a hand on his arm.

"Let's take this from the beginning, Vic, shall we?" he said softly. "I know you feel sore, but that's only because you don't know the full facts. So let me put you in the picture. One, Merlin did not come running to me or to Brad with a complaint."

"Like hell he didn't!" said Goldblatt.

"That door is not soundproofed. We heard you having a trantrum."

"Do you blame me?"

"All I'm trying to do is explain things. One, drop the charges. Merlin Richards is innocent. Two, he was chosen for this job because the clients wanted him. Yes, don't worry," he said quickly as Goldblatt spun around to challenge him, "I put your name forward as well, Vic, gave you a big buildup, even showed them some of your work. Mr. and Mrs. St. John were very impressed, but for personal reasons, they opted for Merlin."

"What personal reasons?"

"I can't breach client confidentiality."

Goldblatt flared. "Are we talking anti-Semitism here?"

"That's a crazy idea!"

"So what are these personal reasons?"

"He who pays the piper, calls the tune."

"Give it to me straight, Gus."

"I just have. I offered them you—and Reed, of course—and

Merlin. They saw examples of work by all three of you. Hobart St. John was particularly struck by your design for the Du Vivier residence out in Berwyn. But he still preferred Merlin."

"For personal reasons?"

"And on my advice," confessed the other. "When he put me on the spot and asked me who I'd recommend, I went for Merlin. And it's no good looking at me like that, Vic," he said as Goldblatt glowered. "You're a more seasoned architect than Merlin, but you don't take criticism lightly, and this job is going to involve a lot of needless criticism. Ask Merlin. He's been forced to take on Mrs. St. John as a codesigner, and she's a very demanding lady. There'll be a heavy call on patience and diplomacy. You're pretty low on both."

"And you're pretty high on bullshit."

"Three," continued Westlake, smoothly. "Merlin did not leapfrog over you. There's another job on the horizon, a much bigger and more interesting one. A new office block for Jerry Niedlander. If it comes off, we'll all be laughing. Brad and I have you penciled in for that but you wouldn't have been available if you were tied up in the Oak Park project. The Niedlander deal calls for our best man, Vic. That's you. We never even considered Merlin Richards."

"Is this on the level?" asked Goldblatt suspiciously.

"I give you my word."

"Brad?"

"It's true, Vic," confirmed Davisson. "The Niedlander deal has been in the offing for months. Gus has to iron out a few last wrinkles, that's all."

"I see. Why didn't you tell me earlier?"

"Because we're not home and dry yet."

"And we didn't want to give you false hopes," said Westlake. "But it's looking good, Vic. Very good. Keep it under your hat, mind. I don't want the others to hear about this until the contract is actually signed."

"Sure," said Goldblatt, and a first smile broke through.

"Tell you what," said Davisson. "When this does get out, I bet that Merlin Richards will be the first to congratulate you. Not an ounce of envy in that guy. So get off his back, Vic. Okay?"

Goldblatt nodded, but he was only partially mollified.

"One last thing," said Westlake with a grin. "You asked me why we don't employ Frank Lloyd Wright to design another house in Oak Park. The answer is simple. He's not too popular out there. Don't forget that he ran off with the wife of one of his clients, leaving his own wife and kids in Oak Park. I know it was a long time ago, but memories linger. He didn't come near Chicago for years." He gave a ripe chuckle. "One thing about Merlin Richards."

"What's that?" said Goldblatt.

"We can be damn sure that *he* won't run off with the wife of this particular client. Just as well, in the circumstances."

"Why is that, Gus?"

"I know Hobart St. John. He's a great friend to have, but I'd hate to have a man like that as an enemy."

THE UNION STOCK Yards occupied a square mile of land to the south of Thirty-ninth Street and the west of Halsted, an area that was originally outside the Chicago city limits. Only six years earlier the slaughterhouses had been operating at their peak, handling over 18 million head of cattle, calves, hogs, and sheep, bringing them in alive in wagons and sending them out dead in refrigerated transport and tin cans. Nothing was wasted. The thirty thousand men employed in the industry were proficient at their interrelated trades. Meat was their main product, but they also tanned and dried skins, washed fleeces, turned heads and feet into glue, used small bones to make fertilizer and large ones as imitation ivory, cleaned and dried bristles for use in hair cushions, turned the rivers of grease into soap and lard, and found a posthumous role for even the most unlikely and repellent parts of the animals' anatomies.

When the stock market crashed the previous year, Chicago suffered as much as anywhere else, and the stockyards saw a drop in output and a reduction in workforce, but they were still a vital component in the city's manufacturing base. And their distinctive aroma still hung over the district like a pall. Hobart St. John was an astute businessman who survived the Great Crash better than most, but that did not induce any sense of complacence. He still worked long hours to keep his enterprise at the forefront, and he was ruthless with any employee who did not show the same wholehearted commitment.

"Take your money and go!" he ordered.

"But I don't want to, Mr. St. John," bleated the man. "I like it here."

"And no wonder. You treat the place as a holiday resort."

"I sneaked one half-day off, that's all."

"One half hour would have been enough to get you sacked."

"Please, Mr. St. John. I need this job."

"Then you should have taken it more seriously. We've been keeping an eye on you for weeks, Pollock. You don't pull your weight around here, and that's that. I can't have a manager with that attitude. What kind of an example does it set for the guys under you? Now take that ugly mug of yours out of here," said St. John, walking around his desk to grab hold of the man. "If you're still on my premises in fifteen minutes, I'll send you home to your wife in a crate of tin cans."

Tom Pollock was a big man, but he was no match for his

employer when the latter was roused. Hobart St. John took him by the scruff of his neck, dragged him across the office, opened the door, and flung him out. Pollock was still mouthing excuses when the door was slammed in his face. St. John went swiftly back to his desk and flicked the switch on the intercom.

"Helen!" he snapped.

"Yes, Mr. St. John?" said a girl's voice.

"Has Donald Kruger arrived yet?"

"He's in his office."

"Send him in at once."

"Yes, Mr. St. John."

Flicking the switch, he sat back in his chair and mused on the shortcomings of the man he had just dismissed. Within a minute there was a tap on the door, and Donald Kruger came in. He was a tall, well-built man in his thirties with thinning fair hair and a handsome but expressionless face that seemed to have been chiseled out of marble. St. John wore expensive clothing, but his assistant looked even more immaculate in a blue pin-striped suit. His shoes gleamed.

"I've just sacked Pollock," announced St. John.

"Very wise."

"Make sure that he leaves the factory."

"I will."

"And shake him up a bit before he goes."

"Leave it to me."

Kruger stepped forward and put a folder on the desk.

"What's this?"

"The information you asked me to get on Merlin Richards."

"That was quick work."

"You wanted it soon."

"I did, Donald," he said, picking up the folder and opening it. "Thank you. When I employ a man, I like to know a bit about him. Especially when he's going to spend so much time in my wife's company. This new house is really exciting Alicia." He glanced at the typed pages. "What did you find out for me about Merlin Richards?"

"Everything," said Kruger.

"And?"

"He won't give you any trouble."

The speed of events took Merlin Richards completely by surprise. Back in Wales, architecture had been an almost leisurely profession, hampered by rules and beset by delays. The construction of a new house was a lengthy process. When the client's approval had been given, there was planning consent to obtain, and there were building regulations with which to comply. The delivery on-site of materials was often a problem that led to much haggling and further postponements. Arranging for tradesmen to work in the correct sequence was another headache, and Merlin lost count of the number of times that eager decorators were held by up tardy plasterers or impatient roofers waited on sluggish carpenters. A snap inspection by a Council official might lead to additional holdups.

It was several months before a house could make the journey from the drawing board to the status of an inhabited dwelling, and larger buildings took even longer. The Methodist chapel Merlin had designed was in construction for the best part of two years, leading to a war of attrition with its minister, who used language not to be found in any Methodist hymnal and which, set to music, would have emptied every chapel in the principality and caused a national scandal. With a pencil in his hand, Merlin could work swiftly and effectively, but once his design was complete, everything seemed to happen in slow motion.

In America, by contrast, there was a greater sense of urgency. Buildings seemed to go up more quickly, with far less interference and delay from officialdom. Saints' Rest looked set to be one of the fastest projects yet. No sooner had terms been agreed upon and a contract signed than Merlin was required to produce a set of sketches for Alicia St. John to study and amend. He incorporated her wishes in the revised versions, adding a first-floor plan, a second-floor plan, a section, an elevation, a detailed layout of the garden, and side sketches of the many idiosyncratic features on which she insisted. Merlin had never worked so swiftly or so fluently as he searched for a compromise between his artistic vision and the perverse requirements of his client.

It was highly exhilarating, but it left him little time or opportunity to repair the rift with Sally Fiske. Desperate to see her again, he found her tantalizingly out of reach. This was especially galling as he had finally taken delivery of the automobile that he had been saving up to buy and which was a necessity to an architect making regular visits to a site in Oak Park. He had vowed that Sally would never again be bothered by amorous cabdrivers, only to realize that that was exactly how she now saw him, a chauffeur to be spurned. When he rang her at the hotel, she refused to speak to him. When he sent her flowers, they elicited no reply. In the short term, at least, burned spaghetti was off the breakfast menu.

Merlin hoped that the passage of time would have its celebrated healing effects. Sally Fiske receded to the back of his mind, and Alicia Martinez took her place. As he drove out to the house on Lake Shore Drive once again, his regrets soon gave way to anticipatory pleasure. His Model A Ford looked like an interloper among the magnificent limousines that cruised effortlessly past him, but Merlin did not mind. He drove his car as if he was behind the wheel of the latest Cadillac or the finest Hispano-Suiza cabriolet, turning into the drive of the St. John mansion with a sense of achievement he had never felt before. He wished that his father, Daniel Richards, who prophesied his son's doom in America, could see him now. Merlin had a car, a career, and the sort of commission that would have been unthinkable in his native country.

He parked his Ford beside a two-passenger Stutz Torpedo and strode toward the front door with a portfolio under his arm. The butler escorted him to the library. Expecting to be met by the lady of the house, he was taken aback to learn that she was not even there. In her place, waiting to receive him, was a young woman who rose from her chair and offered a brisk handshake.

"Hello, Mr. Richards. My name is Clare Brovik."

"Pleased to met you," he said, feeling the coldness of her hand.

"I work for Mr. St. John," she explained. "I'm sorry that his wife is not here today, but she had an urgent appointment. However, she briefed me thoroughly before she left, so your journey has not been wasted."

"That's good to hear."

"Would you like tea, coffee? Or something stronger?"

"Tea will be fine," said Merlin.

Clare Brovik nodded to the waiting butler, and he went off to convey the order to the kitchen. Spread out on the table, Merlin saw, were the sketches he had left on his previous visits. He noticed that they were liberally marked with comments and arrows.

"Mrs. St. John is delighted with what you've done so far,"

said Clare, waving him to a seat at the table, "and I must say that I think you've come up with some beautiful designs."

"Thank you."

"I look forward to seeing the house take shape."

"You won't have long to wait. The site has been cleared, and the O'Brien Construction Company starts work on it next week."

"Ah, that's not strictly correct, I'm afraid."

"There's been a delay?"

"A change of builder."

"But we recommended O'Brien. We've used him many times before."

"Mr. St. John has his own contacts in the construction industry," she explained levelly. "He decided to make use of those. Mr. O'Brien has been informed that he will not be needed."

"Why wasn't I told of this?"

"You just have been, Mr. Richards."

"We were given a free hand to engage builders of our choice."

"Subject to Mr. St. John's approval."

"He made no objection to O'Brien."

"He has now."

The peremptory note in her voice irked him, but he tried to conceal his irritation. The loss of a builder whom he knew and liked was a serious blow, and the way in which he had been informed of it only added insult to injury. Merlin took a moment to appraise Clare Brovik. She was a shapely young woman with a businesslike air about her. Her brown hair was brushed back severely and imprisoned by a large amber slide, exposing to the full a face that was interesting rather than attractive. She had poise, intelligence, and quiet determination. If she was negotiating on behalf of her employer and his wife, they must have great trust in her.

Clare seemed to read his mind. A polite smile surfaced.

"Don't shoot the messenger," she said.

"Messenger?"

"For delivering an unwelcome message. I'm not responsible for the decision to change the builder. I was merely asked to tell you about it."

"It would have been more courteous if Mr. St. John had talked to me directly about it," said Merlin. "Then at least I would have had the chance to speak up for O'Brien."

"It would have been in vain."

"How do you know?"

"I've worked for Mr. St. John for almost five years."

"I see."

"Nobody ever persuades him to change his mind."

"I suspect that his wife might."

Clare suppressed another smile and looked up as a tray of tea was brought in by the maid. When it was set on the table, the maid went out again, and Clare took charge, pouring tea for both of them and leaving Merlin to add his own milk and sugar. He noted that the tray was made of solid silver, and the chinaware was from Limoges. He took his first sip. Accustomed to drinking coffee since he came to America, he was pleased to taste a good cup of tea once more.

"What exactly is your position?" he asked.

"I report directly to Donald Kruger."

"And who is he?"

"Hobart St. John's right-hand man. You'll see a lot of Donald."

"Will I?"

"Yes, Mr. Richards. He will supervise the construction."

"That's my job, Miss Brovik."

"He won't tread on your toes," she said, "and he won't always be there in person. But I will be. Donald wants regular bulletins. It will be my job to send them to him."

"So I've lost O'Brien but gained you and this Donald Kruger. It's going to get a little crowded out there, if Mrs. St. John wants to look over my shoulder all the time as well."

"Oh, she won't come out to the site."

"Why not?"

"All that mess and filth. Mrs. St. John is very fastidious. She simply wanted to be involved in the actual design. Once that's finalized, she'll stay well clear until Saints' Rest starts to look like the house in your wonderful sketches."

"Don't *you* mind it?"

"What?"

"The dirt and chaos of a building site."

"I work down by the stockyards, Mr. Richards. There's no room for ladylike sensibilities down there, I can tell you."

Her eyes smiled at him over the cup as she sipped her tea. Clare Brovik was left-handed, and he saw that there were no rings on her third finger. Her only concession to jewelry was a pair of tiny pearl earrings. She looked too neat and well-groomed to clamber around a building site, but Merlin sensed a toughness beneath the surface gentility. A woman who could survive for five years in the employ of Hobart St. John would need strength of character.

"So who has been taken on to build Saints' Rest?" he asked.

"The Ace Construction Company."

"With whom will I be dealing?"

"Mr. Sarbiewski. The owner. He built a factory for us."

"That's not quite the same thing as working on a project like this. Saints' Rest must be constructed to the highest standards. It will need specialized craftsmen."

"Mr. Sarbiewski knows where to get them."

"When will I be able to meet him?"

"As soon as you wish. I should warn you that he's Polish, and his English is a bit uncertain at times, but he gets things built quickly and properly. I don't think that you'll have any complaints."

"Would it make any difference if I did?"

He threw out the question to test her. The reply was curt.

"No, Mr. Richards. As you know full well."

He bit back a sarcastic rejoinder. Clare Brovik was, as she had reminded him herself, only a messenger. There was no point in striking at her. She was polite, efficient, acting on orders. Alicia Martinez was a more beguiling woman with whom to spend time, but Merlin suspected that he would work more productively with her replacement.

"Shall we start?" asked Clare.

"I'm ready when you are."

"Then why don't we look at your latest revisions?"

"Fine," he said, undoing the ribbon on his portfolio.

"I have to say that I love this," she said, picking up one of the sketches on the table. "It's my favorite."

"And mine. But Mrs. St. John used her veto."

"Most of its features have been retained."

"Not the best ones, unfortunately. Don't you agree?"

"You're the architect."

"I'm glad that someone recognizes that."

"We all do, Mr. Richards."

He took a deep breath. "Miss Brovik."

"Yes?"

"If we're going to be working side by side on this—"

"We are, Mr. Richards."

"Then I'd like to ask you a favor?"

"Well?"

"Call me Merlin. Please."

"If you wish."

"I do," he said. "And I'll call you Clare."

She looked him full in the eye and spoke very firmly.

"Only when we're alone."

"Any special reason?"

"It's the way I want it."

"Then that's the way it will be," he said obligingly. "Brovik. Is that Russian? Czech? German?"

"Norwegian."

"Ah."

"My mother was Irish—from County Clare. My father emigrated from Oslo. They met on American soil. I'm the result."

"Irish and Norwegian, eh? Lethal combination."

"You were going to show me what you've brought."

Merlin took out his drawings, and they got to work.

Clare Brovik was a revelation. She was so well prepared that it was like talking to Alicia St. John herself without any of the posturing and caprice that the latter always inflicted on Merlin. It was all over in less than an hour. Decisions were made, details finalized. Saints' Rest was ratified. Merlin was relieved to be spared another interminable session with his client and heartened that so many of the elements he favored had been retained. The house would not merely be a composite of Alicia's Hollywood fantasies. Saints' Rest would be a house in which the architect could take justifiable pride.

"Well, that just about wraps it up, Merlin," she said.

"It does. In record time."

"Then we can go our separate ways."

"As long as you're satisfied."

"Everything is agreed."

"Thanks to you."

"I'm only acting on orders."

"So what's the drill now?"

"When it's been cleared with Mr. and Mrs. St. John, you'll get the go-ahead from Donald Kruger. He'll ring you at your office tomorrow."

"I'll be waiting, Clare."

She offered her hand again. "It was good to meet you."

"Same here," he said, finding her palm much warmer now.

"Thank you for being so amenable."

He grinned. "I'm famous for it."

She ushered him out of the library, and the butler was waiting to open the front door to bid them farewell. Merlin was sorry to be parting company with her, but Clare Brovik was patently not interested in socializing with him. She climbed into the Stutz, gave him a wave, then drove off without a backward glance. The Model A Ford was facing the house. As he gunned the engine, Merlin looked up at the house and saw a curtain twitch in the master bedroom. A face appeared briefly at the window, then disappeared.

He was fairly certain that it belonged to Alicia St. John.

SALLY FISKE ALIGHTED from the streetcar and walked toward the hotel with a new spring in her step. Though she would be working late that evening, she would be doing so in the knowledge that her days as a hotel clerk might well be numbered. A letter had arrived that morning from her agent in New York, telling her to call him long distance. Only good news would prompt such a request, and Sally willingly bore the expense of the call, getting through at the third attempt and learning that she had, after all, and against stiff competition, secured the commission to work on the illustrated book about wild animals.

Her agent preened himself over the wires and gave her the contractual details. Sally was thrilled. The breakthrough may have come at last.

Unfortunately, there was nobody with whom she could share her triumph. Her father was a fisherman who worked out of Seattle, and her mother, having tired of her husband's long absences, was now living on a farm in Nebraska with a man whom she had met at a prayer meeting and who thought a telephone was the instrument of the devil. Even if she wanted to—and she was not sure that she did—Sally had no means of getting into direct contact with either of her parents. They would have to hear the tidings by letter. There were no friends who would appreciate the importance of her news and no colleagues at the hotel who would feel pleased for her. If anything, the other clerks would be resentful of her talent and envious of her success.

The one person she wanted to tell was Merlin Richards. He would be genuinely delighted for her. Having been unemployed himself, he knew the pain and humiliation of being separated from a profession to which he was dedicated. He was a fellow artist. Merlin would understand. But she could not bring herself to call him at his office. It was too soon. She was not yet ready to forgive and forget.

"Hi, Sal," said a pert voice.

"Hello, Gloria."

"You're early."

"I enjoy this job so much!" said Sally with light sarcasm.

"Don't we all?"

Gloria was a plump girl in her late twenties with a cheerleader brightness and a toothy smile. She looked as if she had been born to work behind the desk in reception. She reached for a slip of paper.

"You had a coupla messages, Sal."

"Did I?"

"You won't like the first one."

"Why not?"

"It was from Mr. McPherson," said Gloria with a grimace. "You know, that creepy guy in 214. Always inviting you up to his room. He asked if you'd be on duty tonight and said he'd stop by to see you."

"Thanks for the warning."

"He's old enough to be your father. Your *grandfather*."

"That doesn't stop them asking. What was the other message?"

"Phone call."

"Who was it from?"

"Didn't give his name. Said you'd know."

"What was the message?"

"Get in touch."

"That all?"

"Yes," said Gloria. "Pity, because he had a lovely voice. Musical. I think he was Welsh or something. Who is he?"

"Nobody you know. Be back in a few minutes."

"Sure."

Sally went across to the public telephone booth on the far side of reception. Stepping inside, she pulled the folding door shut, then rummaged in her purse. Merlin's call somehow cheered her. Though he had been sending the same message in a variety of ways for the past ten days, this was the first time that she felt able to respond to it. She could bask in her good fortune at last. It was early evening, and there was a chance that he might still be at his office. She pulled out her diary and flicked the pages until she found his number. Merlin would be overjoyed to hear from her.

Yet even as she lifted the receiver, she knew that she could not continue. Doubts formed, memories rankled. She recalled the endless wait outside the hotel, the loneliness of the restaurant, the friction with the cabdriver, the needless expense, and the sight of Merlin Richards rising from her doorway. She could still see that foolish smile, still hear those lame excuses, still smell that whiskey on his breath. He did not deserve her. In any case, he was preoccupied with his work on the house in Oak Park. Thanks to the beneficence of a New York publisher, Sally would soon be immersed in her vocation as well.

She put down the receiver with an air of finality.

IT WAS MID-EVENING by the time Merlin reached Oak Park, and there was still enough light for him to inspect the site properly. He was impressed with the choice of location. Saints' Rest would occupy a prime position on Chicago Avenue, and he was surprised that such a coveted plot of land was available for purchase. An earlier dwelling had apparently been built there, but there were no vestiges of it now, and Merlin had no idea why it had been demolished. All he could think about was the residence that would take its place, a sixteen-room house that would blend with the buildings around it yet unassailably overshadow them.

Having parked his car, Merlin stood on the sidewalk in front of the site and visualized the completed building. He felt inspired. He walked up what would be a drive, then followed the imaginary curve to the front entrance. Letting himself into the hall, he went from room to room, admiring each in turn and congratulating himself on the positioning of his windows. When the tour of the first floor was over, he was about to go upstairs to inspect the bedrooms, but a piping voice brought him back to reality.

"What are you doing, mister?" said the boy.

"Eh?"

"You were talking to yourself."

"Was I?" said Merlin.

"I heard you."

"Sorry."

The boy was no more than eleven or twelve, a fresh-faced kid with freckles and a brace on his teeth. His ginger hair was short and spiky.

"Dad does that sometimes," he confided.

"Does what?" asked Merlin.

"Talks to himself. Know when?"

"When?"

"He's had too many beers. Of course, he's not supposed to drink, I know, with Prohibition and that, but nothing stops Dad. If it's not beer, it's gin. Mom drinks that with him. He's a dentist."

"I see."

"Have you been drinking gin?"

"Afraid not."

"So why were you talking to yourself?"

"I didn't realize that I was," said Merlin, amused by the boy's wide-eyed curiosity. "I was looking around the site, that's all."

"Are you going to live here? We heard someone was."

"No, I'm not going to live here."

"Our house is on Euclid Avenue. I walk past here every day."

"Then you'll see them building on this site."

"Is that what you are, mister? One of the builders?"

"Not exactly," said Merlin with a touch of pride. "I'm the architect. I designed the house. I was just taking a look around it."

"But it's not there yet."

"It is in my mind."

"That's weird!" said the boy.

He gave a sudden jerk as if he had just remembered something.

"Do you know who *is* going to live here?"

"Yes. My clients."

"Who are they?"

"Mr. and Mrs. Hobart St. John."

"Where are they from?"

"Lake Shore Drive in Chicago."

"Mr. and Mrs. Hobart John."

"*Saint*," corrected Merlin. "St. John."

"Thanks, mister."

"What's your father's name? They may need a good dentist."

But the boy did not even hear him. He left abruptly and raced off, vanishing around the corner onto Grove Avenue. Merlin shrugged, then resumed his tour of the invisible building. His clients had an inquisitive young neighbor, but the kid seemed harmless enough.

The boy came to a halt beside the first tree in the avenue. A short, thin, swarthy man with a pencil mustache stepped out from the shadow of the tree and made sure that his informer was not being followed.

"Well?" he said.

"Give me the money first."

"No name, no dough."

"Come on, mister. You promised."

"Who was that guy?"

"He's crazy. Talks to himself."

"What's he doing there?"

"Said he's an architect."

The man's interest quickened. "Is he designing a house?"

"Yes."

"Who for?"

"Let me see the money."

"Who for?" pressed the other with a mixture of entreaty and menace. "Did you ask him?"

"I did exactly what you told me to, mister."

"And?"

But the boy's nerve was failing him. The kind man who offered him money in exchange for a simple errand was now glaring at him through narrowed lids. He began to wonder why the nattily dressed stranger did not make the inquiry himself.

"And?" repeated the man. The boy noticed for the first time the livid scar on his neck. "What did that architect say?"

"The house is for someone from Chicago," gabbled the boy.

A dollar was dangled in front of him. "I need a name."

"Mr. and Mrs. Hobart John. No, wait. *Saint*. Hobart St. John."

"Are you sure that was the name you heard?"

"I swear it."

"Hobart St. John?"

"Yes—from Lake Shore Drive in Chicago."

The man's face glowed with pleasure. He handed the money over.

"Take it, kid," he said expansively. "You earned it!"

6

"That's what I like to see, guys," said Gus Westlake. "A hive of industry."

His braying laugh filled the outer office. All in shirtsleeves, Reed Cutler, Victor Goldblatt, and Merlin Richards were bent over their work, each lost in his individual project. There was a sense of quiet dedication.

"Good morning, Gus," said Merlin without looking up.

"Good *afternoon*, you mean," said Goldblatt pointedly.

"Hi, Gus," mumbled Cutler.

"Stay at it, fellas," urged Gus. "That's what keeps Westlake and Davisson afloat in this sea of shit. Combination of hard work and genius. You provide the hard work, I come through with the genius."

"We noticed," said Goldblatt dryly.

"Nice to be appreciated by my staff."

"Like us to take up a collection for you, Gus?" joked Cutler.

"Terrific idea!"

The braying laugh was louder than ever. Gus Westlake favored a white suit and a straw hat on this morning. An unlit cigar was held between his teeth, but it caused no impediment to his speech or his mirth. He went from one drafting table to another, looking over the shoulder of each of them and making approving comments. He was especially flattering about Goldblatt's work.

"That's great, Vic!"

"How would you know?" said the other.

"I haven't forgotten everything about architecture," said Westlake airily. "Believe it or not, I still pick up a pencil myself from time to time. Seriously, Vic. That's swell. The client will be delighted."

Goldblatt was cynical. "Isn't that what it's all about?"

"What do you mean?"

"Delighting the client. Kowtowing to the guy with the dough. No room for artistic inspiration anymore. No freedom to express yourself. A client chooses the kind of box he wants, we just draw the lines."

"There's more to it than that," argued Cutler.

"A lot more," agreed Westlake, "and you know it."

"Come off it," said Goldblatt tartly. "We're not architects anymore. We're robots. The client presses a button, we click into action. Look at the design for Saints' Rest," he continued, indicating the first-floor plan on Merlin's drawing board. "How much of that can you describe as the brainchild of an architect who's been given a completely free hand?"

"A fair bit of it," defended Merlin.

Goldblatt hunched his shoulders. "Who are you kidding? I've watched you chop and change and sacrifice most of your best ideas. Saints' Rest will be one percent Merlin Richards and ninety-nine percent Alicia Martinez. What's that going to do for the reputation of Westlake and Davisson?"

"To hell with reputation!" said Westlake. "It will keep this practice in business. That's the name of the game these days. Survival."

"I call it architectural surrender."

"Call it what you like, Vic. It feeds your family."

"Just about."

"Oak Park is going to have a palatial new home built out there. And the architect of record will be Merlin Richards."

"Not from where I'm standing."

"Look," said Westlake, shedding his customary bonhomie, "I don't have time to discuss the relationship between artistic integrity and the state of the nation, but it's there for all to see. When work is scarce, you can't afford to be high-minded. You take what you can get, or you go to the wall. Okay, Vic?"

"Yeah," said the other wearily.

"Talk it over with Bill Marion. Or George Wybrand. Or any of the other poor guys who fell by the wayside."

"I get the message."

"Remember it. And stop rocking the boat."

Westlake distributed a smile among all three of them before going into the inner office. Merlin was stung by Goldblatt's comment but did his best not to let it show. Reed Cutler acted as the peacemaker.

"What's got into you, Victor?" he asked.

"I had an attack of honesty."

"It sounded like stupidity to me."

"I'm entitled to my opinion, Reed."

"Not when it stinks the place out. Sure," he said reasonably, "it's tough. We know that. We're all in this together. But it doesn't help if you piss over a colleague's work. I'd say you owe Merl an apology."

"There was nothing personal in my remarks."

"Oh, yes, there was."

"Forget it, Reed," suggested Merlin.

"Victor needs to say that he's sorry."

"But he isn't."

"I said nothing to be sorry for," insisted Goldblatt.

"We've got to have mutual respect around here," said Cutler.

Merlin tensed. "How can I respect asshole remarks like Victor's?"

"I was only telling the truth," said Goldblatt.

"Your *version* of the truth," corrected Cutler gently, "and where has it got us? You upset Gus, insulted Merlin, and created a nasty smell around here. We can do without that kind of truth, Victor. I think that Merlin's done a terrific job on Saints' Rest and—whatever you say—it's got his signature all over it. Now, how about that apology?"

There was a taut silence. It was broken by Gus Westlake.

"Hey, Merl," he said, putting his head around the door, "can you come in here for a minute, please?"

"Of course."

Glad to escape, Merlin went into the inner office and closed the door after him. Wearing an eyeshade, Brad Davisson was perched on a stool at his drafting table. Westlake put an arm around the newcomer and conducted him to a seat.

"What are you doing on Saturday night, Merl?"

"Nothing in particular."

"You are now," said Westlake, resting against the edge of the desk. "Invitation from on high. You're going to a party on Lake Shore Drive."

"Since when?"

"Since Hobart St. John called me. I'll be going, so will Brad. But Hobart was very keen to include you in the invitation." His eyebrows rose meaningfully. "It's not one you ought to refuse, Merl."

"No, no," said Merlin. "I'll be there. Thanks."

"I didn't want to tell you out there in front of the others," explained Westlake. "Not with Victor Goldblatt in that mood."

"How are you getting along with him now?" asked Davisson.

"Much better over the last few days."

"Good."

"He's been almost friendly toward me."

"Until today," noted Westlake.

"Oh, I'm not going to pay any attention to that, Gus," said Merlin with a dismissive gesture. "Water off a duck's back. I feel sorry for Victor. He's worried sick at the moment. Reed told me. Wife in hospital, kids playing up, legal wrangle over a boundary line with his neighbor. That kind of thing would fray anybody's nerves."

Davisson scowled. "Victor's nerves are always frayed."

"He'll be fine when he starts work on the Niedlander office block," said Merlin. "He's talked about nothing else. It's given him a real boost to his confidence. When he's up to his eyes in that, he won't have time to make waves for the rest of us."

Westlake traded a rueful glance with his partner.

"I'm afraid that he will," he said. "Tidal waves, probably."

"Why, Gus?"

"The deal fell through, Merl. I had a call from Jerry Niedlander last night. He's decided to engage another firm of architects. So much for promises! Westlake and Davisson are out."

Merlin's head turned involuntarily toward the outer office.

"Don't breathe a word of this to Vic," warned Davisson. "He doesn't need to know about it just yet. Let him go on dreaming dreams. We have to break the bad news at the right time."

"Until then," said Westlake, recovering his grin, "we keep him in a state of blissful ignorance. Anyway, forget Victor Goldblatt. Think Hobart St. John. Put that date in your diary, Merl.

Eight o'clock on Saturday. Lake Shore Drive. It's party time!"

Merlin was curious. "Any chance that Clare Brovik will be there?"

"They'll all be there. Including Donald Kruger. He's very keen to meet you, Merl. Important guy. He'll be riding shotgun on Saints' Rest. So you be especially nice to Donald Kruger."

"What sort of a man is he?"

Westlake chuckled. "I think you'll figure that out for yourself."

HOBART ST. JOHN finished dictating the letter to his secretary, then asked her to read it back to him, standing close behind her while she did so and admiring the view down the front of her blouse. He was making a few alterations to the letter when, after a tap on the door, it opened to admit Donald Kruger. St. John's manner changed at once.

"That's all for now, Jane," he said brusquely.

"Shall I type out the letter, Mr. St. John?" she asked.

"Just leave us alone, will you?"

The girl folded her pad, rose from the chair, and gave the newcomer a submissive smile before going out and closing the door behind her. Hobart St. John sat down heavily in the chair behind his desk and subjected his visitor to a long and disapproving stare. Kruger waited calmly for the expected rebuke.

"What the fuck is going on, Donald?"

"I don't know, Mr. St. John."

"But I *pay* you to know."

"I set everything up. It went like clockwork."

"Until now."

"Let me speak to him," suggested Kruger.

"Well, *I* certainly don't want to hear that voice again," said

St. John grimly. "I shouldn't have heard it at all, Donald. It was supposed to be nothing to do with me. How did he get hold of my name? I pick up the telephone, I want to do business with an associate or talk with a friend. I do not want to have that kind of poison poured into my ear."

"I'm sorry, Mr. St. John."

"So you should be."

"It won't happen again."

"It mustn't happen again, Donald."

"What exactly did you say to him?"

"Nothing. I acted dumb. What else could I do?"

"Do you think he bought it?"

"No. He sounded too smart for that."

"I'll talk to him at once, Mr. St. John."

"You do that. Or I may start to lose my temper." He looked down at the framed photograph of his wife. "There's a lot riding on this, Donald. I gave my word to Alicia. Nothing must be allowed to get in the way. This is to be a dream house for both of us, and someone is trying to turn it into a nightmare. Do something about it."

"Right away."

"Clean up your mess."

"Yes, Mr. St. John."

Donald Kruger winced inwardly. He was so accustomed to getting praise from his employer that the biting criticism hurt far more than it might have done. Kruger rarely made mistakes, least of all when it came to delegation. He was a shrewd judge of character and knew how to choose the right person for a particular assignment. That is what he assumed he had done in this case, but there were repercussions. They needed to be dealt with promptly and ruthlessly.

"No other problems, I hope?" said St. John quietly.

"None."

"Everything is in hand?"

"They're laying the foundations today. Right on schedule."

"Have you spoken to Sarbiewski?"

"A couple of times. He understands the position."

"I'm glad that someone does."

He let the reproof hang in the air while he sifted through some papers on his desk. Kruger was kept waiting deliberately. St. John pretended to read through a letter.

"Donald."

"Yes, Mr. St. John?"

"You're coming out to the house on Saturday, I believe."

"I hope so."

"Let's make sure we have something to celebrate at the party."

"I will."

When he looked up, Hobart St. John's eyes were blazing.

"Bring me good news."

MERLIN RICHARDS ACCEPTED that he had to apply some of his design skills to himself for a change. He would be on public display at the party, and Gus Westlake had warned him that many influential people would be there. It was a roundabout way of telling him to have a haircut and put on his best suit. Merlin did both, even buying a new shirt and tie for the occasion, but the end result still fell well short of conventional smartness. There was something about his physique that defied the most cunning tailor. Instead of being long and unruly, his hair was now short and willful. Improvement was marginal.

Gus Westlake and Brad Davisson would be taking their wives to the party, and it was made clear to Merlin that his invitation also included a partner of his choice. Unfortunately, he no longer seemed to be the partner of *her* choice, so he did not even bother to contact Sally Fiske, fearing yet another rejection and uncertain, in any case, whether he wanted to be seen with a girlfriend in tow. Though he had met her only once, he was intrigued to see Clare Brovik again, and he could hardly get to know her better if he had Sally on his arm. He opted to head to Lake Shore Drive on his own.

Judging from the noise coming from the house and the number of vehicles parked outside it, the party was in full swing by the time he arrived. Merlin parked the Ford between a Minerva landaulet and an SSK Mercedes-Benz. He could hear dance music being played by a small band. The front door was open, and the butler was on duty to welcome and announce him. Guests thronged the hall, their champagne glasses topped up by cruising waiters. The great and the good of Chicago were breaking the law with cheerful abandon.

Hobart St. John came out of the mass of bodies to pump his arm.

"Hi, Merl. Welcome to the party!"

"Thank you for asking me."

"Alicia is around somewhere. Now, who else do you know?"

"Gus Westlake," said Merlin, catching sight of him in the middle of the crowd. "And Brad Davisson, of course."

"Forget them," said St. John with mock contempt. "Hell, you don't come to a party to talk to your bosses. You're here to enjoy yourself. Come on. I'll introduce you to some of the folk here."

"Oh, right."

"We might even find an unattached lady or two."

"Let's go," said Merlin with a grin.

Someone thrust a glass into his hand, and he took a first sip of champagne. It removed the last traces of his shyness. Leading him by the arm, his host wended his way across the hall, performing introductions, allowing Merlin to exchange handshakes and niceties, then whisking him off to the next guest. The Welshman was confronted with so many names and faces in such a short time that he was quite bewildered. He was grateful when he finally encountered someone familiar.

Alicia St. John had regressed to her days on the movie lot. Attired in a long, body-hugging black dress with a tasseled hem, she stood on the steps that led up into the living room and performed in front of an adoring audience. Poses and gestures that would have been dramatic on a large screen seemed absurd and exaggerated in a domestic setting, but Merlin was the only person who dared to notice. When she saw him emerging from the crowd, she used his appearance as an excuse to play yet another little scene.

"Darling!" she said, swooping on him to bestow a kiss on his cheek.

"Hello, Mrs. St. John!"

"This is Merlin the Magician," she announced.

"Your favorite architect, honey," said her husband.

"Go away, Hobart," she ordered, taking Merlin by the hand. "He's all mine now. You circulate. It will help your blood pressure."

"I got a gorgeous wife to do that for me!"

He collected a giggle from the people surrounding her, then went off to greet the latest newcomers. Still holding Merlin's hand, she introduced him to her cronies. Her praise was so fulsome that he had to take another sip of champagne to prevent himself from blushing. She then began to describe Saints' Rest to her assembled fans, highlighting her own contribution to the design and calling upon Merlin to add his comments. He was duly succinct, recognizing an actress's need to hold center stage and monopolize the dialogue.

Gus Westlake eventually came to his rescue, detaching him from the group and leading him into the living room. Older guests had already migrated there to find somewhere to sit and to escape the blaring music. Resplendent in a tuxedo, Westlake looked completely at home.

"Well, Merl," he said, "now you know how the other half lives."

"A lot better than I do."

"Your time will come."

"That's what I keep telling myself."

"The cream of Chicago society is here tonight. You have to be able to mix with them. Brad has never managed that."

"Why not?"

"Heaven knows. Stick him in a tux, and he loses his voice."

"I caught a glimpse of him earlier. He looks very ill at ease."

"Terrified, Merl. He only agreed to come because he's got his wife to hold his hand. Eleanor blossoms at a party, Brad shrivels up. Now you know why I didn't want *him* to take on this commission."

"Saints' Rest?"

"He should have had first refusal. Way ahead of Victor."

"So why didn't he get it?"

"Her name is Alicia Martinez." He nudged Merlin's elbow. "Can you imagine Brad Davisson trying to cope with a woman like that? When she batted those eyelids at him, he'd break out in a cold sweat. Alicia would put the fear of death in him. Whereas you charmed the pants off her."

"I'm not so sure about that."

"I am. That's why I chose you. Instead of Brad. Instead of Victor."

"What about Reed Cutler?"

"He was never in the running. Ah!" he said, pointing through the window. "Looks as if Donald Kruger is arriving."

Merlin looked out to see a tall, elegant figure in a white tuxedo, getting out of his Packard and coming around to open the passenger door so that his companion could get out. Offering his hand, Kruger helped her out, said something that made her laugh, then kissed her on the cheek. They strolled side by side toward the house. Merlin felt a strange surge of jealousy. He had been hoping that Clare Brovik would be there alone.

A waiter refilled their glasses, and Westlake sipped happily. "How many houses as big as this back in Merthyr Tydfil?"

"Dozens!" lied Merlin with a grin.

"What would you be doing if you were back there now?"

"Downing a pint of beer at the Rugby Club."

"I'd forgotten you played that violent game."

"Rugby's not violent, Gus. It's very civilized beneath the surface."

"The opposite to architecture, then?"

"Opposite?"

"Yes, Merl," said the other. "We're civilized on the surface, but we fight each other tooth and claw in reality." Two elderly men drifted past them, and Westlake's eye kindled. "I sniff a possible client. Excuse me while I go and work my wonders."

Happy to be left alone, Merlin went back into the hall in search of Clare Brovik, but there was no sign of her. Her chauffeur, however, was very much in evidence, descending on the Welshman at once and giving him a firm handshake.

"Mr. Richards?" he said. "I'm Donald Kruger."

"Glad to meet you at last."

"Are you enjoying the party?"

"Very much. What will happen to this place when they move?"

"Move?"

"Mr. and Mrs. St. John are going to live in Oak Park."

"Yes," said Kruger easily, "but they won't sell this house. They'll keep it on. Mr. St. John plans to run his business from here in time."

"Oh, I see. So they'll have two houses?"

"Three altogether."

"Three?"

"They have a holiday home in Key West as well."

"I must be in the wrong business," said Merlin cheerfully. "All that I can afford is a two-room apartment."

"I know."

"It's reassuring to hear that someone is making money."

"We survive."

Merlin was slightly disconcerted by Kruger without quite knowing why. He was excessively polite, but there was also something faintly intimidating about him. He had a penetrating gaze and an aura of unforced authority. Merlin observed the complacence in his reply.

We survive.

Donald Kruger sounded like part of the family.

"Anything you need," offered Kruger, "come straight to me."

"I will."

"You've met Mr. Sarbiewski, I hear?"

"We had a long chat out on the site."

"He's a good man."

"Yes," agreed Merlin. "He seemed to know his stuff. I was sorry to lose O'Brien, but it looks as if the Ace Construction Company will be an able deputy."

"It will, Mr. Richards. I'll make certain of that."

"How have you managed to move things along so swiftly?

Don't you have any building regulations?"

"Dozens of them. But there are always shortcuts."

"Who finds them?"

"I do."

Kruger gave a thin smile and sipped his drink. Merlin saw that it was orange juice. Hobart St. John bore down on them, gave Kruger a backslapping welcome, then eased him off into a corner. The two men grew serious, and Merlin could see the suppressed anger in his host's face. Leaning forward to whisper in his ear, Kruger drew a series of nods out of him. St. John was reassured. He beamed again, patted his employee on the shoulder in gratitude, then melted into the crowd.

Merlin managed a brief conversation with Brad Davisson and his wife before the double doors of the dining room were opened to reveal a sumptuous buffet. Guests immediately began to stream in. Davisson's hunger got the better of his embarrassment, and he joined the queue. As the hall slowly emptied, Merlin hung back and enjoyed simply watching and listening to the others. There was something endlessly fascinating about the tribal habits of the rich. The band continued to play.

When almost everyone had disappeared, he decided to follow them, but a tap on the shoulder halted him. He turned to see the smiling face of Clare Brovik. Dressed in a turquoise dress and with her hair down, she looked much more striking than at their first meeting.

"Hi there," she said.

"Hello," he replied, pleased to see her at last. "I was wondering where you disappeared to."

"Mr. St. John and I had business to discuss."

"At a party?"

"He's never off duty."

"What about you?"

"I do sign off from time to time."

"Good."

"Have you met Donald yet?"

"Yes," said Merlin. "He made a point of introducing himself."

"He hates these occasions."

"Really? He seemed so relaxed."

"He is. But then, Donald would be relaxed anywhere. He's urbane, intelligent, and attentive to women in the right way. But he's a very private man, really. He avoids crowds."

"Then he came to the wrong place. This is worse than Soldier Field." The hall was almost empty. "Shall we go into the dining room?"

"Not yet."

"We don't want to miss our share of the food."

"There's more than enough for all of us, believe me. I should know."

"Why?"

"I engaged the caterers. And the band."

"They're good," noted Merlin. "Top-notch."

"Does this music make you want to dance?"

"It does, actually."

"Me, too."

Clare Brovik put her purse on a nearby table. Slipping an arm around his waist, she held his other hand in a gentle grip. Her warm smile swept away all resistance.

"So what are we waiting for, Mr. Richards?" she asked.

The party finally began to break up around midnight. After expressing their thanks to their hosts in a series of hugs and handshakes, guests drove off contentedly in their automobiles. The band departed, but someone started playing Chopin nocturnes on a distant piano. Brad Davisson was among the first to leave, seizing the opportunity to end long hours of discomfort in a house full of strangers whose language he could never quite master and whose easy sophistication unnerved him. Gus Westlake, by contrast, lingered to the very end, working on new contacts with practiced guile and cementing old friendships with equal diligence. He was in his element. Merlin Richards found it an education to watch him in action.

"How on earth do you do it, Gus?"

"Do what?"

"Keep going all night. You never seem to flag."

"Someone has to advance the cause of Westlake and Davisson."

"I thought I was doing that."

"You are, Merl. Simply by being here. Hobart was pleased."

"It was kind of him to invite me."

"Let you into a secret," said Westlake. "He didn't. Alicia did."

"Oh."

"I was on his list, you were on hers."

"How do you know?"

"Ask her if you don't believe me."

Merlin glanced across at their hostess, who had slipped back into her role as Alicia St. John as she stood beside her husband to wave off another batch of guests. With the aid of her hairdresser, beautician, and designer dress, she had outshone every other woman at the party, and she was still an arresting sight, her laughter tinkling, her vivacity undimmed. Compared with her, even Clare Brovik seemed a little dowdy.

"Remarkable lady!" commented Westlake.

"I agree with you there, Gus."

"But not the kind you marry."

"Why not?"

"She's high maintenance. That can be wearing."

"They seem happy enough together."

"Take another look in eighteen months. Different story then."

"Alicia told me that the new house would bring them together."

"It will. When her husband wants to get laid."

The two men were reclining on a sofa in the living room. Merlin drained his glass of water and rose to leave. Having drunk too much whiskey on his first visit to the house, he had been careful to control his intake of alcohol at the party. The problem was that the occasion itself had been intoxicating, and it left him feeling light-headed. His dance with Clare Brovik was the undoubted high spot, and he was disappointed that he never had any time alone with her after that. After bidding his farewells, he looked around the hall for Clare, but she was no longer there. Merlin felt vaguely cheated. A mazurka had replaced the nocturnes, but he did not hear it. He left the house and trudged toward his car. His gait was unsteady in the cool night air. Footsteps pursued him.

"Wait!" called Clare. "I haven't said good-bye yet."

Merlin halted. "I couldn't find you," he said, turning to face her. "Where have you been?"

"In the powder room with some of the stragglers."

"Girl talk, eh?"

"Afraid so."

"Men never go in for that kind of thing."

"Everyone likes gossip."

"They prefer nudges and innuendoes. Some men, anyway."

"But not you, I take it?"

"No, Clare."

"Why not?"

"Because I value privacy."

"You mean that you're afraid to show your feelings."

"Not afraid. Just selective in my choice of audience."

She smiled. "Thank you for the dance."

"I ought to be thanking you, Clare. It was your idea."

"Why waste a good band like that? You're very light on your feet, I must say. Is it true that you go out running every morning?"

"Who told you that?"

"It was the talk of the powder room."

"Pull the other one!"

"Is it true?"

"As a matter of fact, it is," he admitted. "Every morning I run at least three miles. But it does no good. They always catch me and bring me back." She laughed. "I've never heard you laugh before."

"It's something I do at parties."

"What else do you do?"

Their eyes locked for a few moments, and he had to resist the temptation to reach out for her, knowing that it would be a serious mistake. Clare Brovik looked entrancing in the moonlight, but there was an invisible barrier between them, and she was making no effort to move it. She was safer on the other side. And she already had an escort.

"Did you know that he was coming to Chicago?" she said.

"Who?"

"Frank Lloyd Wright. He's giving a lecture at the university."

"Yes. He wrote to tell me about it."

"Will you be going yourself?"

"Wild horses wouldn't keep me away."

She looked wistful. "Will you tell me about him one day?"

"Frank Lloyd Wright?"

"When we're in Oak Park together. Show me his work. I feel terribly ignorant about architecture. But I do know that he was one of the best in the business."

"Was and still is, Clare."

"I thought he'd retired."

"Men like that never retire. He's ageless. So is his work."

"Will you explain why someday?"

"With pleasure."

"Next Saturday, perhaps?"

"It's a date."

"Not in that sense," she clarified. "I'm interested, that's all."

Her curiosity was serious, and he found it rather touching. Clare Brovik had such an air of control that he never expected her to admit to any deficiencies. Merlin had a sudden urge to drive her out to Oak Park at once, notwithstanding the late hour and the darkness. But someone else was taking care of her travel arrangements.

"There you are!" said Donald Kruger, coming out of the house.

"I was waiting for you," she explained.

"I thought you'd already left," said Merlin. "Where were you?"

"Playing the piano."

Clare nodded. "Donald has a thing about Chopin."

Merlin was impressed. Donald Kruger did not strike him as a musician. The nocturnes had been played with precision and feeling.

"We must be on our way," decided Kruger.

With a nod to Merlin, he escorted Clare to his car and opened the passenger door for her with studied gallantry. Merlin watched until the Packard shot away. Then he drove back to his apartment. Very slowly.

HOBART ST. JOHN'S stamina never waned. When the last of his guests had been dispatched, he was still pulsing with energy. He summoned the servants to clear everything away, then went off upstairs. The party had been Alicia's idea, and she was gratified by his willingness to hold it. By the terms of their tacit contract, an obliging husband could now claim his reward. His wife had not forgotten. Her shoes had been left on the staircase, her dress discarded on the landing. Underclothing lay just inside the master bedroom, and jewelry was scattered on the bed itself.

The sound of running water took him across to the bathroom, from which steam was already beginning to issue. Alicia was inside, stark naked, bending invitingly over the water to test its temperature with long, sensuous fingers, pretending to be unaware of his presence behind her, holding her pose so that he could take maximum pleasure from the curve of her haunches and the glimpse of pubic hair between her thighs.

Her husband was on fire. Peeling off his tuxedo, he tugged at his bow tie until it hung loose, then worked at the studs in his shirtfront. His eyes never left his wife as she climbed slowly into the circular bath and beckoned him after her. He was scrambling out of his trousers when the telephone rang in the bedroom.

"Shit!" he exclaimed.

"Let it ring, sweetie."

"It will put me off."

"Ignore it."

"I can't."

"Let someone else answer."

"There's no extension on this line."

"Get rid of them. Quick. I'll wait."

"What a time to ring!"

One leg still in his trousers, Hobart St. John hopped into the bedroom and snatched up the receiver angrily from the bedside table.

"Who the hell is this?" he demanded.

"We spoke once before," said a man's voice.

"You!"

"I have a warning to give, Mr. St. John."

"This is my home, goddammit!"

"Listen carefully."

He was puce with rage. "Who gave you this number?"

"You were very stupid," said the voice. "Threatening me like that. The price has doubled. If that prick tries to scare me off again, it will go up even higher. Good night, Mr. St. John."

"Jesus fucking Christ!"

"Sweet dreams."

The line went dead.

THE ACE CONSTRUCTION Company had a reputation for honoring its commitments. Instructed to work fast, it obeyed the command to the letter and transformed the site in Oak Park in record time. When the new foundations had been laid and the wine cellar dug out, the bricklayers turned their attention to the exterior walls. Plumbers installed their pipe runs beneath the floor joists. Stonemasons were already working on the marble pillars for the portico. Carpenters, joiners, plasterers, decorators, glaziers, and roofers were poised to make their contribution. Electricians were studying the plans to decide on the elaborate wiring system. Deafening machines were helping to landscape the garden. Materials were delivered in bulk, stored on-site, and protected behind a high perimeter fence topped with barbed wire. The tranquillity of Chicago Avenue was shattered by the noise, but neighbors could only speculate on what was actually happening behind the fence.

Jan Sarbiewski, the taciturn owner of the company, was a giant of a man with fists as big as hams and a face as large and inscrutable as a watermelon. Thirty years in the trade had acquainted him with all its shortcomings, and he knew how to circumvent them. Since he had been enjoined to keep the building of the house under close supervision, he came to Oak Park every day, assessed progress, issued advice, admonished any hint of inferior workmanship, and when the mood took him, stripped off his coat and labored alongside his men for an hour or two. A large house for a wealthy client was a coveted commission at a time when the construction industry was being decimated. Sarbiewski was grateful. He wanted a personal stake in the construction of Saints' Rest.

Merlin Richards found Sarbiewski uncommunicative at first, but he gradually coaxed complete sentences out of the laconic Pole, and a business association soon developed into a kind of friendship. The house was an unqualified bonus for Merlin. Not only did it give him the chance to design a residence in a suburb made famous by Frank Lloyd Wright, it gave him a reason to leave the office on a regular basis and escape the sniping of Victor Goldblatt. Still under the illusion that he was going to design the Niedlander office block, his colleague was tolerably unpleasant. What would happen when the truth leaked out, Merlin did not know, but he promised himself that he would be carrying out a site inspection when it happened. Even from the safety of Oak Park, he suspected, he might hear Goldblatt's anguished protests.

Greater freedom conspired with his increased mobility to give him a sense of power. He felt good about himself and happy in his work. There was only one dimension missing in his life. Merlin decided to make a last effort to regain it. Where phone calls and flowers had failed, a Model A Ford might yet succeed. He was parked outside the hotel when Sally Fiske arrived for work that evening. Merlin tooted the horn.

"Hello, Sally," he called.

She was startled. "Merlin? What are you doing here?"

"Hoping to have a word with you."

"We've got nothing to say to each other."

"Like the car?"

She hesitated. "Is it yours?"

"No," he teased. "I stole it. Fancy a ride?"

"I'm just going to work."

"I don't mean now. Later on, perhaps."

"No, thanks."

"Tomorrow, then?"
"No."
"That takes us on to next week."
"I won't be here."
"Why not?"
"I've quit my job. Finish tomorrow."
"Does that mean you landed that commission?" He saw the half-smile. "Sally, that's fantastic news! Well done! I knew you'd get a break sooner or later. Illustrating a book for a New York publisher! It's no more than you deserve."
"I have to go. I'll be late."
"It has to be tomorrow, then."
"No, Merlin."
"Last day as a hotel clerk. We can celebrate your escape."
"No! We're through."
"Let's talk it over."
"Leave me alone, will you?"
"Can't I at least give you a lift home?"
"Good-bye, Merlin."
"I'll be waiting out here tomorrow. Just in case."
"Waste of time," she said, going up the stairs.
"There's no charge."
"It's over. Period."
"See you tomorrow, Sally."

She went in through the revolving door without another word. He waited hopefully for her to reappear and announce his reprieve, but she stayed resolutely out of sight. Merlin was saddened at first, but, after reviewing their brief meeting, he eventually came around to a much more optimistic view of it.

"At least she talked to me!" he said. "That's progress."

Then he tooted the horn again and drove off.

⋯

CLARE BROVIK BELIEVED in giving clear signals. When Merlin picked her up outside her apartment on Kinzie Street, her hair was swept up into a bun, her dark green suit decidedly sober, and her manner businesslike. She was not the kind of woman who would be found at a party, still less one who would actually invite a man to dance with her. Evidently there were two Clare Broviks. Even on a Saturday afternoon, the version who accompanied him to Oak Park was manifestly on duty. It simplified their relationship.

Her interest was genuine and her patience inexhaustible. She wanted to see everything. She was especially struck with the Arthur Heurtley house; she rhapsodized over Frank Lloyd Wright's former home and studio; and she gazed long and hard at the Edwin Cheney house, ignoring the scandal of the architect's elopement with his client's wife and commenting instead on its use of glass and overhangs. Clare was surprised that its front door was such a minor feature that it took her a while to locate it. Merlin Richards conducted her with pride from building to building, indicating its salient features and tossing in an anecdote each time about his hero.

"Now I know what a Prairie House really is," she said.

"Of course," he reminded her, "Oak Park was much smaller then. More open. When he moved here in 1889, the population was only four thousand. Now it's well over sixty thousand."

"Mr. Wright probably wouldn't recognize it now."

"It's certainly changed since his day. He told me that he owned one of only three cars in the whole town. A Stoddard Dayton sports car. They used to call it the Yellow Devil because he drove it so fast. The speed limit in Chicago was twenty-five miles an hour, so Mr. Wright collected a regular supply of tickets for speeding." Merlin smiled nostalgically. "He's always loved fast cars. When I first met him in Arizona, he was driving this Packard straight eight touring car."

"Donald likes Packards."

"So I noticed."

The tour was concluded with a visit to Unity Temple, which occupied an unpromising corner site on busy Lake Street. Constructed of poured concrete for reasons of economy, the building had a powerful simplicity. Its entrance was cleverly screened from the road, and once inside, Clare was amazed how the noise of traffic faded away. Unity Temple was a haven of calm in the Saturday pandemonium. After securing permission from the janitor, Merlin guided her around the building and answered her questions with knowledgeable eagerness. They sat in the back row of the balcony and looked down at the pulpit.

"It's so quiet in here," said Clare.

"An atmosphere conducive to prayer."

"And so intimate."

"That was the intention. Wherever you sit, you feel close to the pulpit. Involved in the service. Not like the Methodist chapel I once designed. That was a long, narrow building. Latecomers had to sit right at the back, well away from the action. Here the congregation is on three sides. So much better. It bonds them."

"How many people does it hold?"

"Four hundred."

"It's the quality of light that fascinates me."

"Those glass panels create a canopy of colored light for the entire room. Do you see?" he asked, pointing upward. "Each panel is recessed in the crossed ceiling structure and composed of four glass modules, set at different angles. Frank Lloyd Wright was years ahead of his time. And such attention to detail!"

"You're pretty hot on detail yourself."

"Only because he taught me, Clare."

"There are touches of Frank Lloyd Wright in Saints' Rest."

"He's usually there somewhere in anything I design."

There was a long silence. They sat there side by side and looked around the temple again, admiring its subtleties and luxuriating in its serenity. It was twenty minutes before Clare came out of her trance.

"I could stay here all day," she said.

"They'd kick us out."

"Maybe we should push off, in any case. I've taken up far too much of your time as it is."

"Not at all, Clare. It's been a labor of love."

"I gathered that."

"Thanks for suggesting it."

"I have another suggestion."

"What's that?"

"Dinner," she said. "I insist on treating you by way of gratitude."

"There's no need to do that."

"It's the least I can do. You've just given me a crash course in American architecture. How many other students have a personal tutor like Merlin Richards?"

"Is that what you are—a student?"

"For today, at any rate."

Merlin needed little persuasion. It was early evening, and there was no danger that he would be delayed in Oak Park again and forced to miss a rendezvous with Sally Fiske. She would not finish at the hotel until midnight, and he was determined to be waiting outside for her in his car, even though she had refused his offer of a lift. Dinner with Clare Brovik was an enticing preliminary.

They found a restaurant within easy walking distance on Oak

Park Avenue and ordered from an alluring menu. After hours spent in his company, Clare was still on a business footing with Merlin, unfailingly pleasant but slightly detached. He tried to break through the formality.

"Do you live alone?" he asked.

"Why do you ask that?"

"Idle curiosity."

"I don't see that it's any of your business."

"Is it a state secret?"

"No. Just a personal matter."

"I see."

"You're a great believer in privacy," she said. "So am I."

"Fair enough. Let's drop the subject." He cast one more line in the water. "I just wondered if you shared an apartment with Donald Kruger, that's all."

"No, I don't."

"But I assumed—"

"Quite wrongly. That's all I'm prepared to say."

"Didn't mean to pry."

"Eat your soup."

They retreated to neutral topics for the bulk of the meal. Merlin was puzzled by her. The more time he spent with Clare Brovik, the less he seemed to know her. She was like the human equivalent of the Edwin Cheney house, replete with interesting features but having a concealed entrance. He simply could not find the way in. It made him wonder exactly what was hidden away behind the walls.

"Do you like working for a meat baron?" he asked.

"I'm grateful to have any job at a time like this."

"That's not what I asked."

"You got the only answer I'll give you."

"Hobart St. John looks like a tough employer."

"You should know. He's employing you."

"Indirectly," said Merlin. "I answer to his wife. And now there's you and Donald Kruger to take into account. Quite a chain of command."

"It's the way Mr. St. John wants it."

"Then that is how it will be."

She gave a nod. "Tell me about the Robie House," she said.

"Why that?"

"You said it was the most beautiful house in America."

"That's only my opinion."

"I respect that opinion," she said. "I also feel ashamed that I live in the city where this house was built and I never even knew it was there. Where did you say it was? In Hyde Park?"

"Yes," said Merlin. "Number 5757 South Woodlawn. Built for Frederick Robie in 1908. It's the quintessential Prairie House. Some people prefer the Dana House in Springfield, but I always cite Robie. Let me explain why."

Merlin was away, blending enthusiasm with lucidity and keeping her captivated. He was still singing the praises of his master as they left the restaurant and stepped out under an overcast sky. The meal had taken far longer than either had realized. Merlin was about to escort her back to his car when she remembered something.

"There's one house in Oak Park I haven't seen."

"It's not built yet, Clare."

"They've made a start. Can I see what they've done so far?"

"Is this for your progress report to Donald Kruger?"

"No, Merlin," she said levelly. "This is for me."

He grinned. "In that case, let's go."

The site was deserted, and the high perimeter fence looked forbidding, but Merlin had a key to unlock the steel door. They went through it, to be confronted by a mixture of order and chaos.

Building materials lay around in haphazard piles, but the smooth symmetry of Saints' Rest was rising slowly out of them. Even in its early stages, the house had a definite presence. Clare was impressed.

"Take me around it," she said.

"It's a bit muddy. Your shoes will get dirty."

"So what?"

"Yes," he said, dodging an upturned wheelbarrow. "So what?"

He took her around the curve of the drive and up the steps to the front door. Picking their way between stacked bricks and timber, they went from room to room to get a feel of the place, creating imaginary walls, windows, floors, staircases, and roofing. Saints' Rest would give Alicia St. John what she desired. Its exterior made a bold architectural statement, while its interior offered luxurious sanctuary. Merlin had found a balance between prospect and refuge.

"It looks even more striking than it does on paper, Merlin."

"Thanks."

"You must be delighted with what the builders have done."

"The real thrill for me is to design a house on Chicago Avenue. I mean, what a wonderful coincidence! Only blocks away from Frank Lloyd Wright's home and studio."

"Would *you* like to have a home and studio here?"

"That would be my idea of heaven, Clare."

"I'm sure. Oh, we haven't seen the wine cellar yet."

"It'll be dark down there."

"I've got matches in my purse," she said, searching for them. "And I can't leave until I've seen the cellar. It was the one feature that Mr. St. John insisted on himself."

"Who else would want a wine cellar when the sale of wine is illegal? I could be accused of aiding and abetting a violation of Prohibition."

"Not by me."

"Give me the box."

He took the matches and lit one before descending the stone steps to the cellar. It was built in a series of bays, each with a vaulted ceiling. There were alcoves in every wall for the storage of wines and spirits. It was gloomy but dry. Their voices echoed in the gloom.

"We can't see all that much, I'm afraid," he apologized.

"We can see enough."

"Stay close."

"I hadn't realized it was so big."

"It goes right under the house. The largest bay is at the far end."

When the first match spent itself, he dropped it to the floor and lit another, taking her deeper into the cavern and casting an appreciative eye over the brickwork. The last bay had special features incorporated into it, but Merlin had no time to explain what they were. As they groped their way along, the tiny flame of the match conjured the intruder out of the darkness.

A rope around his neck, he was dangling lifelessly from a hook.

Clare screamed in horror. The match burned Merlin's fingers.

Everything went pitch-black.

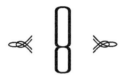

Merlin reached out involuntarily to comfort Clare, and she came willingly into his arms. She felt warm and frightened. He shuffled her slowly away from the bay. She recovered quickly and resisted him.

"You can let go of me now."

"Are you sure?"

"I'll be fine. It was the shock."

Merlin released her, then fumbled for another match.

"Look away."

"What are you going to do?"

"See if the poor devil is still alive."

"Who is he?"

"He didn't say."

He lit another match and went back into the last bay. Clare Brovik cowered behind him, watching with trepidation. Merlin held the flame close to the man's face and made a swift diagnosis. The eyes stared, the mouth was agape, the cheeks bloated. Blood streamed from a wound on his temple, covering much of his face and staining the jacket of his suit before sending tributaries down both legs. When he tried to check the pulse, Merlin found that both hands were tied behind the man's back. The stiffness of his limbs confirmed that he had been there for some time. The noisome smell suggested that he had defecated. He was comprehensively dead.

As another match flamed, Merlin turned away from the corpse.

"We're too late, Clare."

"Let's get out of here."

"I'll light another match."

"Just come!"

She lurched off, feeling her way along the walls, ignoring the pain as she bumped into a pillar, then caught her knee against a wooden crate. Merlin preferred a degree of illumination, striking a match to guide him past any obstacles and catching her up as she was scrambling on all fours up the stone steps. When they reached fresh air again, they both gasped for breath.

"That was terrifying," she said.

"I'm sorry I took you down there."

"It was my idea."

"That was the last thing I expected." Merlin tried to collect his thoughts. "Right," he decided at length, "we need to call the police."

"I'll do that," she said, putting out a hand to stop him.

"Why can't we go together?"

"You stay here, Merlin. Guard the site."

"Nobody can get in when the door in that fence is locked."

"He did."

Merlin glanced back down the steps and nodded.

"Sure you can manage?" he asked.

"Quite sure."

"You've gone white, Clare. And you're trembling."

"It got to me."

"That makes two of us."

She gave a pale smile and offered her hand. He squeezed it gently.

"I'll get the cops," she said.

"Hurry!"

Letting her out, he locked the steel door behind her, then went slowly back toward the cellar. His stomach was heaving, his brain racing. He was not merely shaken by the discovery of a murder victim. He was appalled to find it in the cellar of a house he had designed. It was a bad omen. Saints' Rest had been defiled.

Common sense told him to stay well clear of the body, but he was too outraged to listen to reason. He scoured the site until he found an empty cement bag. Tearing it into strips, he twisted each into a long taper, then went back to the cellar. He lit one with a match, stuffed the rest of the tapers into his pocket, then went down the stairs. The bigger flame gave him clearer direction, and he reached the last bay within seconds. He could now take a more detailed inventory.

The man was in his late thirties. He was short and slim. The blood that obscured much of his face had also ruined what had been an expensive suit. The tie was silk, the shoes made of patent leather. There were rings on both hands, and he wore a gold wristwatch. Merlin could not bring himself to search the body for identification, and his makeshift torch was, in any case, burning low. Grabbing another taper from his pocket, he lit it from the flame of the other and dropped that to the floor, noticing for the first time the footprints in the thin film of dust. There were dozens of them, often overlapping. Evidently there had been a struggle.

A thorough search of the bay revealed no other clues. He took a last look at the tortured face of the victim. It seemed to be pleading for release, but Merlin overcame the urge to lower the body to the floor. He would be disturbing evidence at a murder scene. It was time to hand it over to the police now. A third taper was needed to take him back up into the open air. Tossing it to the ground, he stamped it out. Clare had made a telling point. The intruder had somehow found his way onto the site, and so, presumably, had his killer. Since the lock on the steel door had not been tampered with, they must have gained access by other means.

Merlin walked slowly around the inside of the perimeter fence, searching for signs of forced entry. The fence was high and solid, the barbed wire intact. He was baffled. Making a second circuit, he looked for footprints in the soft earth or any other indication that someone might have scaled the fence and jumped onto the site. The fruitless exercise forced him to consider another possibility. Perhaps the man had sneaked on-site when the Ace Construction Company was there and the steel door open. He could have used the cellar as a hiding place. Yet it seemed unlikely that such a well-dressed man would venture into such a filthy place, and the theory did not explain how his killer also managed to trespass on private property.

As he stood there and pondered, Merlin became aware of how long Clare had been gone. It seemed an eternity. He chided himself for letting her go alone, fearing that she might have been overcome by the shock and gone astray somewhere. He took out his key and trotted across to the steel door. The moment he unlocked it, he heard the wail of police sirens and saw two vehicles hurtling down Chicago Avenue toward him. They screeched to a halt, their arrival fetching anxious neighbors out onto their terraces. Clare Brovik clambered out of the first police car, accompanied by two men in dark suits. Three uniformed policemen leaped out of the other vehicle.

Merlin rushed to greet Clare. She looked harassed.

"What took you so long?" he asked.

She shrugged helplessly. "I couldn't find the police station."

"Why didn't you go to the nearest house and ask to use the phone?"

"I was too confused."

"Mr. Richards?" said the detective with the thick eyebrows.

"Yes?"

"We'll take over now, sir. Why don't we all go inside?"

While one of the uniformed policemen was left on sentry duty, the rest of the party went in through the steel door. Most of the newcomers were carrying battery torches. The man with the thick black eyebrows was perfunctory in his introductions.

"I'm Sergeant Hogan," he said. "This here's Detective Ziff."

His companion, a stringy man in a shapeless hat, gave a nod.

"Miss Brovik tells us you found a dead body," said Hogan.

"That's right," said Merlin. "In the cellar. I'll show you."

"We'll find it, sir," replied the other. "You stay here."

He glanced at one of the uniformed policemen, and the man moved in to stand beside Merlin and Clare. Hogan, Ziff, and the third policeman went off toward the house, switched on their torches, and vanished down the steps of the wine cellar. Merlin was concerned about Clare.

"Are you sure you're okay?"

"Yes, Merlin," she whispered.

"What did you tell them?"

"The truth."

"Who did you speak to?"

"Sergeant Hogan."

"Did you say what we were doing in Oak Park?"

"Of course."

"Did he believe you?"

"Why shouldn't he?"

"Because we found the body, Clare. That raises a question mark."

"They surely can't suspect *us*!"

"They're coppers. They suspect everyone."

Their uniformed companion gave a grunt of amusement.

"Who on earth can he be, Merlin?" she wondered.

"He doesn't work for the construction company, I know that. I went back down there to take a closer look. He's a flashy dresser. Obviously has money. And he's still wearing a gold wristwatch, so the motive couldn't have been robbery. No thief would have left that watch behind."

"What else did you find down there?"

"Nothing."

She shivered. "I'm beginning to wish we never came to Oak Park."

"Everything was going so well until then. Calm before the storm."

"Yes."

"I don't relish telling Mr. St. John about this."

She lowered her head but said nothing.

"I hope it doesn't jeopardize the building of the house," he said anxiously. "That would be a tragedy for everybody."

"Saints' Rest will be built," she said, looking up.

"But a man has been murdered on the site, Clare."

"We can't be sure about that."

"You saw him."

"Only for a split second."

"He was hanged down there," he reminded her. "Some house owners are very superstitious about things like that."

"Not Mr. St. John."

"What about his wife?"

A momentary hesitation. "Mrs. St. John will come to accept it."

"I'm not sure that I would, in her position."

"Look, why don't we just hand it all over to the cops?"

"Because we're *involved*."

"Only by accident."

"Clare, this is my house."

"You won't have to live in it."

"I designed it!" he said with feeling. "You saw the plans. If I'd wanted a dead body in the cellar, I'd have drawn one in!"

"There's no need to be sarcastic, Merlin."

"Then stop trying to minimize what's happened."

She lapsed into silence and kept glancing over her shoulder. He tried to draw her into conversation again, but she shook her head and turned away. Hogan reappeared from the cellar with Ziff and the uniformed policeman, the last of whom remained at the top of the steps. Deep in discussion, the two detectives strolled across to them.

"Who is he?" asked Merlin.

"I'll ask the questions, Mr. Richards," said Hogan.

"Did he have a wallet on him?"

"No, sir."

"Any form of identification in his pockets?"

Hogan was blunt. "You conducting your own investigation here?"

"I want to know, Sergeant."

"So do we, Mr. Richards. So do we." He looked back at the house. "Not much more we can do here. Time for the ME to take over. And the guys from forensics. Get on that, Larry."

"Right, Sarge," said Ziff.

He sauntered across to the steel door and let himself out.

"He's not exactly in a hurry, is he?" complained Merlin.

"You a cop, sir?"

"Of course not."

"You ever worked in a police department?"

"No, Sergeant."

"Then don't tell us how to do our job. We got routines, we stick to them. I wouldn't tell you how to design a house now, would I?"

Horace Hogan was a chunky man of medium height with an air of someone who could acquit himself well in a brawl and a squashed tomato of a nose that suggested that an assailant had hit him when he was not looking. Tiny black eyes were embedded in the sockets beneath the two bushy outcrops. Receding black hair was turning gray. His voice was deep and unhurried.

"So what's your story, Mr. Richards?" he said.

"We went into the cellar and found the body."

"I need more detail than that."

"Clare has told you what happened," said Merlin.

"I'm interested in your version, sir. And any discrepancies that may arise between it and Miss Brovik's."

"There *are* no discrepancies."

"Let me be the judge of that."

"We stumbled on the body together."

"Reel it back a bit, Mr. Richards," suggested the other. "What were you doing in Oak Park in the first place? This where you always spend your Saturdays off?"

"No."

"So why come here today?"

Merlin glanced at Clare, controlled his irritation, then gave his account of events. Hogan made desultory notes on his pad with a pencil that seemed to need a regular lick to keep it in service. It was very laborious. Merlin's impatience was growing visibly.

"What happened when Miss Brovik left you?" said Hogan.

"I went back down to the cellar."

"Now, that wasn't in her statement."

"How could it be? Clare wasn't here at the time."

"So we have no witness to confirm your version of events."

"No, Sergeant," said Merlin.

"Why did you go back down there?"

"Why do you think?"

"Tell me. And don't rush. I write slowly."

Merlin gave as concise an account as he could. Hogan questioned him about a few details, then thanked him for his help. An automobile was heard arriving at speed in the street outside. Merlin expected it to be Detective Ziff with the medical examiner, but the man who came striding purposefully through the steel door was not from the police station.

It was Donald Kruger.

He waved at Merlin, enfolded Clare in a token embrace, then took Hogan aside for a private discussion. The newcomer did most of the talking and the detective did all of the nodding. Merlin was bewildered.

"What is Donald doing here?"

"The police contacted him," said Clare.

"Why?"

"Because I asked them to. Donald is in charge now."

"But we're the ones who discovered the body."

Clare Brovik sighed with relief. The appearance of her colleague seemed to have lifted a huge weight from her.

"Leave it to him, Merlin," she advised. "He'll sort everything out."

THOUGH HE WAS sorry to lose such an efficient clerk, the hotel manager congratulated Sally Fiske on securing a contract from a publisher and wished her well. Since it was surprisingly quiet for a Saturday night, he handed over her wage packet and suggested that she leave half an hour earlier. Sally was grateful, but it put her in something of a quandary. If she left now, she might miss Merlin Richards, who had promised to be there at midnight. On reflection, she decided that she had perhaps been rather harsh on him, and his persistence merited some reward. If he could endure a series of rebuffs yet still pursue her, then his fondness was deep and sincere. At the very least, she would agree to talk to him.

Instead of leaving when she could, therefore, she hovered in the lobby and kept one eye on the front window. It was not long before a Model A Ford glided into view and parked under a lamp on the opposite side of Randolph Street. Sally gave a valedictory wave to the night porter behind the desk, then skipped out. She was surprised how much she was looking forward to seeing Merlin again. Old doubts vanished, new hopes took their place. After waiting for traffic to pass, she tripped across the street and tapped on the driver's window of the Ford.

"I didn't think you'd turn up!" she teased.

The window was lowered by a bald-headed man in his sixties.

"Why!" he said, leering at her. "I'd turn up for you any night!"

THE OAK PARK Police Department was situated in a municipal building on the corner of Lake Street and Euclid Avenue. Since it was so close to the site in Chicago Avenue, Merlin was surprised that it had taken the police so long to reach the murder scene. He and Clare Brovik had been taken there for further questioning, then left to cool their heels in an airless office that looked like a glorified broom closet. Clare was remarkably calm, but Merlin was mutinous.

"Why are they keeping us here?"

"Ask them."

"We've been here for hours, Clare."

"Donald is speaking with the police chief."

"What for? How does Donald Kruger fit into all this?"

"Saints' Rest is his responsibility, Merlin."

"And mine. I designed the house, remember."

"I know," she said, putting a soothing hand on his arm. "This is a terrible thing to happen. Everything was perfect until now. I do feel for you, honestly. It must be shattering."

"It is, Clare," he said, "but it would be easier to bear if the coppers showed any sympathy. They've been so offhand with me." He got up from his chair. "What are they doing out there?"

"They'll tell us when they're ready."

"I have somewhere else to be."

When he checked his watch, he recoiled as if from a blow. It was almost midnight. There was no way that he could honor his promise to pick Sally Fiske up from her hotel. It was the second time in a row that Saints' Rest had come between the two of them. His one hope was to catch her before she finished work.

"Excuse me," he said, opening the door.

"Where are you going?"

"To make a phone call."

But the duty officer was not amenable to the suggestion. The telephone was for official police business, not for members of the public to talk to their girlfriends. Merlin cajoled him, pleaded with him, and even offered to pay for the call, but the man was adamant.

"If she loves you, she'll forgive you," he said flatly.

"The call will take less than a minute," reasoned Merlin.

"We got rules."

"Bloody stupid rules!"

He went back to the waiting room and sat down heavily.

"Who did you want to speak to?" wondered Clare.

"Nobody you know."

"I thought it might be Gus Westlake."

Merlin had forgotten him. Both of his bosses would need to be told about his misadventure, as would his colleagues. Monday morning at the office would be an uncomfortable place to be, but not as maddening as the Oak Park Police Department at midnight on a Saturday. He tapped his foot. Clare opened her purse and took out a packet of Chesterfields. She offered him one, but he shook his head, mildly shocked that she smoked. It explained the box of matches. He took it from his pocket and lit a match as she slipped a cigarette between her lips. Before he could ignite it, the door opened and Donald Kruger stood in the doorway. He gave Clare a smile.

"We can go now," he announced.

"Thank God for that!" said Merlin, getting up.

"Not you, I'm afraid. Sergeant Hogan wants another word."

"But I have to drive Clare home."

"I'll take care of that, Merlin."

"She was my guest."

"Circumstances have changed."

"Clare would rather come with me."

He turned to her for confirmation but got an apologetic look instead. Donald Kruger took precedence. He reinforced the point by giving Merlin a steely smile. Then, with an arm around her shoulder, he escorted Clare out. As soon as they had gone, a bleary-eyed Hogan wandered in, sipping a cup of coffee. His coat was off, exposing his holstered gun and his substantial paunch. He yawned. He leaned against the doorjamb and lifted his cup.

"Want some coffee, sir?"

"No, thanks. I've tasted it."

"Yeah, I know. Camel piss. But you get used to it."

"Why are you keeping me here?"

"I'm not, Mr. Richards."

"You could have fooled me."

"Just wanted to give you a little friendly advice."

"What's that?"

"Ease up."

"Ease up?"

"Don't try to do our job for us," said Hogan, rubbing at an eye. "I went through that statement you gave us. Half of it is fact and the other half is supposition. Stop guessing, Mr. Richards. Stop jumping to conclusions that may turn out to be erroneous."

"A man was murdered in a building I designed."

"There you go again! Suppositions." Hogan spread his arms. "How do you know he was murdered? How do you know the crime took place there? How can you assess the cause of death accurately when you're not a pathologist? See what I mean?" He gave a tired grin. "Ease up."

"Is that all you kept me here to tell me?"

"We needed you on hand in case your story didn't tally."

"With what?"

"Mr. Kruger's account."

"But he wasn't *there*. I was."

"Mr. Kruger's employer has a huge stake in that house, sir."

"So have I."

Hogan drained his cup, then lumbered across to Merlin.

"Oak Park is a nice place to live," he said fondly. "Decent people, good facilities, clean streets. This is not Chicago. We don't have gang warfare here, Mr. Richards. We don't have vice rings and gambling joints. You want that, go next door to Cicero. They got all kinds of shit going on down there. It's hell. I know, I used to work there. Oak Park is how a town ought to be. I aim to keep it that way."

"Why tell me? Do I look like a serial murderer?"

"No, sir. But you sound like a guy who talks too much."

"Sergeant Hogan, we found a dead body in the—"

"We heard your story," snapped the other, cutting him off. "And it doesn't quite match what Miss Brovik tells us. But, then—hell, let's face it—she's a woman, and they get rattled in situations like that. So I'll give you the benefit of the doubt. Only don't go shouting this from the rooftops, is all I say."

"Am I supposed to pretend it never happened?"

"No, of course not."

"Then find out who that man was."

"We're pursuing it, sir."

"And catch whoever murdered him."

"I think it's time for you to go home, Mr. Richards."

"What have you done with the body?"

"That needn't concern you."

"I'd like to know, Sergeant."

"Talk to Mr. Kruger."

"Don't bring him into it again."

"He's a key player here."

"Why?"

"Ask him."

"We're going around in circles."

"Then let's break it up, eh? Good night, sir."

"What was Donald Kruger saying to you in there?"

"I got a bed to go to even if you haven't."

Merlin gave up. He was battering his head against a wall of silence. Horace Hogan was giving nothing away. Donald Kruger had ordered Clare Brovik back into the fold, and they had the power of Hobart St. John behind them. Merlin was on his own. He had no chance.

Hogan took pity on him and tossed an unexpected bone.

"Duty officer says you wanted to make a call."

"It's against the rules."

"Depends. How important is it?"

"Very important."

"Sweetheart?"

"Not anymore," groaned Merlin. "I said I'd pick her up."

"Ring her."

"She'll have gone by now."

"Worth a try. Call her on the phone in my office."

"What about the rules?"

"I'm going to the john," said Hogan, moving off. "Phone is on my desk. Get in there and keep it short." He flicked a final remark over his shoulder. "Sometimes, in this game, you have to make up your own rules."

Merlin did not hesitate. He crossed the passageway and went into the office directly opposite. It was spectacularly untidy. Seizing the telephone, he lifted the receiver, dialed a number, and waited as it rang out. The voice of an old man eventually came on the line.

"Beauregard Hotel," he said.

"Can you put me through to Reception, please?"

"This *is* Reception, sir. Switchboard closes down at ten. All calls are put through to here. I'm the night porter."

"Is Sally Fiske still there?" asked Merlin.

"No, sir. She quit."

"Are you sure she isn't on the premises?"

"Certain," said the old man. "I'm the one what takes over from her. You want little Sally, you're too late. Way too late."

"What time did she leave?"

"Forty minutes ago. Be safe and sound in bed by now."

Merlin's day of woe was complete.

Jan Sarbiewski came out of the Church of St. Alban with his wife and his three children. He looked incongruous in a suit, too big for its inadequate cut, too uncouth for the respectability it conferred. His attractive wife was surprisingly small, his three daughters surprisingly young, yet they somehow formed a homogeneous family group. Sarbiewski's watermelon face was creased into solemnity. A devout Roman Catholic, he never missed mass on a Sunday morning. As the crowd swept down the steps of the church, he was lost in contemplation. His wife's arm was looped in her husband's; the three girls walked behind them in a row.

Merlin Richards got out of his car to accost the builder.

"Good morning," he said, blocking their path on the sidewalk.

The Sarbiewski family came to a collective halt.

"I wondered if I could have a word with you, Mr. Sarbiewski."

The giant Pole was dumbfounded. *"Now?"*

"Please. It's rather important."

"We've been to mass," said the other, as if it absolved him of conversation for the rest of the day. "It's Sunday, Mr. Richards."

"I know that."

"Who is this man?" asked the wife suspiciously.

"My name is Merlin Richards," he said, wishing that she and the three girls would stop staring at him. "I'm an architect. I designed a house that your husband is building." He turned to Sarbiewski. "Look, there's been a slight problem."

"Tell me tomorrow," grunted Sarbiewski.

"It won't keep."

"My husband doesn't work on Sundays."

"What does he want, Dad?" asked one of the girls.

"Why hasn't he been to mass?" challenged another.

Merlin's appearance did not suggest a dedicated churchgoer. A button was missing off his jacket, his trousers were baggy, his shoes dirty. He had forgotten to put on a tie, and his hair was disheveled. When he viewed himself through the eyes of the Sarbiewski family, he was not an appealing sight. What they saw was a scruffy intruder. It was clear that he had no chance of speaking with the builder alone, and he could hardly pass on news of a gruesome murder in front of the whole family. Nothing would separate them on a Sunday.

Merlin was defeated by the Roman Catholic Church.

"I rang you at home, Mr. Sarbiewski," he explained, "and the lady who answered told me that you'd gone to mass."

"My mother."

"She said that you'd be at St. Alban's."

"It's Sunday."

"I'm more interested in Saturday," he said, trying to wrest something out of the awkward encounter. "I was out at the site last evening. I just wondered what time you and your men left?"

"Left?"

"Finished work for the day."

Sarbiewski blinked. "You came here to ask me that?"

"Please," said Merlin. "I need to know."

"Why?"

"Because I do. What time did you finish?"

"No time."

"I don't follow."

"We did no work on-site yesterday."

"But you were supposed to be there."

"We were stood down."

"When?"

"First thing yesterday morning."

"What happened?"

"Got a call. Stop work for the day."

Merlin was incredulous. "Stop work?"

"I got to the site first. Sent my men home."

"But why?"

"Those were my orders."

"Who gave them?" pressed Merlin. "Who rang you yesterday?"

"Big boss."

"Boss?"

"Mr. St. John."

It was all that Sarbiewski was prepared to say. He used a massive palm to ease Merlin out of the way and walked off with the rest of his family. His wife and daughters continued to make unflattering remarks about the architect until they were out of earshot. Merlin smarted under their criticism. He felt that he had just committed blasphemy.

WHY SHOULD HOBART St. John suspend work on a house he wanted built as soon as possible? It did not make sense. It did, however, explain why none of Sarbiewski's men had discovered the body in the wine cellar, and it raised the possibility that the corpse may have been there at least twenty-four hours before Merlin and Clare Brovik chanced upon it. When the autopsy was completed, the police would have a clearer idea of the exact time of death, but Merlin suspected that Sergeant Hogan would not feel obliged to divulge that information to him. He had to make his own estimate. What he now knew was that the site had been unoccupied from four o'clock on Friday afternoon, when the Ace Construction Company stopped work. It gave him something to work on.

When he got back to his apartment, his landlady was cleaning the hallway with a mop. Nobody had told her that the Sabbath was a day of rest. She was a slovenly woman of fifty in a working dress and a pair of moth-eaten carpet slippers. Smoke curled up from the cigarette in her mouth. She gave her lodger a cursory glance.

"You had a call," she said without pausing in her work.

"Who was it, Mrs. Romario?"

"Number's by the phone."

Hoping that Sally Fiske might have relented, Merlin rushed to the telephone on the wall and snatched the slip of paper that had been slid in behind the fixture. He did not recognize the number. There was no name. All that his landlady had written was one word. ERGENT. He found coins in his pocket and started to dial.

The receiver was picked up immediately at the other end.

"Is that you, Merlin?" she asked.

"Clare!" he said, recognizing her voice and wondering why it was so breathy. "Are you all right?"

"Fine, fine."

"You sound funny."

"Do I?" Her voice steadied. "It must be this line. I'm in good shape. Well, put it this way. I feel a lot better than I did last night."

"It was a disaster!"

"That's why I rang, Merlin. To see how you were."

"Still in one piece."

"You got back safely, then?"

"Just about. Sergeant Hogan gave me the Dutch uncle treatment."

"Dutch uncle?"

"Never mind."

"I also wanted to apologize for leaving you there. Donald had a lot to discuss with me, that's why I had to go with him. I didn't mean to dump you like that. It must have seemed very rude."

"I would have preferred it if we'd driven back together."

"So would I."

"Apart from anything else, I'd like to have compared stories."

"Stories?"

"Sergeant Hogan reckons there were discrepancies between your version of events and mine. Can't think why. Can you?"

"No," she said firmly. "Of course not."

"What did you tell him?"

"What I saw. It was scary. Spoiled what had been a lovely day."

"Yes, it was lovely," he recalled. "Sitting in Unity Temple with you like that. I felt—I don't know, Clare—sort of at peace. We should have quit while we were winning."

"It was my fault, Merlin."

"No, it wasn't."

"I was the one who asked to look around Saints' Rest."

"You weren't to know what we'd find there."

"That's true."

"Anyway, I solved one mystery," he told her. "It was bugging me. Why had nobody else found the body before we did? Seemed odd when the builders were due on-site all Saturday. I caught Jan Sarbiewski as he came out of church this morning."

"You've spoken to Mr. Sarbiewski?" She sounded worried.

"Yes. I wanted some answers."

"Merlin, this is police business now. Back off."

"But I needed to know, Clare."

"And what did Mr. Sarbiewski tell you?"

"Very little. He had his wife and kids with him. They looked at me as if I'd just tried to steal the cross off the top of their church. Anyway," he continued, wishing that his landlady would make less noise when she moved her bucket of water, "what I did learn was this. There was no work done on-site yesterday. Sarbiewski's boys were stood down. And do you know who told them to take the day off?"

"Merlin—"

"Your lord and master."

"I'm not sure that this gets us anywhere."

"Hobart St. John."

There was a long pause. He was disappointed by her apparent lack of interest. He waited until Mrs. Romario had dragged the bucket a few yards down the hallway.

"Doesn't that surprise you, Clare?" he asked.

"No, it doesn't."

"Why not?"

"Because I already knew about it."

"You *knew*? And you never bothered to mention it?"

"Mrs. St. John was having second thoughts about the design of the bay window at the front," she explained smoothly. "They were due to start work on it yesterday. She wanted the weekend to think it over and go through your sketches once again. So Mr.

St. John suspended work for the day. That's all that happened."

"Why wasn't I brought in on this?" His voice rose.

"Calm down, Merlin."

"You can't just change a central feature in the facade on a whim. If Mrs. St. John fiddles about with the size or the shape of that bay window, everything else will have to be altered. Doesn't she realize that?" He ran a fevered hand through his hair. "I spent hours talking to her about that window. I must have come up with six or seven variations. And she finally found one that she liked."

"That may still be the one she goes for in the end."

"So what's all this about second thoughts?"

"Mrs. St. John is a little capricious at times."

"The plans were submitted for approval. They've got an official seal. We can't start hacking them about now, Clare. This is lunatic!" he said, working himself up into a mild rage. "I need to speak to the lady herself. We can't have her putting a spoke in the wheel at this stage. I'll give her a ring and see if I can drive out there today."

"No, Merlin!" she ordered.

"I'm not letting anyone else redesign my house!"

"It may not come to that. This is just a temporary hitch, that's all. Ignore it, and it will probably go away of its own accord. My guess is that Mr. Sarbiewski will be back on-site tomorrow morning, building that bay window exactly the way you've specified."

"And what happens next time?"

"Next time?"

"Yes," he said, wincing at the grating of the bucket as it was pushed within feet of him. "Hold on a minute, Clare." Cupping a hand over the mouthpiece, he turned to his landlady. "Mrs. Romario," he said sweetly, "I'm trying to hold a conversation here."

"Floor's got to be cleaned," she said.

"Could you just take a break for a few minutes, please?"

She was unrepentant. "You and the others bring all the dirt in here. I got to wipe up the mess. Who else would do this?"

"I will," he volunteered recklessly. "Anything to stop that noise."

She paused long enough to shift the position of her cigarette and assess his offer. Then she lifted her bucket, carried it to the far end of the hallway, and resumed her mopping. Grateful for the partial relief, Merlin spoke into the mouthpiece again.

"Sorry about that, Clare. What was I saying?"

"Something about next time."

"Ah, yes," he said, picking up the thread. "What happens next time Mrs. St. John has second thoughts about some aspect of the house? Will the Ace Construction Company get laid off again while she plays about with my design? Is this going to be the pattern from now on?"

"No, Merlin. I can guarantee that."

"You told me that she'd handed everything over."

"She did."

"Until yesterday."

"Don't keep on about it, Merlin."

"Well, you can hardly expect me to shrug it off. For heaven's sake, Clare. When we were on-site, I stood there and described that bay window to you in loving detail. And you didn't say a single word about it. Why didn't you warn me that it was under review?"

"Listen," she said softly, "we both had a rotten night. It's left me wiped out, and you must feel the same. Try to get some rest, Merlin. We'll talk again tomorrow. Everything will have calmed down a bit by then."

"I want to see you today."

"Why?"

"Because we've got a lot to talk about, Clare. Starting with what you told Sergeant Hogan. I won't be palmed off like this. Let's get together soon." He checked his watch. "Why don't we meet for lunch?"

"Because I can't, Merlin."

"Can't or won't?"

"I've made other arrangements."

"Oh, I see. Going out to Lake Shore Drive to help Mrs. St. John make some more changes to my design, are you? Whose side are you on here?" He made a decision. "Sit tight. I'm on my way over to you right now."

"But I'm not at home."

"Then where are you?"

"In Donald's apartment. I'm having lunch here."

Merlin felt a prickly sensation at the back of his neck.

"Has Donald been listening in on this conversation?" he said.

There was a long pause. Merlin had his answer. He hung up.

GUS WESTLAKE WAS regular in his devotions. All over Chicago and throughout its burgeoning suburbs, bells of every denomination had called the faithful to their respective places of worship that Sunday morning. While thousands knelt in prayer, Westlake preferred to crouch over a tricky putt and send up a silent plea for divine assistance. The Church of Latter-Day Saints of the Holy Green lay to the north of Lincoln Park, and there was no more assiduous member of the congregation than Westlake. Though a passerby might mistake it for a golf course, it was in reality an al fresco shrine at which the converted paid dutiful homage. Open for worship throughout the week, its full religiosity shone through only on the Sabbath, and its exclusively male membership flocked through its portals to hear the almighty shout "Fore!"

It was early afternoon by the time Westlake tore himself away from the eighteen consecutive altars. He was in a somber mood. Having played well yet lost badly to his partner, he had forfeited a hefty wager and been forced to buy refreshments for the victor. The presence at the club of Jerry Niedlander had soured him even more, though nobody would have guessed it from the way Westlake went up to the man, slapped him familiarly on the back, and thanked him for pulling out of the prospective deal because it liberated Westlake and Davisson to handle an even bigger commission in the offing. The braying laugh was at its highest pitch, but the trademark smile vanished as soon as Westlake left the clubhouse.

He was not pleased by what he saw in the parking lot. Merlin Richards was sitting in his Model A Ford, reading a newspaper. His baffled employer strode across to him.

"What in God's name are you doing here, Merl?" he said.

"Waiting for you."

"This club is for members only."

"That's why I didn't come in. Did you win?"

"Almost."

"What was your score?"

"Never mind about that," said Westlake irritably. He looked at the car and shuddered. "You'll have to get a better automobile than this, Merl. It creates a bad impression."

"What's wrong with it?"

"Look around you. It's a donkey among thoroughbreds."

Merlin was hurt. "This is the very latest model."

"It's a Ford!"

"So?"

"The car for the masses."

"I'm one of them, Gus."

"Well, I wouldn't buy a windshield wiper from Henry Ford. Hell, the man is a temperance fanatic!"

"Did your car come with a crate of whiskey?" He became serious. "I needed to see you, Gus. Urgently. And I wanted you to hear this before Brad. In fact, I'd like you to be the one to break it to him, because it's not a task I'd enjoy." He put his paper aside. "I was in Oak Park yesterday."

"So I hear."

"Who told you?"

"Hobart St. John. Called me first thing this morning."

"What did he say?"

"That you and Clare Brovik had a nasty shock out there."

"You know about it?" Merlin was surprised. "A murder takes place on a site that has a Westlake and Davisson board outside it, and you come here to play a round of golf?"

"It's what I do on Sunday mornings."

"That's why I came here. I assumed that you knew nothing about what happened at Saints' Rest. How on earth can you behave so calmly when this is hanging over us?"

"We'll talk about it tomorrow."

"Now, Gus. We need to thrash this out."

"Why?"

"Because it affects the whole future of the project."

"No, it doesn't. Saints' Rest goes ahead."

"Who says so?"

"Old Hobart. That's why he called."

"What about his wife? Doesn't she mind?"

"Mind what?"

"The fact that a man was hanged in her new home!" said Merlin excitedly. "It would spook most people. Every time she goes down to the wine cellar, Mrs. St. John will be haunted by bad memories."

"No, she won't."

"She's bound to be, Gus."

"Alicia won't *have* any bad memories, Merl," said Westlake. "Besides which, can you imagine a woman like that ever going to fetch her own booze when she can send one of the servants? She never does anything on her own. They probably have a roster to wipe the shit off her ass."

"What was that about not having bad memories?"

"You can't fear what you don't know."

"Her husband hasn't *told* her about the murder?"

"Let's just call it an unfortunate incident, shall we? And no, Merl. Hobart hasn't said a word to her, and he's not going to, either."

"But she's bound to find out."

"How?"

"From a radio broadcast. From the papers."

"You see any mention of it in there?" asked Westlake, pointing to Merlin's newspaper. "It wasn't in any of the papers I read today. And you can forget the radio. The only thing that Alicia Martinez listens to is the sound of her own voice. She's a movie star, and you're confusing her with a human being. Movie stars don't live in the real world. Alicia wouldn't notice if the Wrigley Building collapsed during the rush hour into Michigan Avenue." He chuckled. "When she moves out to Oak Park, she'll simply be shifting from one ivory tower to another. They haven't even told her that Woodrow Wilson is dead yet."

"Mr. St. John can't keep his wife ignorant of something like this."

"Oh, yes, he can. So don't you go spilling the beans to her." He wagged a stern finger. "Hobart was most particular about that. You speak to his wife about this, you're off the site."

"Gus, this is ridiculous!"

"It's the way he wants it."

"Keeping his wife in the dark? That's disgusting!"

"Wait till you get married," said the other with easy cynicism. "You'll find it's perfectly normal behavior for a husband. Now stop getting yourself all het up, Merl. And don't embarrass me again by bringing this heap you call a car into my golf club. Someone might have seen you."

He patted Merlin on the shoulder, then walked away.

Merlin was shaken. Anticipating a reaction of horror, he was appalled to find that Gus Westlake was instead treating the events as a minor matter. This was a callous streak that he had never seen before. As he watched the yellow-and-black Lincoln roll away, he felt like the victim of some weird conspiracy. Everyone else—including the police—seemed to be playing down the discovery of a hanged man in a wine cellar. Merlin began to wonder if there was anyone apart from himself who really cared about what had happened in Oak Park.

ALICIA MARTINEZ COULD not contain her anguish. Weeping copiously and clutching at her hair, she wailed in distress. She looked once more at the body of her prince, stretched out on the floor of the palace ballroom, then bent down impulsively to snatch the curved dagger from his belt. Holding it high and trembling with emotion, she plunged the dagger into her breast and fell dramatically on top of her dead lover. When she vanished from the screen, a caption came up with her final line.

>I COME TO JOIN YOU IN AN UNTIMELY
>GRAVE, MY LOVE.

Alicia reappeared, still showing a fair amount of life as she writhed around on top of Prince Achmed until, with a final spasm, she expired.

>THE END.

Hobart St. John led the applause and Donald Kruger joined in obediently. Seated between them in the darkened living room, Alicia preened herself, accepting their plaudits graciously.

"It was always my favorite," she admitted.

"You were so moving," said Kruger. "I wept with you."

"I didn't," said her husband. "I was too busy being jealous of that guy who played Prince Achmed. I wouldn't mind getting paid to lie on the ground with Alicia on top of me. It was great, honey."

"Thank you for sitting through it again."

"Anytime."

"You're sweet," she said, kissing him on the cheek. "But I won't hold you up any longer. I know that you need to speak to Donald. And I want to take a nap before dinner." She waggled her fingers. "Good-bye, Donald."

"Good-bye," he said.

The butler switched the light back on again so that he could remove the film from the projector. The two men rose quickly and headed for the library.

"Alicia is a brilliant actress," said Kruger.

"I know. Such a pity she never got the lead in that movie. She's got such class. You could see that from the screen test. The way she stabbed herself at the end. So realistic."

"Hollywood's loss is your gain."

"Let's forget Hollywood and talk Oak Park."

St. John closed the door of the library behind them. His joviality was usurped by a quiet rage. He stepped forward to confront Kruger.

"I told you to clean up your mess, Donald."

"I thought that I had."

"That's not the way it looks to me."

"It's all under control now."

"Is it?"

"Yes," said the other confidently. "I've covered all the bases. Spoken to all the right people. We'll have no more worries now."

"I hope, for your sake, that's true."

"It is, Mr. St. John. You have my solemn oath."

"If Alicia ever got wind of this, there'd be hell to pay."

"There's no reason why she should ever know. By the time you move into the house, the whole thing will have faded completely away. I've made sure of that. Nothing will besmirch Saints' Rest for the St. Johns."

"Unless some fool opens his trap."

"They won't."

"Think we can trust that architect?"

"Richards? I'm certain of it."

"He worries me. I spoke to that cop. What's he called?"

"Hogan. Sergeant Hogan."

"Got his home number from the chief of police and gave him a call. Hogan had doubts about Merlin. A cop's intuition. That worries me."

"I'll speak to Mr. Richards tomorrow."

Hobart St. John walked across to the table, on which a sketch of Saints' Rest was laid out. He stared down at it for a long time while he pondered. Then he turned back to Kruger.

"No," he said. "I'll talk to him myself."

10

Ignoring the light drizzle, Merlin Richards ran at a steady pace through the streets of South Side in a pair of shorts and a grubby old rugby shirt. He kept to his usual route and collected the usual array of waves, jeers, and stares from passersby. A dog chased him at one point, barking furiously at his heels, but it lost interest after a hundred yards and transferred its attentions to a streetlamp. Merlin's stride was low and economical. He moved fluidly. When he was close to home, he put in a burst of speed that took him all the way to the end of the street and left him breathing more heavily.

The wizened old news vendor was in his stall on the corner.

"You're early this morning, Merl," he noted.

"Lots to do."

"How far you been?"

"Three, four miles."

"That'd kill me," said the man, coughing throatily. "I stopped running the day I got married. There's better ways to exercise."

"I like to suffer," joked Merlin.

He took a copy of the *Chicago Tribune* from the man and handed over the money. Glancing at the front page, he expected to see at least a mention of a murder in Oak Park. Instead, he was looking at a banner headine about the latest shooting in Little Italy. More bad news about the financial markets occupied the rest of the space. He decided that the unsaintly discovery at Saints' Rest had been relegated to an inside page.

"Take it home to read," said the news vendor. "You'll get soaked."

"I already am. See you tomorrow."

"I'll be waiting, Merl."

Folding the paper, Merlin tucked it under his arm and trotted around the corner. Within a minute, he was letting himself into the little apartment block. Mrs. Romario was in the hallway, bending to pick up the milk bottles. She was wearing a tattered dressing gown and the moth-eaten slippers. Her hair was a petrified forest.

"Good morning, Mrs. Romario," he said.

She sniffed. "You been out running again?"

"I like to keep in trim."

"Be the death of you."

"It blows away the cobwebs."

She clicked her tongue. "Did you see the man?"

"What man?"

"The one who was asking after you."

"When was this, Mrs. Romario?"

"Ten, fifteen minutes ago," she said uncertainly. "Maybe longer. He got me out of bed. Wanted to know the number of your room."

"Why?"

"Search me."

"Did he leave a name?"

"No name."

"What did he look like?"

"I can't remember."

"You must be able to tell me something about him."

"I was only half awake."

"Was he tall or short? Thin or fat?"

"Sort of average."

"Age?"

"Older than you, younger than me."

"You're not being very specific here, Mrs. Romario."

"He was wearing a suit. A dark suit. And a hat."

"Is that all you can tell me?"

"He was only here for a minute."

"Did he say he'd call back?" She shook her head. "Did he give you the impression that he knew me?" The headshake was more vigorous. "Isn't there *anything* else you remember about him, Mrs. Romario?"

"No," she said, ruminating. "Except that he was very polite."

"Polite?"

"Spoke to me in Italian."

The landlady retreated into her room to make her husband's breakfast. Merlin became conscious of how wet he was. He went up to his room to collect a towel, then dived into the bathroom before any of his neighbors beat him to it. While the water was filling the tub, he leafed through the pages of the *Tribune* in search of the report that he felt sure would be there. It took him some time to locate it. The item occupied less than a square inch of space. It rocked Merlin.

OAK PARK SUICIDE

The body of a derelict was found by police on Saturday night at a building site in Oak Park. The man, who has not been identified, apparently hanged himself.

Sergeant Horace Hogan of the Oak Park Police Department said that there was no evidence of foul play. Investigations continue.

BRAD DAVISSON PACED his office like a caged tiger. The morning mail lay unopened on his desk. His brow was corrugated; his ulcer reminded him that it was still around. It was Monday morning with a vengeance. As soon as Gus Westlake came in through the door, Davisson pounced.

"What the hell is going on, Gus!"

"You're just about to perforate your ulcer, Brad," said his partner, holding up both hands. "That's what's going on. Now, why don't you just take a seat and try to calm down? Let's discuss this in comfort."

"Comfort!" yelled Davisson with a hollow laugh. He snatched up a copy of the *Chicago Tribune* from his desk. "Have you read this report? A dead body is found on our site. That's supposed to be comforting?"

"I came here to explain."

"Start by explaining why you *didn't* explain."

"Brad—"

"This guy is found hanging on Saturday night, and I don't get to hear about it until I open the paper on Monday morning!"

"I didn't want to spoil your weekend."

"For chrissake, man—I'm your partner!"

"I tried to spare you the *angst*."

"Gus, I had a right to be told."

"That's why I've come in early this morning before the others get here. If they see you in this state, they'll call an ambulance. When you phoned me before breakfast, you sounded as if you were having a seizure."

"I am. His name is Gus Westlake!"

His partner grinned. "That's more like the Brad Davisson I know!"

"What exactly happened out in Oak Park?"

"That's what I came here to tell you."

"I'm amazed you remembered where the office was."

The braying laugh gave Westlake time to rehearse what he was going to say. Guiding his partner around the desk, he eased him into his chair and waved away his protests. He took the paper from Davisson's trembling hand and glanced at the news story. Then he perched on the edge of the desk.

"There is a bit more to it than this, Brad."

"Surprise, surprise!"

"So let me fill you in. Why didn't I call you over the weekend? I only heard about it myself yesterday morning, and I wanted to know more details before I brought you in on it. Also, I'm very fond of Eleanor. And you wouldn't have been fit to live with if I'd dropped this bombshell in your lap. Your wife was entitled to a restful Sunday."

"And I was entitled to the facts."

"You're getting them."

"Stop lying, Gus. You deliberately kept this from me."

"Of course I did," said the other, putting the paper on the desk. "I knew you'd get overexcited. Make a mountain out of a molehill."

"A dead body on our site? That's a molehill?"

"See? You're off again. The bulging eyes, the pounding heart. Now you just sit there and listen while I explain it to you. The questions can wait until afterward. Okay?" He took Davisson's brooding silence for consent. "Good. Here it comes. Merlin Richards took that girl out to Oak Park on the Frank Lloyd Wright trail. You remember her. Clare Brovik. One of Hobart's underlings. I introduced you to her at his party. Anyway, she and Merlin go out there to see a few architectural sights, and they end up—you guessed it—at Saints' Rest. When they go down to the wine cellar to see if Hobart has laid in a supply of booze yet, they find this guy down there, swinging from the end of a rope. They call the cops, who say that everything points to suicide." He gave a shrug. "End of story."

"What about the bits you left out?"

"There are none. I tell it like I heard it."

"Who from?"

"Hobart St. John."

"Who told him?"

"The cops."

"I'd like to speak to them myself."

"There's no need, Brad. I've already talked to Sergeant Hogan. He confirmed the details, and that was that. Now listen up, because this is very important. We got two choices here. Either we try to put this behind us, get on with building that house in Oak Park and keeping this practice solvent. Or"—he raised an eloquent eyebrow—"we make a song and dance about it, get a lot of bad publicity in the papers, annoy the cops, and piss off Hobart so much that he'll pull the plug on the whole deal. Is that what you want?"

"No, Gus."

"Then let's leave it at that."

"I can't."

"You have to, Brad. Or it will blow up in your face."

"Is that a threat?"

"Would I ever threaten my beloved partner?"

Davisson held back a snide comment and sulked for a moment.

"How did you spend yesterday?" he said at length.

"On the golf course."

"Nothing is ever allowed to interfere with that, is it?"

"This is your office, that's mine."

"Weren't you even upset by the news?"

"Sure, who wouldn't be? Last thing we need is some hobo crawling onto one of our sites to kill himself. Leaves a nasty taste. I was livid when I first heard." He beamed. "But when I chipped in from a sand trap on the sixth green, I felt a lot better about it. Took the sensible view."

"And what's that?"

"No use moaning over something you can't change. It happened. It was bad luck. Let's try to forget it." He chuckled. "I was far more upset when I saw that treacherous bastard Jerry Niedlander in the clubhouse afterward. Wanted to sock him on that big nose of his. But I also want to stay in business, so I killed him with kindness, made out he'd done us a favor by cutting us out of the deal, and walked away." He stood up and spread his arms. "Now you know it all."

"All that you're prepared to tell me."

"Learn to trust your partner."

"No comment."

"We're in this together, Bradley."

"That's what worries me." He looked down at the *Tribune*. "There's something you're hiding from me, Gus. Your story has got more gaping holes than a whorehouse. I want to hear it from Merlin."

"He won't be in this morning."

"Why not?"

"Hobart St. John sent for him."

"Sent for him?"

"Yes," said Westlake. "To have a little talk."

・・・

"YOU'VE NEVER BEEN sailing on Lake Michigan? You're kidding me, Merl."

"No, Mr. St. John. It's an experience I've missed out on."

"You'll be telling me next that you've never seen Niagara Falls."

"I haven't."

"What have you been *doing* since you got to the States?"

"Either working or looking for work."

"No vacations?"

"I did manage a week in California once."

"A week—in all the time you've been here? That's not even long enough to get a decent tan on Santa Monica beach."

"I didn't go there to sunbathe, Mr. St. John."

"Then why did you go? Let me guess. To look at architecture."

"Some of Frank Lloyd Wright's most interesting work is there."

"That's your idea of a vacation? We'll have to change that."

Hobart St. John was in an affable mood. He welcomed Merlin Richards to his office with a smile and a zealous handshake. Tea and biscuits were waiting for the visitor. His host was disarmingly friendly.

"Tell you what, Merl," he said. "Next time I take my yacht out on the lake, you'll be aboard. That's a promise. Wait till you feel that wind blowing through your hair and hear the flap of that canvas. I love sailing, and so will you. The *Alicia* is a swell craft."

"The *Alicia*?"

"I named it after my wife. Renamed it, actually," he confessed with a grin. "It used to be called the *Cornelia Rose* after my third wife, but she insisted that I take her name off it as part of the divorce settlement. Not that I'd want to keep it there, anyway, but women are finicky." He sat back in his chair. "Which brings me very neatly to Alicia. I believe that Gus had told you the score."

"Yes," said Merlin. "Mrs. St. John is to know nothing about this."

"She is even more finicky than Cornelia Rose was. Alicia will have a fit of screaming if she finds the tiniest defect in Saints' Rest. If she hears that someone actually hanged himself there, she won't go near the place."

"Mrs. St. John won't hear that from me."

"I knew I could count on you."

"I wouldn't lie to her, Mr. St. John."

"Lie?" echoed the other, stiffening.

"The man didn't hang himself. He was murdered."

"Now, hold on a minute!"

"I saw him with my own eyes."

"So did Clare Brovik. So did the cops."

"His hands were tied behind his back, Mr. St. John."

"I've heard all the details," said the other easily, "and I don't need to hear them again. Sergeant Hogan conducted a thorough investigation, and I accept his findings. So must you."

"How can I?"

"Because you're being invited to do so."

Hobart St. John spoke with chilling simplicity. He reached out for the silver coffeepot on his desk and refilled his cup. After spooning in some sugar, he stirred the coffee with slow deliberation. Merlin was given time to let his companion's words sink in. St. John eventually looked up.

"You happy with Westlake and Davisson?" he asked.

"Most of the time," said Merlin.

"They give you a fair shake?"

"Very fair."

"Times are hard in your game. You're lucky to be in work."

"I know that, Mr. St. John, and I'm deeply grateful."

"Then maybe you should direct some gratitude toward me," said the other gently. "Because I'm helping to keep your bosses in business. I'm providing you with the most exciting opportunity you've had since you hopped on a boat and came over here. I'm trusting you, Merlin, with something that is very dear to me and to my wife. Chicago is full of architects who'd give their balls for a commission like this. I looked at dozens before deciding on your firm. When I asked for the best man in the office, Gus Westlake recommended you."

"I appreciate that."

"There have been irritations, I know. Alicia can be a trial sometimes. She got you to change your design a dozen times or more. But I like to think that it was all worth it in the end, Merl."

"It was, Mr. St. John."

"The benefits are endless."

"Benefits?"

"I always reward good service. When someone does a job well for me, I make sure that they have another pretty soon. Take that lump of Polish granite, for instance. Sarbiewski. I like what he does, so I put lots of work his way. I could do the same for Westlake and Davisson. These would not just be commissions from me," he stressed, taking another sip of his coffee. "You came to my party, you saw my friends. The people who make things happen in this city. When they want something built, they may well take my advice about architects."

"I'm sure that your opinion carries a lot of weight."

"Oh, it does. You'd be amazed."

"We'd be thankful for anything you did for us, Mr. St. John."

"I want more than thanks, Merl. I expect loyalty."

"That's reasonable."

"So don't contradict me again."

Merlin saw the folly of trying to argue with him. He elected to bide his time until he could establish the full facts about what had happened. He gave a nod of assent. St. John smiled.

"Ask old Gus to tell you about the bonus," he suggested.

"Bonus?"

"If the house gets built on schedule, there'll be an extra five grand in it for Westlake and Davisson, and the same for the Ace Construction Company. And by the way," he said with a wink, "I told Gus that a chunk of that bonus must go to the architect of record."

"Thank you."

"I'm sure you could use it."

"That's certainly true, Mr. St. John."

"As for what you saw in Oak Park on Saturday," said the other casually, "only you can know. I wasn't there myself, so I have to rely on the police report. That seemed conclusive to me. If you still have doubts, take them up with Sergeant Hogan. But don't wave them in front of me again," he warned, "and don't even drop the slightest hint to Alicia that there was a spot of bother out at Saints' Rest. Understood?"

"Yes, Mr. St. John."

"The cops rarely make mistakes about these things."

"No, Mr. St. John."

Merlin held his gaze for a full minute without flinching. Confident that his words had been heeded, Hobart St. John rose to his feet and straightened his jacket.

"What are your immediate plans?"

"I was hoping for a word with Clare Brovik," said Merlin. "She said she'd be in touch today. Since I'm actually on the premises, I wondered if there was any chance of seeing her."

"Afraid not, Merl."

"Oh?"

"Clare was pretty shaken up by what happened," said the other with apparent concern. "Donald spent most of yesterday helping her through it, but the kid is still a bit groggy. We gave her the day off."

"I see."

"She'll bounce back tomorrow, I'm sure. Clare is very resilient."

"I'll give her a call."

"No," said St. John. "Don't do that. She needs a rest. When she's good and ready, Clare will get hold of you." He looked around. "Well, no point in wasting a chance like this, is there? Let's go."

"Where?"

"To look at the Hobart St. John empire. It may not compete with Lake Michigan or Niagara Falls, but at least it will tell you something about the man who's employing you to build his new home. You ever seen a slaughterhouse before, Merl?"

"No, Mr. St. John."

"Ours is the most efficient one here."

"Is it?"

"See for yourself. Our guys kill those animals like shelling peas. They're real artists. I could watch them for hours." He crossed to the door and opened it. "But then, I've got a strong stomach. How about you?"

Merlin followed him. "I won't faint on you."

"Good. I want you to see the whole process from start to finish." He led the way along a corridor. "Wagons bringing the livestock in, meat being dispatched all over the world. Huge operation, Merl."

"I can't stay too long, I'm afraid."

"I insist."

"But I must get out to the site this morning," said Merlin. "Apart from anything else, I owe an apology to Mr. Sarbiewski. I'm afraid that I rather upset him yesterday."

"Forget Sarbiewski. Donald will smooth his feathers."

"Donald Kruger?"

"He's on his way to Oak Park right now."

"Why?"

"Bit of unrest out there."

"Unrest?"

"Yes," explained St. John. "Jan Sarbiewski called us. Some of his men are superstitious about what happened. They think the site is spooked. They've got cold feet. Not to worry. Leave it to Donald. He'll know how to calm them down."

"What's he going to do?" said Merlin. "Play Chopin at them?"

WHEN HE WALKED on-site, Donald Kruger was annoyed to see that no work was being done at all. The men were standing around in disconsolate groups, and Sarbiewski was engaged in a heated argument with his foreman. Kruger took the owner of the Ace Construction Company aside.

"What seems to be the problem?" he asked.

"They're not happy, Mr. Kruger."

"They're not here to be happy. They're here to work."

"That's what I told them."

"And what did they say?"

"They'd like to think it over."

"Think it over!" repeated Kruger with high irony. "This is a building site, not a philosophers' convention. They've already lost two, almost three hours' work."

Sarbiewski nodded. "And Saturday."

"That was an unavoidable mishap. We can't afford another delay like that. There's a schedule to keep to. Surely the men realize that?"

"Yes, sir."

"So what's holding them up?"

"The rumor."

"What rumor?"

Sarbiewski shifted his feet and licked his lips in discomfort.

"What rumor?" pressed Kruger.

"About the dead man."

"Well?"

"Was it really suicide?"

"You saw the report in the paper, Mr. Sarbiewski."

"I did."

"There's your answer, then."

"My foreman has this hunch."

"Hunch?"

"Wonders if it might have been murder."

"Whatever gave him that idea?" said Kruger, treating the notion with polite contempt. "I was here when the police searched the premises and removed the body. I talked at great length with the investigating officer. There's no margin for error here, Mr. Sarbiewski. It was suicide."

"Oh, I believe you."

"Then why don't they?"

"It's my foreman, really."

"Let me have a quiet word with him. I'm sure that I can convince him where his best interests lie. And I need to nip this stupid rumor in the bud before it does any more damage."

Donald Kruger detached the foreman from his conversation with the other men and chatted to him in private. His voice was calm, but his manner was forthright. Five minutes later, on the instruction of their foreman, the others went back to work with a new urgency. Kruger strolled back to the watching Sarbiewski.

"We won't have any more trouble now."

"What did you tell him, Mr. Kruger?"

"The facts of life."

THE GUIDED TOUR at the Union Stock Yards was harrowing, but Merlin knew that it was intended to be. Hobart St. John wanted to show him the orchestrated brutality at his command in the slaughterhouse. In their own way, the factories had been almost as disturbing, vast buildings where grim-faced employees worked at the unvarying pace set by the clanking machines and where carcasses were dismembered with cruel precision. The slaughter of the hogs was the most disquieting for him, and he vowed that he would think twice before eating ham again. When he saw what went into the sausages, he struck them off his diet for the foreseeable future.

Merlin concealed his feelings carefully from his host, thanking him for taking the trouble to show him around and telling him what a valuable insight it had given him into the world of meat. He drove away from the stockyard with great relief and headed for his apartment, keen to change out of a suit that was impregnated with a fearsome stink and to take another bath. He wondered how such a fastidious person as Clare Brovik could bear to work in those surroundings. Hobart St. John belonged there. She did not.

Parking in the street, he went swiftly upstairs, glad that he did not meet anyone on the way and offend their nostrils. He let himself into his room and began to tear off his clothes. Then he stopped dead. The room was in disarray. Papers and books were strewn everywhere. Drawers had been pulled out and emptied. The wardrobe had been ransacked, the bed stripped; even the threadbare carpet had not escaped attention. It was rolled up to expose the bare floorboards.

Merlin was horrified. His room had been searched.

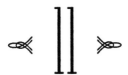

Horace Hogan liked being a cop but hated the paperwork that went with the job. He seemed to spend more time jabbing away at the typewriter with two wayward index fingers than he did out on the street catching the bad guys. Indeed, there were occasions when he let minor offenders off with a stern warning and a kick up the ass in order to save himself another grueling session in front of the infernal machine. There was nothing like an hour of piano practice on the Remington to bring out the iron in his soul. When the tap came on the door of his office, he was less than welcoming.

"Stay out!" he yelled.

"It's me, Sarge," called Larry Ziff from the passageway.

"I'm writing this report."

"The guy insists on seeing you."

"What guy?"

"That architect."

"The awkward one?"

"That's him. Merlin Richards."

"Tell him to come back next week. Next month. Next year."

"He's kind of persistent."

Hogan's fingers erred, and he invented new letters in the alphabet.

"Damnation!"

"I knew you'd want to speak to him?"

Hogan tore the sheet of paper out and flung it into the wastepaper basket after his other failures. When Merlin was shown in, the detective glowered at him, then pointed resignedly to the other chair in his office. Merlin cleared the set of files off it and sat down.

"You're late," said Hogan.

"What do you mean?"

"I expected you here first thing this morning with a copy of the *Tribune* under your arm. You let me down."

"I had somewhere else to go first, Sergeant Hogan," said Merlin. "Then I was held up at my apartment. It was burgled."

"Don't come to me. Chicago South Side's out of my jurisdiction."

"I know."

"So why bring your sob story to Oak Park."

"I'm wondering if the crimes are related."

"What crimes?"

"The murder here and the break-in there."

"We had no murder here. Don't you read the *Tribune*?"

"I prefer my fiction between the covers of a novel."

"That was good, honest reporting, Mr. Richards."

"It was a pack of lies," said Merlin sharply, "and you know it. You'll be telling me next that Abraham Lincoln committed suicide."

"Metaphorically speaking, he did."

"Let's go back to Saturday night."

Hogan moaned. "I'd rather not. Too many unpleasant

memories. My wife bit lumps off me when I got back so late. She hates it when I climb into bed and wake her up like that. Why can't cops work daylight hours like everyone else? You, for instance."

Merlin swept aside his prevarication with a direct question.

"Who was the man we found in that wine cellar?" he asked.

"No idea, Mr. Richards."

"Are you sure?"

"He had no identification on him."

"There are other ways to find out his name."

"We're still working on it."

"You must have some clue who he is."

"Thousands of transients pass through Illinois."

"He was no transient."

"Then what was he?" said the other. "Help a dumb cop out here."

"Some kind of professional man. That suit of his wasn't cheap."

"It could have been stolen."

"Along with the patent leather shoes and the gold wristwatch."

"Nothing is safe these days. You just been burgled yourself."

"They didn't take anything."

"Eh?"

"Whatever they were looking for in my apartment, they didn't find. Not for want of trying. The place had been turned over good and proper. It took me ages to get everything straight."

"Did you call the cops?"

"No, Sergeant Hogan."

"Why not?"

"There's an issue of trust involved."

Hogan rode the punch in silence and fed another sheet of paper into the typewriter. His fingers pecked away at the keys for a full minute. He pretended to be surprised to find Merlin still there.

"I thought you'd gone."

"Why should I do that?"

"Because you have such a low opinion of cops. You don't trust us, why are we having this conversation? Might as well tell you, I'm not mad about architects either. Especially big-city architects."

"Is that what I am?"

"What you are is a pain in the pubic region, Mr. Richards."

"I'm glad I'm getting through to you at last."

Hogan leaned forward. "Okay, wise guy. Let's have it. You got a beef, lay it on the table and we'll look at it together. Get smart with me, I book you for wasting police time unnecessarily."

"Fair enough."

"And make it snappy, Richards."

"Why are you trying to brush this case under the carpet?"

"Next question, please."

"What did Donald Kruger say to you on Saturday night?"

"And the next."

"How many derelicts wear smart clothes?"

"I haven't done the math."

"Then perhaps you can tell me how many people bash themselves over the head before they crap in their pants and hang themselves."

"We're riding the Supposition Trail again, sir," warned Hogan with a world-weary sigh. "How do you know the deceased sustained the head injury *before* putting the noose around his neck? He might just as easily have swung against the ceiling and cracked his skull open that way. You looked properly, you'd have spotted bloodstains on the stonework."

Merlin was scornful. "That's a ludicrous suggestion!"

"Is it? How many suicides you seen? I been called to dozens, and there's something different in each case. Take this one, for example. This guy obviously didn't realize it's not that easy to hang yourself. You want it over quick, you need a long drop." He jerked a thumb in the direction of Chicago Avenue. "No chance of that in your wine cellar. When he was strung up, his feet were barely six inches off the floor. So, the poor mutt tries to hang himself, discovers it'll take him ages to strangle to death, and swings about in the hope of knocking himself out."

"Do you expect anyone to believe that?"

"The autopsy report said that death was caused by the blow to the head and not by strangulation. You figure it out."

"I already have, Sergeant Hogan. He was murdered."

"When your own autopsy report is ready, send it in."

"I *saw* the man!"

"By the light of a match."

"I had a closer look at him the second time."

"You were still suffering from shock."

"It didn't stop me from seeing that his hands were tied behind his back," argued Merlin. "How do you explain that? What was he trying to do? Set a new trend in hanging. Look—no hands!"

"I thought we closed the book on wisecracks."

"I'm sorry, Sergeant Hogan. But it is a factor in the equation."

"Sure."

"So what's your answer?"

"That the guy's hands were not tied behind his back," said the other dryly. "They were only made to *look* as if they were." He rode over Merlin's objection before he could put it into words. "Hear me out, sir. You said in your statement that you only saw that rope. Did you touch it? No. Did you try to untie it? No. We did, Mr. Richards. And we found that it was only twisted into place. Consistent with the deceased wanting to appear bound and thus the victim of foul play."

Merlin was mystified. "Did we go into the same wine cellar?"

"No, sir. You went in with a match in your hand and got a scare. I went in with a battery torch and two other cops, knowing what we'd find. You're an unreliable witness. The three of us saw it like it was."

"What about Clare Brovik?"

"Her testimony was even shakier than yours. Kid was upset."

"Let's go back to the man's hands. He tied them up himself."

"We believe so."

"But there's no possible motive."

"To the layman, no," said Hogan, hitching up his trousers. "To a trained cop, there are quite a few. Obvious one is sexual gratification."

"That's bizarre."

"Plenty of bizarre people out there, believe me. I don't want to rob you of your innocence, Mr. Richards, but the way it works is this. When guys want to jerk off, they sometimes heighten the pleasure by putting a noose around their neck, cutting off the blood and oxygen supply to the brain. Turns up the flame of pleasure no end, I'm told. When they shoot their wad, off comes the rope, and there they are. Panting in midair with sticky fingers. You never tried that."

"No, Sergeant!"

"Well, don't. Easy to get it wrong. I've cut down three or four guys who hanged themselves by mistake while in the throes of ecstasy. Me? I'll settle for my wife. There's still a high risk element, but two people are usually happy at the end of it."

"Why should anyone sneak onto a deserted building site to

get his kicks? He could do that at home or go to a hotel room."

"Know many hotels with hooks in the ceiling?" countered Hogan. "As for having his fantasies at home, maybe he was afraid his wife might catch him at it. They're not all inadequate single men, you know. Two of the guys I saw strung up were married. One of them was in his wife's panty hose. She knew nothing about his strange personal habits. Told me their sex life was wonderful."

"We're straying a bit off the point here, Sergeant."

"You asked me for possible motive. I gave you one."

"A transient in a hundred-dollar suit hangs himself and ties his hands up to get sexual pleasure?"

"Don't forget the head wound. Inflicting severe pain on himself. Type of flagellation. That's typical, according to the shrinks. To do with guilt. Punishing himself for being naughty."

"Is all this in your report?"

"My report concludes that it was suicide."

"In defiance of all the evidence."

"The *Chicago Tribune* never lies."

"Only its contributors."

"So, Mr. Richards," said the other with a bland smile, "coming back to the question with which you started, my answer is no. The two crimes are not related. The deceased did not break into your apartment, because he was on ice in the morgue."

"Even you must see the coincidence."

"You find a dead body, someone burgles you. Just bad luck."

"I have this feeling, Sergeant Hogan."

"Well, maybe you could have your feelings somewhere else, sir. I got work to do. I gave you plenty of rope. But I'm out of patience now."

Merlin studied him carefully as he tried to work it out.

"Donald Kruger is behind all this, isn't he? That's why you were so slow getting to the scene of the crime. You were giving him time to get across from Chicago. He told you to whitewash the whole thing. A murder in that cellar would send shock waves through Oak Park. As you told me, it's a nice, safe, law-abiding town. You just don't have men getting tied up, beaten, and hanged around here."

"We might make an exception in your case, Mr. Richards."

"I think that Kruger somehow gagged you."

"Is that an accusation?" demanded the other. "If it is, put it in writing, and we'll take the matter up in court. Though I suggest that you speak to Mr. Kruger himself before you do that. He's a gentleman. He also knows the way the law works around here. In favor of the innocent. Mr. Kruger might save you from ending up with egg all over your face. Now beat it, will you?"

"One last thing—"

"No, goddammit!" roared Hogan, on his feet. "There's no last thing! We're through here! Want to know why Mr. Kruger showed up Saturday night, I'll tell you. The body was found on the property of a Mr. Hobart St. John, and his designated representative is Donald Kruger. Like I said, we got our routines. Something like this happens, we need to talk to the owner of the property in question or someone who speaks on his behalf. On account of the fact that the said owner might have a vested interest. You see anything sinister in that, keep it to yourself. But stay out of my face, Mr. Architect. I'm just doing my job the best way I know how." He reined in his temper and contrived a smile. "Tell you what. I'll make a bargain with you."

"A bargain?"

"Yes, Mr. Richards. You stop hassling me, I won't report this conversation to anyone. Not to Mr. Kruger. Not to Mr. St. John. Not to my chief. Or maybe you'd like them to hear what you've been saying in here?"

Merlin remembered his earlier meeting with Hobart St.

John. There was no point in antagonizing the man when the future of Saints' Rest was at stake. There was also nothing to be gained by getting embroiled in a long dispute with the Oak Park Police Department. They held the whip hand over him. To get to the bottom of the mystery, Merlin would have to work more discreetly. Hogan's squashed tomato of a nose twitched.

"Well?" he said.

Merlin nodded. "It's a bargain."

IT WAS ONE of those rare moments when Brad Davisson realized why he had become an architect. He was having a coffee in the outer office that afternoon with Victor Goldblatt and Reed Cutler when the talk turned to a new hotel that was being built on Dearborn Street by a rival firm of architects, Hengest and Munroe. Approaching completion, it was now revealed in all its glory and excited great controversy. Cutler enthused about it, Goldblatt thought it hideous, and Davisson occupied a middle stance between the two, praising some features while condemning others. Three architects were sharing their opinions in a lively discussion that never strayed anywhere near acrimony. It was informative, invigorating, and sheer fun. Davisson had not felt so good about himself or his profession in years.

Merlin's arrival interrupted the debate.

"The prodigal son returns at last!" mocked Goldblatt.

"That's no joke, Vic," said Merlin. "Hobart St. John took me around his factory this morning. I've seen enough fatted calves to last a lifetime."

"Where've you been?" asked Davisson.

"Here, there, and everywhere. Down to the Union Stock Yards, back to my apartment to find that it had been burgled, then out to Oak Park."

"Burgled?" said Cutler. "What did they take?"

"And what's all this about a corpse on a building site?" said Goldblatt, keen to exploit a sensitive subject. "I saw that item in the *Tribune*. It has to be the house you've designed, Merlin."

"It was."

"That will put the curse of death on it."

"Literally," observed Cutler.

"No, it won't," said Davisson fussily. "Everything will go ahead as planned. We have the client's assurance on that, so let's not waste any breath talking about it. I'm glad you're back, Merlin. You had a call from Clare Brovik. She's most anxious to speak to you."

"Clare? When did she ring?"

"About an hour ago. Use the phone in our office."

"Thanks, Brad."

"Before you go," said Cutler. "Settle an argument."

"About what, Reed?"

"The Excelsior. That new hotel on Dearborn. I think it's the best thing that Hengest and Munroe have ever done, and Vic claims it will set Chicago architecture back fifty years. Where do you stand, Merl?"

"I like it."

"I knew you would!" said Cutler.

"Bits of it, anyway," added Merlin. "The concept is terrific. You won't find a better example of art deco anywhere else in the city. Problem is that it sells itself short. It should be four stories higher and have a much more imposing entrance."

"That's exactly what I said!" asserted Goldblatt.

"It's a masterpiece," claimed Cutler.

"It's a civic eyesore."

"They surpassed themselves, Vic. No wonder Hengest and Munroe edged us out for the Niedlander job."

There was a strained silence. Goldblatt colored, Davisson put a hand to his brow, Merlin felt embarrassed, and Cutler realized that he had spoken catastrophically out of turn. He gestured apologetically.

"Sorry, Vic. I thought you knew."

"Is this true?" said Goldblatt, rounding on Davisson.

"Yes and no," mumbled his boss.

"Reed sounded pretty certain about it to me."

"I know one of the draftsmen at the firm," said Cutler. "He told me about it. They're going to build the Niedlander office block."

Goldblatt looked at Merlin. "Did you know about this?"

"It was . . . mentioned as a possibility," he admitted.

"So everybody in this fucking office knows that Jerry Niedlander has dumped us except the man who's supposed to be designing the building!" Goldblatt was fuming. "Why didn't anyone have the grace to tell me? I've been dining out on that job, and it's been taken behind my back. What kind of colleagues are you? It's a fucking conspiracy."

Davisson writhed in discomfort, Cutler was purple with shame.

Merlin thought it a good moment to make his phone call.

THE APARTMENT BLOCK on Kinzie Street was undergoing renovation. Its first three stories were half hidden by scaffolding that jutted out over the sidewalk and which was festooned with warning notices for pedestrians, urging them to look up before they ventured into the maze. When he picked her up on Saturday in his car, Clare Brovik had been waiting outside the building, so Merlin had little time to appraise it. He could repair that omission now. Arriving back there that evening, he took the trouble to study the apartment block from the other side of the street.

It was impressive. Employing the same skeletal-frame construction as the Monadnock Building, it climbed to ten stories and was fronted by a series of projecting bays built of contrasting red and black brick. The interior was equally striking. It made Merlin's own accommodation seem meager. As he took the elevator up to the top floor, he wondered how Clare could afford such a comfortable pad. The corridor that led to her door had a fitted carpet and ornate lighting fixtures at regular intervals. It was worlds away from the bare boards and dangling naked bulbs of Mrs. Romario's establishment. Clare's apartment even had a bell.

"Good evening," he said as the door opened.

"Come on in."

"This is quite some place, Clare."

"Thank you."

She seemed at once pleased and apprehensive. Her hair was down and she wore a dress, but the barrier between them was still there. Merlin could see that it was not a social visit. The apartment was large and well-appointed, with a sense of luxury that took him by surprise. It was not only the Turkish carpet, the big semicircular sofa, the velvet drapes, and the carefully chosen prints and ornaments that astonished him. It was the femininity of the apartment. When she was at work, Clare Brovik cultivated a brisk impersonality. Her home was all woman.

She looked tense. It crossed his mind that she had been crying.

"Are you okay, Clare?"

"Yes. Much better now."

"You sounded a bit anxious over the phone."

"I was keen to talk to you, that's all," she said, waving him to a seat on the sofa. "Thanks for coming over, Merlin."

"I'm glad you invited me. We have a lot to straighten out."

"Yes," she said quietly. "Can I get you anything?"

"No, thanks."

"I've got beer, if you want it. Or wine."

"Later, perhaps."

She nodded and sat in the armchair opposite him.

"First of all," she said seriously, "let me apologize for what happened yesterday. I just wanted to get in touch. Explain."

"You might have mentioned that Donald Kruger was listening."

"That's not strictly true."

"You were in his apartment, Clare."

"Yes."

"Telling me what he told you to say."

"No, Merlin."

"You and Donald were giving me your ventriloquist's act."

"That's not true."

"It makes a change from his Chopin nocturnes."

She bit her lip and lowered her head. Her hands were clasped together in her lap. He waited until she raised her eyes again. There was a mixture of fear and anger in them.

"Let's go back to Saturday evening," he suggested. "You rang him first, didn't you? That's why you took such a long time calling the police. You had to get in touch with Donald Kruger first. Am I right?"

"Yes," she admitted.

"Go on."

"I went back to the restaurant where we had that meal and used their telephone. Donald was wonderful. So calm and reassuring. He told me exactly what to do. I *had* to ring him, Merlin," she explained. "Don't you understand? Saints' Rest is his responsibility. He'd never have forgiven me if I'd rushed off to the cops without telling him what we'd found out there."

"At least I know what the sequence of events was now," said Merlin. "You ring Donald, and he probably gets straight onto the Oak Park Police Department. By the time you get there to raise the alarm, they've already been told what to do, so they drag their feet while Donald is haring across from Chicago in that Packard of his."

"That's not quite how it happened."

"But near enough. Is this all his doing as well?"

"This?"

"Getting me here. Hoping to shut me up. Giving me the story that you and Donald have worked out between you. Is that what's going on?" He looked around him. "Have you got him hidden away somewhere?"

"No."

"Oh, I see. You'll just ring in your report afterward."

"You're wrong, Merlin!"

"Then why do I get the feeling I'm being set up?"

"Donald has no idea that you're here, and he must never find out."

"Why not?"

"Because I'm not supposed to fraternize with business associates."

"What about Saturday?"

"That was different."

"Did you tell him I was taking you to Oak Park?"

"No, I didn't."

"Was he annoyed when he found out?"

"Very annoyed," she said. "He told me to stay away from you for a while. That's why he must never discover that you actually came here to my apartment. He'd be livid."

"Why? Donald Kruger doesn't *own* you."

"It's difficult to explain."

"You're free, white, and over twenty-one. You can do what you like."

"Not when Saints' Rest is involved."

"It's not Donald's house. It belongs to Hobart St. John."

"There are wheels within wheels here."

"So I can see."

"Just accept that I took a big risk in inviting you here."

"What would Donald do if he found out? Fire you."

"And the rest!" She got up and headed for the kitchen. "I need a drink, even if you don't. Sure I can't get you something?"

"A glass of wine, maybe," he said, following her, "but don't open a bottle especially for me, Clare."

"It's already opened."

They went into the kitchen, and she took a bottle of white wine from the refrigerator. He noticed the wineglass on the table. Beside it was an ashtray full of cigarette stubs. Clare took a fresh glass from a cupboard and poured the wine, handing it to him before she refilled her own glass. She took a long sip. Merlin raised his glass to her, tasted his wine, then flicked an approving glance around the kitchen and dining area. Clare Brovik lived in style. His own tiny kitchen ran to a couple of gas rings and a cracked sink.

"Let's go back in there," she said.

Merlin went out first. She joined him on the sofa this time.

"Tell me about those wheels within wheels," he said.

"I can't, Merlin."

"Then what can you tell me? I'm out on a limb here, Clare. Last Saturday I showed you around the site in Oak Park and we found the body of a murder victim in the wine cellar. Now I learn," he continued with sarcasm, "what I really saw was a transient who wandered into that cellar to hang himself. That's what Hobart St. John wants me to believe. And Donald Kruger. And the police themselves. Was I hallucinating on Saturday? You were there with me, Clare. What did you see? A murder victim or a suicide?"

"That's beside the point, Merlin."

"It *is* the bloody point!" he exclaimed, then raised a penitent palm. "Sorry. Didn't mean to swear. It's been a trying day. Apart from anything else, my apartment was burgled."

"That's terrible! What did they steal?"

"The only thing of value that I had. My peace of mind."

"What did the cops say?"

"I've rather lost my faith in policemen."

"You poor thing!" she said with real concern. "On top of everything else, getting burgled. You must have felt sick."

"It didn't exactly improve my health, I'll admit that. But we're straying a bit here. Now," he said, fixing her with a stare, "just answer one simple question. Murder or suicide? Whose side are you on, Clare?" He leaned in close. "Mine or theirs?"

There was a long silence. He could see the reserve slowly draining out of her face. It allowed the affection and the sympathy to show through. She took a sip from her wineglass, then set it aside on the coffee table. She eventually reached a decision. Holding his gaze, she put a gentle hand on his knee.

"Your side, Merlin," she said.

He kissed her.

It was over quickly. Clare Brovik was an uninhibited lover. She gave herself completely, reached her climax early, and at its peak went into such a wild paroxysm that his own release was sped along and shot out of him like molten metal. The pleasure was devastating. Merlin had never known a woman who bit him so hard on the chest or scratched his back with such penetrating nails. Passion spent, tension relieved, Clare was curled up contentedly in his arms. As they lay side by side, it never occurred to him to wonder why a single young woman owned a king-size bed with silk sheets.

How exactly had they ended up there? He could not remember. The first kiss started it, but what followed was a confused jumble of images. A kiss, an apology, a second kiss, an accusation, an argument, a push from her, another kiss, a fourth, a fifth, tears from her, questions from him, more argument, his offer to leave, her plea for him to stay, doubts, confessions, stopping, starting, recriminations, more tears, bed. Was that the sequence? He was certain that he had left something out, and it made him reflect on the unreliability of evidence. It was sobering. Something very important and very enjoyable had just happened to him, yet he could not even hold the details in his mind.

Had the same thing happened in Oak Park? Had the intensity of an experience blurred its edges? Did he really see a murder victim at the end of a rope, or was it the embroidery of an excited imagination?

"Clare?" he murmured.

"Yes?"

"Thank you." She snuggled up to him. "I never expected this."

"Nor me."

"Do you regret it?"

"Shut up."

"I don't. I wasn't even sure if you liked me."

"Don't spoil it."

"What do you mean?"

"Shhhhhh!"

She burrowed deeper into his arms, her face nestling under the side of his chin. Merlin let a hand run down the undulating smoothness of her back and gently caressed her buttocks. Clare had a beautiful, firm body, and her hair had a fragrance that made him tingle, but he was suddenly struck by a thought. He preferred Sally Fiske. Even with her burned spaghetti for breakfast. In a single bed with squeaky springs, Merlin could feel totally at ease with Sally. Lying on silk sheets in a ritzy apartment, he was like a privileged interloper.

Clare dozed off, and it was some time before she opened her eyes again. When she did, she was instantly awake. Stiffening with surprise, she moved his arms and eased away from him.

"What's wrong?" he said.

"Nothing."

"You're pushing me away, Clare."

"Am I?"

"Didn't you want this to happen?"

"I'll make a coffee," she announced, hopping off the bed and slipping into the bathroom. She came out in a kimono. "Then you must go home."

"Go?" He was disappointed. "Can't I stay?"

"No, Merlin."

"Why not?"

"It's too dangerous."

"Are you expecting somebody else?"

"Of course not!"

"Then where's the danger?"

"Get dressed. I'll put that coffee on."

"Clare!"

"Hurry up!"

She left the bedroom, and Merlin felt even more like an interloper. His privileges had been revoked. He was being ejected. When he tried to find his things on the floor, he realized that there were whole stages of their love-play that had slipped his mind. His clothes were scattered along a meandering path that led all the way back to the sofa in the living room. As he was pulling on his shirt, he recalled that her apparel had been discarded in installments along with his, but there was no sign of it now. Clare had hastily removed it as if wanting to obliterate all evidence of their encounter. That hurt him.

Merlin had put on everything but his shoes and his jacket when he noticed the prints. Glimpsed on arrival, they had looked expensive and tasteful, carefully arranged along three walls. Curiosity led to a closer inspection, and he was mildly shocked. The prints were reproductions of ancient Egyptian pornography, suggestive drawings that worked subtly on the senses rather than crude and explicit obscenity that assaulted them. Coffee cups clattered out of sight. He put on his shoes and went into the kitchen. Clare Brovik was now dressed.

"You've put your things back on!" he said in dismay.

"I have work to do, Merlin."

"Is that why I'm being booted out?"

"You're not being booted out."

"I didn't hear you begging me to stay."

"You can't stay."

"Any particular reason?"

"It's not a wise thing to do."

"From where I'm standing, it's a very wise thing to do," he said with a grin. "Under the circumstances, I think it's the *only* thing to do, but it's your apartment, and I'll play to your rules."

"It's not a question of rules."

"Then what is it a question of? Guilt?"

"Don't be silly."

"Remorse? Regret? A headache?"

She opened the refrigerator. "You take milk, don't you?"

"I take what I'm offered, Clare," he said with an affectionate hand on her arm. "And I'm grateful for it. Very grateful."

She lifted his hand, kissed it softly, then pushed it away.

"Back on a business footing, are we?"

"That's the way it has to be, Merlin."

"You could have fooled me."

"I don't want to get you into trouble."

"Why not?" he sighed. "Trouble is my natural milieu. I seem to have had nothing else in the past couple of weeks. I've had trouble from you. Trouble from Mr. St. John. Big trouble from his finicky wife. Trouble from Donald Kruger. Trouble from Sergeant Hogan. Trouble in triplicate from Victor Goldblatt at the office. And trouble at my apartment."

"I still think you should report that to the cops."

"What would they do, Clare?"

"Help."

"Please!" he protested.

"They would, Merlin."

"Not if the Oak Park Police Department is anything to go by. They'd probably try to persuade me that I wasn't burgled at all. A passing hobo left my window open by mistake and the wind blew everything over the floor. No thanks, Clare. I'll do my own detecting."

"Do you have any idea who it might have been?"

"Yes," he said. "Though it's a bit of a long shot."

"Long shot?"

"According to Mrs. Romario, my landlady, a man called this morning to ask the number of my room. Didn't give a name, didn't stay."

"Did he come back?"

"Not while I was there. But he may have done so while I was out."

"There you are, then," she urged. "You've got something to work on. Give his description to the cops, and they can track him down."

"I don't have his description."

"Your landlady does. She saw him."

"All she can remember about him is that he's Italian. Anyway," he said, thrusting his hands into his pockets, "I may be barking up the wrong tree. The burglary may be nothing to do with him. In fact, it may not even have *been* a burglary. Just an excuse to trash my room."

"Why should anyone do that?"

"To let me know that he doesn't like me."

"That's spiteful."

"It's human nature. And there are one or two suspects."

"Such as?"

"Victor Goldblatt."

While the coffee was percolating, Clare set everything out on a tray. She avoided his eyes. The invisible barrier had dropped down between them again. It was impossible to believe that she had been naked in his arms less than ten minutes earlier. Merlin felt a pang of regret.

"Maybe I should just push off."

"Have the coffee first."

"You don't want me here, Clare. I'm in the way."

"No, you're not," she said. "I'm just worried for you."

"I can look after myself."

"Only up to a point. Beyond that—"

He took her by the shoulders and turned her to face him.

"It's Donald Kruger, isn't it?"

"What do you mean?"

"You and he have got something going between you?"

"We haven't. I told you that."

"All right," he decided, "you *did* have, but you split up. Donald is the possessive type. He gets jealous if you take an interest in anyone else. He doesn't just employ you. Donald Kruger wants you." She stifled a laugh. "What's the big joke?"

"You are, Merlin. Can you be that naive?"

"What do you mean?"

"Donald is not interested in any woman."

When he realized what she was telling him, he came close to blushing and chided himself for not being more perceptive. A number of things now fell into place. His envy of Kruger turned to mockery.

"Much rather live happily ever after with Chopin, would he?"

"Donald is very discreet about it."

"So why would he object to my being here? No skin off his nose."

"He wouldn't like it, Merlin."

"Tough!"

"You'd be the one to suffer."

"How?"

"Look," she said. "Let me lay it on the line. We were in the wrong place at the wrong time. It would have been far better if we hadn't gone down into that wine cellar. We saw something that we must try to forget, Merlin. Pretend it was never there. Otherwise, the whole house may come tumbling down around your ears."

"You don't mind that the police are doing a cover-up?"

"It's none of my business, Merlin."

"They're passing off a murder victim as a suicide."

"That's up to them."

"We saw him, Clare. Covered in blood."

"Don't remind me!"

"We were there together. You have to back me up."

"Sorry, Merlin. I work for somebody else."

"Does that mean they own your self-respect?"

She slapped him hard across the face.

GUS WESTLAKE POURED the last of the whiskey into the three glasses, then dropped the bottle into the wastepaper basket. He and Brad Davisson were still in their office, devoting the whole evening to the difficult task of placating a distressed employee. Long hours yielded scant progress. Sobbing quietly, Victor Goldblatt sat in a chair with his head in his hands. Violent rage had given way to cold vengeance, which was now being washed away with pathetic tears. Davisson felt like crying with him. He shot his partner a look of disgust and emptied his glass in one fearsome gulp.

"Here, Vic," said Westlake, taking out a handkerchief. "Borrow this."

"Leave me alone."

"We're only trying to help."

"Big joke!"

"Victor!"

"Get lost!"

"You have to learn to take these setbacks in this profession."

"I certainly have plenty of practice at it, Gus," said Goldblatt, looking up in another fit of rage. "Working for this crummy outfit, I've had setback after fucking setback."

"You've also had your share of triumphs."

"I didn't notice any."

"We did, Vic," said Davisson proudly. "That's why we kept you on when we had to let other guys go. You're our top man. Our star."

"So why am I sitting in your office, crying like a baby?"

"You had a disappointment."

"Oh, that's all it was!" sneered Goldblatt. "A disappointment. A great big hole opens up in front of me, I fall headfirst into it, and you brush it off as a mere disappointment."

"You shouldn't have found out that way," said Westlake.

"Left to you, I wouldn't have found out at all. You knew, Brad knew, Merlin knew, and even Reed Cutler knew. But me? Not a clue. What was I supposed to do? Wait until that office block had been built, then walk past it one day and say, 'Oh, look. Jerry Niedlander didn't give us that commission, after all. What a disappointment! Never mind. I never really wanted the job in the first place!' You stabbed me in the back."

"No, we didn't," insisted Westlake.

"We were on the point of telling you," said Davisson.

"Yes, Vic. I was coming in today for that very purpose."

"Like hell! You were too busy playing a round of golf at the club." He turned his glare on to Davisson. "You're the one I really blame, Brad."

"Me?"

"Yes. I thought you were my friend."

"I am, Victor."

"I actually believed you looked out for me."

"I do, I do."

"Then why didn't you tip me off about this?"

"You don't make it easy."

"Why didn't you call me into your office, pour me a shot of bootleg liquor, then break it to me? It wouldn't have hurt so much then. I mean, I expect Gus to be two-faced, but not you."

"Hold on!" complained Westlake. "I'm not two-faced."

"Come off it, will you?"

"There's no need for insults, Vic."

"You send plenty my way."

"I am *not* two-faced."

"Three-faced, then. Four!"

"Speak up for me, Brad!"

"We don't want to get into a shouting match here," said Davisson.

"Take that back, Vic!" demanded Westlake. "I'm not two-faced."

"Okay, okay," relented the other. "Maybe I shouldn't have said that. You are not two-faced, Gus. But you're the only guy I know who can swallow nails and shit screws."

"I'm not going to put up with this!"

"Calm down, Gus!" said his partner.

"Did you hear what he just said about me?"

"I've heard worse opinions of both of us."

Goldblatt grinned wildly. "You will if you stick around."

"This is getting us nowhere," said Davisson. "All I can say is that I'm deeply sorry, Vic. And so is Reed Cutler, blurting it out like that. Poor guy didn't know where to put himself."

"I could tell him!" said Goldblatt.

"The whole thing was a terrible mistake."

"Brad is right," said Westlake, picking up his cue. "A terrible and regrettable mistake. And it wouldn't have happened if I'd been here. We lost the job, and that's that. Even though Niedlander as good as offered it to me on a plate. Call *me* two-faced?" he howled. "Jerry Niedlander could give me lessons in deception. That creep led me by the nose for weeks. Still," he continued, "let's forget all that. Water under the bridge. We must look to the future. And I tell you this, Vic—Brad will bear me out here—we'll make this up to you. That's a promise. Right, Brad?"

"Yes, Gus. A promise."

"Next big job that comes along, it goes to Victor Goldblatt."

"No question about it."

"You've earned it, Vic."

Goldblatt grew sorrowful and looked from one to the other. "When do you anticipate this bonanza coming along?"

"Difficult to put a time scale on it," said Westlake evasively.

"You mean it depends when the next blue moon is due? Or are we talking about the next eclipse of the sun here?" Tears were forming in Goldblatt's eyes again. "What I really wanted was to design that house in Oak Park, but you give it to Merlin Richards instead. To stop me yelling, you tell me about the Niedlander contract and assure me that it's more or less signed. I really came to believe that it was. Months and months of work with the chance of a hefty bonus."

"That was all built into the contract," argued Westlake.

"Except that it went to Hengest and Munroe instead."

"Crying shame!"

"It's worse than that, Gus. I was counting on that work. All I'm doing at the moment is marking time over here. But a commission like that, a client with Niedlander's prestige. Those are things I can take to my bank manager. So I did." He gave a helpless sigh. "Rachel needs that operation. It won't cure her, but the doctors say that it will slow things down. Buy her more time. You hear what I'm saying? On the strength of that job, I borrowed money from the bank to fund my wife's medical bills. A lot of money. There's no way I can pay off the loan out of what I get doing run-of-the-mill stuff for you." He turned hollow eyes on Davisson. "That what you call a disappointment, Brad?"

"We didn't know anything about this, Vic," said Davisson.

"Well, now you do."

"You did rather jump the gun here."

"I know, I know."

"And your bank manager should have waited until the contract with Niedlander was actually signed."

"He's a personal friend. He knows Rachel. Appreciates that she needs the operation now. So he was prepared to take a chance." He opened his arms in despair. "What am I going to do? They've set a date for the surgery. It's too late to cancel, and I promised my wife that it would go ahead. What am I going to do?"

Davisson had a silent conversation with his partner.

"I tell you what you'll do, Vic," said Westlake, putting an arm around him. "You'll drive out to the hospital to see Rachel, then go on to your sister to pick up the kids. You keep your chin up and your head high because you got a family that depends on you, and they don't need to know about all the heartache that's going on down here. As for the loan," he said, pausing to think it over, "don't worry about it. You get into trouble, come to us. Davisson and Westlake will help out."

"Would you?" said Goldblatt, touched.

"If you don't mind taking dough from a two-faced architect."

"Every cent you can give me, Gus!"

Davisson was more cautious. "We don't have all that much to give."

"We'll manage somehow," said Westlake.

"Have you seen the accounts?"

"Lighten up, Brad. Spare me the Jeremiah routine. We're owed thousands of bucks, and there'll be fresh commissions coming in. And don't forget Hobart St. John. We stand to make a real killing on that house in Oak Park."

"My job!" said Goldblatt wistfully. "And Merlin got it."

"I don't think he's too pleased about that right now," said Davisson with a grimace. "It's not been plain sailing out there. My guess is that Merlin probably wishes he'd never heard of Hobart St. John!"

IT HAD BEEN a long but productive day. Sally Fiske spent most of it at the zoo, walking around with a sketch pad and drawing every animal that caught her fancy. Lions, tigers, and leopards were there in profusion. So were giraffes. A lone hippo was surfacing from the water. A camel was caught drinking from a trough. Elephant and rhino were included, and so was every species of bear, but she spent the most time watching the antics of the monkeys. They gave her endless inspiration. Ideas dropped onto her cartridge paper like confetti.

The contract with the publisher had been signed, and although the advance was yet to come through, she was keen to begin work on the illustrations. When she got back to her apartment, she was pleased to see that her sketchbook was almost filled. There would be other visits to the zoo and several to the library, but she felt she had made a promising start. She had managed to find the vast majority of the animals mentioned in the text of the book. The reptiles could wait for another day. Sally cooked herself a meal, listened to the radio, and basked in the freedom of the artist.

The evening was well advanced when she finally settled down in her armchair with the *Chicago Tribune*. She had given it a mere five minutes' attention over breakfast and now wanted to read it in more detail. The front-page story only depressed her, so she opened the paper and began to work her way through the items inside. When she came to the mention of a suicide in Oak Park, she paid no heed at first and read the article on a robbery in Berwyn that was beside it. Then a bell rang faintly in her memory, and she went back to the report of a man's body being found on a building site.

Merlin Richards had designed a house in Oak Park. Construction was under way. She wondered if there was any connection between the news item and her discarded boyfriend. Then she remembered how he had let her down and lost interest in the speculation. The item in the paper was probably nothing to do with him. Sally turned a page.

She was soon laughing out loud at a cartoon strip.

MERLIN RICHARDS SAT outside the apartment block in his car for the best part of an hour, debating whether or not to go back up to apologize to Clare Brovik. Her behavior was strange. She wanted him, she took him, then she cast him aside. His pride was wounded. Clare moved from intimacy to detachment with no intervening stage. He was baffled. What had he done wrong? The sex was great for him. Had she faked her pleasure? Once again, he found himself thinking fondly of Sally Fiske. She was open and guileless. She might not live in a luxury apartment, but at least he knew where he stood with her—until she dropped him. But even then, she was obeying the laws of cause and effect.

Clare Brovik did not seem to have heard of such things.

Still musing on his fall from grace, he abandoned his vigil and drove away from Kinzie Street. He suspected that he would have no call to visit it again. Since he had no food in his larder, he stopped at a cheap restaurant to eat a late dinner. He toyed with the idea of buying an evening paper to see if it gave more details of the alleged suicide in Oak Park, but he knew that he would only be courting disappointment. There would be no more publicity about Saints' Rest. Its owner would see to that. At the Lake Shore Drive party Merlin had met a senator, a congressman, two judges, a police commissioner, a district attorney, and no fewer than three newspaper editors.

Hobart St. John could rewrite history with impunity.

It was getting dark by the time Merlin came out of the restaurant. He drove back to his apartment, found a space for his car, then let himself into the hallway. Merlin paused outside Mrs. Romario's door, wondering if he should report the earlier break-in and deciding, once again, that it would only upset her unnecessarily and prompt her to call the police. He did not savor the idea of explaining to the local Sergeant Hogan why a burglary he discovered that morning was not being reported until the end of the day. Besides, nothing had actually been taken, and his room had now been tidied.

The burglary had one beneficial effect. It had sharpened his instincts. He approached his room much more warily. As he stood outside his door, he thought he heard the sound of movement inside. Turning his key in the lock, he opened the door far enough to see through the crack between its two hinges. A dark shape lurked behind his door. Merlin used his full force to push the door right back, knocking the intruder hard and drawing a gasp of pain from him. He then dived into the room, slammed the door shut behind him, and grappled in the darkness with a short, wiry man who was cursing under his breath.

Merlin was strong, toughened by his years on the rugby field. He threw the man to the floor, flung himself on top, and got in a relay of punches. Then his fist struck something hard and metallic. He winced and rubbed the injured knuckles. His adversary took quick advantage of the respite, rolling Merlin over onto his back and clubbing him once on the head to stun him. There was a searing pain where the scalp opened and blood began to ooze. Merlin's eyes filmed over, and his strength seemed to fade away.

When he could focus his eyes again, he was looking at the barrel of a gun. The man sitting astride him dispensed with introductions.

"What happened to my brother?" he demanded.

13

The proximity of the gun concentrated his mind at once. Merlin forgot all about the pain from the blow and the slow trickle of blood down his cheek. They were irrelevancies. The nose of the weapon was jammed against his forehead as the question was repeated. "What happened to my brother?"

"I've no idea who your brother is," said Merlin.

"Don't lie, friend."

"I swear it."

"Where is he?"

"I haven't a clue."

"I think you do. I watched you."

"You're making a mistake. You've got the wrong man." The gun was oppressively heavy against his brow. "Let me tell you who I am."

"I know who you are, Mr. Richards."

Merlin guessed how. "You broke in here this morning!"

"Answer my question."

"I know nothing about your brother—honestly!"

"Then what were you doing out in Oak Park? Talking to the cops."

Merlin's mind was working overtime. He could see his captor only in outline, but the voice gave him some idea of age and education. The man was short, lithe, and powerful. He handled the gun as if he knew how to use it. Merlin did not wish to provoke a demonstration.

"We found a dead body on the site," he explained.

"We?"

"Clare Brovik and me. I designed a house in Oak Park—but you probably know that if you've been through my things. Clare works for the man who owns the house. She wanted to see what progress had been made, so I showed her around. We finished up in the wine cellar."

"Go on."

Merlin was certain that the facts would be highly unpopular, but he did not dare to lie to his listener. Truth was the only card he could play.

"We found a man's body down there."

"A tramp? Like it said in the paper?"

"No, that was a cover-up."

"So who was he?"

"I don't know. I didn't search him, and the police say they found no identification on him. Though I wouldn't trust their word on that. But he was no tramp," said Merlin firmly, "and he didn't commit suicide."

"How did he die, then?"

"Someone killed him."

The man was smoldering, his anger almost tangible.

"Was he hanged?"

"Yes."

"My brother was *hanged*?"

"I'm not sure if it was your brother, but . . . yes, I'm afraid so."

"Describe him."

"What?"

"Describe the man you saw hanging there," ordered the other.

Merlin decided against mentioning the blood and its disfiguring effects. The less detail he could give about the state of the corpse, the better. He was the pressure of a trigger finger away from death. He needed to be obedient and helpful.

"He was short and slim. Dark hair. In his thirties, I'd say. He was wearing a smart suit, black patent leather shoes. Oh, and a wristwatch. A solid gold wristwatch."

"A mustache? Thin mustache?"

"Yes. A pencil mustache."

The man's body sagged for a second, and he brought his other hand up to his face. Relief for Merlin was temporary. The gun was pressed so hard against his forehead that he thought it would bore a hole.

"Did you kill him?" demanded the man.

"No. We just stumbled on the body."

"Do you know who *did* kill him?"

"Not yet, but I intend to find out."

"Why?"

"Because I don't want to see his murderer get off scot-free," said Merlin with passion. "For some reason, the police want to bury this crime and pass it off as a freak suicide. You saw that nonsense in the *Tribune*. When I complained, they told me to keep my mouth shut. But I know what I saw down in that cellar. A victim of murder."

"Benito."

"Who?"

"Benito. My brother, Benito."

"How can you be so sure?"

"It has to be him."

"Go to the police and ask to view the body."

"I did."

"What did they say?"

"They told me to take a powder."

"But they can't do that," said Merlin. "You have rights."

"Cops don't think so."

"Find a lawyer. He'll make them cooperate."

"No need. His body has been identified now. By you."

He stood up very slowly but kept the gun trained on Merlin.

"Stay there, friend. I want to see your face."

"My face?"

"To see if you're lying to me."

He moved backward until he could reach out for the switch on the bedside lamp. It threw a sudden glare into Merlin's eyes, making him squint. The man stood beside it and looked down at him, scrutinizing his face carefully. After a long pause, he snatched the towel that was hanging over the end of the bedstead and tossed it to Merlin.

"Put that on your head."

"Can I sit up, please?"

"Slowly, friend. Very slowly."

"Thanks for the towel."

"No funny business, mind."

Merlin sat up and pressed the towel against his scalp. It was not a deep wound, but it still throbbed painfully. He took his first look at his assailant and saw the resemblance immediately. The man, in his early forties and dressed in a nondescript brown suit, was completely bald; it was his facial characteristics that were so distinctive. Merlin was looking at the same eyes, nose, chin, and pencil mustache as those on the man in the wine cellar. His visitor was Benito's older brother.

The gun was still trained on Merlin, its owner still suspicious.

"Why did you go to the cops today?" he asked.

"In Oak Park?"

"I followed you."

"It was that report in the *Tribune*," said Merlin. "It made my blood boil. It was a pack of lies. I told Sergeant Hogan that it was a whitewash, but he gave me the runaround."

"So what are you going to do now?"

"Find out who the murderer really was and why the Oak Park Police Department is shielding him."

"I can answer the second question."

"Can you?"

"They don't care, is why."

"Don't care?"

"About my brother. Benito was no angel. He's wanted in three different states, and there was a federal warrant issued against him. The cops are not interested in who rubbed him out. They figure the guy performed a public service. One more hood off the streets, that kind of crap." He pursed his lips and pondered. "Some ways, you got to agree with them. Except they're committing a crime in not trying to solve a murder."

"Sergeant Hogan doesn't see it like that."

"He sees it the way he's told."

"And what about you?"

"Benito was my brother," he said simply. "Someone has to answer."

"Have you any idea who that someone is?"

"I thought you were involved somehow."

"I am," said Merlin ruefully, using the towel to wipe some

of the blood from his face. "All I did was to go down into the cellar of a house I designed, and what happens? I get pissed on by the police, strong-armed by the owner of the house, lied to by his employees, burgled by you, and now roughed up into the bargain. I'd call that involvement, wouldn't you?"

The man held his gaze as if looking into his soul. Merlin thought of the staring eyes of the hanged man in the cellar. They had the same manic glint. His companion reached a tentative decision.

"I think you may be on the level, friend."

"Thank goodness for that!"

"Might even consider putting this gat away."

"At least point it in another direction."

"How do I know I can trust you?"

"I've got a kind face."

"What would you do if I walked out right now?"

"Breathe a sigh of relief."

"And then?"

"Take a bath, get myself cleaned up."

"And then?"

"Sleep like a baby, probably."

"You won't go to the cops?"

"Why should I?"

"Intruder in your room. Slugs you. Threatens to shoot you. Most guys might think that worth a mention to the cops." He looked around. "Did you tell them someone broke in?"

"No," said Merlin. "I'm not exactly enamored of police uniforms at the moment. I didn't report the break-in, and I won't report this."

"Awkward for me, if you did."

"Awkward?"

"My brother's lying on a slab in the morgue out in Oak Park.

They got *his* name, they know mine." His face puckered with distaste. "I don't want cops banging on my door again. Ever. I put all that shit behind me. I been clean as a whistle. Until now."

"Clean?"

"It's a personal matter."

"I won't go running to the police. You have my word."

"Would you swear on the Holy Bible?"

"A stack of them."

The man grew solemn. "You a committed Christian?"

"I'm Welsh," said Merlin with a half-smile. "Baptized in the River Taff. Live in Wales, and you carry a chapel around on your back like a snail shell. We quote Scripture by the yard. Don't ask me if I'm a Christian. I even designed a place of worship."

"That's okay, then," said the other as if a secret sign had just passed between them. "I'm going to put this gat away. You can get up, friend, but don't come any closer. Is it a deal?"

"Best I've had all day."

The man edged across to the door and stood where he could make a quick exit. He put the gun into a holster on his belt. Merlin hauled himself up and crossed to an upright chair. He lowered himself gingerly into it. There was real sympathy in his visitor's voice.

"Sorry I had to slug you."

"So am I," said Merlin, still holding the towel to the wound.

"You shouldn't have tackled me like that."

"Force of habit. I played rugby for several years."

"I was just going to hold the gun on you. Ask a few questions."

He gestured to Merlin to remove the towel. Merlin did so. The bleeding had stopped. The man took a step forward to peer at his head.

"You might need a coupla stitches."

"I'll live."

"You pack a good punch, friend. Only way to stop you."

"Stop apologizing."

"I have to live with this," said the other sadly. "I hoped I'd finished with it. Violence. Putting the squeeze on a guy. I can just imagine what Father C. would say to me."

"Father who?"

"But it's a means to an end. I had to do it. For Benito's sake."

"I'm very sorry about what happened to your brother."

"He took one chance too many. I warned him."

"What was he doing on that building site?"

"Getting himself killed. I want the man who did it."

"So do I!" said Merlin with feeling.

"This is not your fight, Mr. Richards."

"It is now."

"Leave it to me."

"But I may be able to help you."

"How?"

"The police are not hushing this up of their own accord," said Merlin. "They're acting on orders. I have access to the man who gave those orders. His name is Hobart St. John."

"I know that."

"You do?"

"Yeah. I know lots."

"Then why don't we pool information?"

"You dig up what you can, pass it on to me."

"How do I contact you?"

"I'll be in touch."

"Isn't there anything you can tell me?"

"No. I'll work on my own theories."

"What made you think that dead body could be your brother?"

"He didn't show up for dinner on Saturday night."

"But how did you connect him with Oak Park?"
"Told me he'd be out there on Friday."
"Why?"
"That's between me and him. You tackle this other guy. Hobart St. John. Patron saint of the meat trade. I'll get back to you."
"But I don't even know who you are."
"Benito's older brother."
"Don't you have a name?"
"It's not important."
"But I'd like to know who I'm dealing with," argued Merlin. "And I'd like to know why you suspected me. And I'd also like to know what you were searching for when you broke in here."
"Oh, I can tell you that, friend."
"Can you?"
"Yeah," said the man. "The money."
And he was gone.

HOBART ST. JOHN was buzzing with contained anger. Restlessly circling his office, he punched a hand into the other palm. Donald Kruger did not try to interrupt him. He stood there impassively and took the criticism.

"That's what I keep coming back to, Donald," said his employer. "None of this need have happened. If it had been handled properly in the first place, we'd have had no problems. Instead of which, we end up in a swamp of shit. What's wrong with you?" he asked, stopping to aim his question into the other's face. "You're my troubleshooter. Your job is to come running when the alarm goes off. But you're supposed to quell any trouble, not start it. You know how much I hate it when things don't go exactly according to plan."

"Yes, Mr. St. John."

"I want a quiet life. Is that too much to ask?"

"No, Mr. St. John."

"Then let this be the last time."

"I can guarantee it."

"If I so much as hear a whisper of trouble, you walk. Permanent."

Kruger's face betrayed no emotion, but he quailed inwardly. He was paid handsomely, trusted completely, and given privileges that nobody else in the organization enjoyed. To have it all taken away from him would be a savage blow to his pride, and he knew that Hobart St. John's displeasure would not end with mere dismissal. It was important to win back his employer's goodwill.

"The matter is over and done with, Mr. St. John," he promised.

"I sincerely hope that it is."

"You won't be disturbed again."

"I'd better not be, Donald. Keep the lid on this one."

"It's done. I called in a lot of favors and spread a few more around. I also put an end to some loose talk among Sarbiewski's men. His foreman will play ball now. While I was out in Oak Park, I took the trouble to call in on Sergeant Hogan and keep him sweet. He's handling this investigation in precisely the way you'd want."

"If it was the way I wanted it, there'd *be* no investigation."

"The site has been cleared. In every sense. As soon as the builders leave at the end of the day, the night watchman takes over. With two guard dogs. Saints' Rest is completely protected."

"That's what I thought before."

"I've learned my lesson, Mr. St. John."

"Remember it." He sat behind his desk. "What about Clare?"

"She's calmed down now."

"We don't want her singing out of tune on this."

"Clare knows what her obligations are."

"Send her in."

"Yes, Mr. St. John."

"And Donald—"

"Yes?"

"Enough is enough."

Kruger gave a submissive nod and strode out of the room. St. John drummed his fingers rhythmically on the desk and meditated. His eye fell on the photograph of his wife. A romantic impulse stirred. It was cut short by Clare's arrival. Poised and businesslike, she came into the room after knocking and stood in front of his desk. He studied her for a moment before giving her an indulgent smile.

"How are you, Clare?" he said softly.

"I'm fine, thank you, Mr. St. John."

"Donald tells me that you were a bit rattled at first."

"At first."

"But all that's past. Good. You understand the position?"

"Donald explained it to me."

"I don't want any more hiccups on this. You know how much time Alicia spent on this project. She went through the drawings with you. It means everything to her. Lake Shore Drive has associations she'd rather forget, and who can blame her? Cornelia Rose was the same. She wouldn't go anywhere near the bedroom I'd shared with my second wife. I respect those feelings." He looked down at Alicia's photograph, then back at Clare. "So tell me," he said. "What exactly were you doing out in Oak Park on Saturday?"

"Looking at the work of Frank Lloyd Wright."

"With his greatest fan. Merlin Richards."

"He explained everything so clearly. It was a revelation."

"And was that the only revelation that happened out there?"

"Yes," she said with categoric firmness.

"Are we certain about that, Clare?"

"I went there to look at buildings."

"Why didn't you tell Donald in advance?"

"I didn't think it was necessary. I was really interested to find out more about Wright's work, and I thought that it might help."

"Ah! That's different. Another motive."

"I was only doing what you asked me to do, Mr. St. John."

"Were you?"

"Yes."

He narrowed his lids to watch her. She held her composure under his scrutiny, but her heart was pounding. He stood up and came around the desk to stand beside her, searching her face for telltale signs. When he found none, he let out a wheeze of satisfaction.

"Carry on doing what I ask, and everything will be fine, Clare."

"SAINTS ALIVE!" EXCLAIMED Gus Westlake. "What happened to you, Merl?"

"I walked into a brick wall."

"A brick wall?"

"Yes, Gus. The one built by you and Donald Kruger and Hobart St. John to keep out prying eyes. It's high and solid, and it hurts like hell when you walk headfirst into it. The three of you ought to be working for the Ace Construction Company. You're nifty bricklayers."

They were in the offices of Westlake and Davisson, and the others had not yet arrived. The meeting was at Merlin's insistence. When he called his employer to arrange it, he did not mention that he would arrive with his head swathed in bandages. Westlake walked around him in awe, as if viewing the Hanging Gardens of Babylon.

"What really happened?" he asked.

"The doctor got carried away."

"Doctor?"

"All I needed was three stitches, but he insisted on bandaging my head as if I was an Egyptian mummy. As to how I got the injury," said Merlin, "I slipped on the soap in the bathroom."

"In other words, mind my own business."

"This *is* your business, Gus! It's the latest memento from that house I'm supposed to be bulding out at Oak Park. I didn't know there were so many occupational hazards attached to architecture."

"Did somebody hit you, Merl?"

"People have been hitting me ever since I took on the commission."

"Now, that's not fair."

"No, it isn't," said Merlin angrily, "and I'm fed up with being the victim of unfairness. So let's have everything out in the open, Gus. None of your usual flannel. I want the truth."

"About what?"

"This mess you dropped me into!"

"Not you as well," groaned the other, flopping into a chair. "Brad and I were in this office for hours last night trying to soothe Victor Goldblatt. Now it's your turn. Reed Cutler will be next in line."

"They're both implicated in this."

"What are you talking about?"

"Dodgy deals, Gus. Like the one you made for me."

"How was I to know you'd find a dead body on-site?"

"Let's go right back to the start."

"What start?"

"Your first barefaced lie."

"There were no lies, Merlin!" protested Westlake. "What's gone wrong with your guys? Yesterday, I got Vic calling me two-faced. Now another man whose career I've nurtured and whose wages I pay slings some mud at me." He stood up to confront Merlin. "You calling me a liar?"

"Don't try to browbeat me, Gus."

"Are you?"

"Yes!"

"Prove it!"

Merlin held his ground and met his hostile glare. He was fond of his boss, but it was time to put personal feelings aside and speak out, whatever the cost might be. It was too late to turn back now.

"Why did you choose me for this job?" he asked.

"You know damn well. Because you were the obvious choice."

"No, Gus. Victor Goldblatt was. Yes, I know he can be nervy and temperamental, but he's had far more experience than I have. So has Reed Cutler. And that's what ruled them out, isn't it?"

"What are you on about?"

"The real reason you picked me. I'm the greenhorn here. You knew that I'd be so grateful to take on this job that I wouldn't notice things that Vic and Reed would have been onto like a flash."

"Such as?"

"Such as the odd behavior of the client."

"Go on."

"Such as unwarranted supervision. Sacking one construction company and employing another. Inviting the architect to a party to soften him up. Tying him hand and foot. Keeping him under constant surveillance. Making sure that he runs the whole race in blinkers." Merlin hit his stride. "The real giveaway was that Hobart St. John retained our services in the first place. Why us? Why a small operation like Westlake and Davisson, when they could have had the pick of the big boys? I've just given you the answer. The big boys would be too smart. They'd lift up stones to see what was underneath them. They wouldn't let a client push them around. That's why St. John went for you, isn't it?"

"No, Merl."

"Because he knew you'd be so grateful for the money that you wouldn't ask where it came from. And you in turn picked me because I wasn't as streetwise as the others. You could butter me up."

"That doesn't make me a liar, Merl."

"Well, it won't win you the Honesty Prize, either."

Westlake flared up and seemed to be on the point of striking him, but he thought better of it and retreated to his chair instead. He ran both hands through his hair in desperation before making an effort to pull himself together. His bonhomie was miles away.

"Go easy on me," he pleaded. "All I'm trying to do is to keep this firm in business, so don't turn the thumbscrews too hard. You've hit a few rocks on this project, I know. I sympathize. But before I come to you, let me tell you what else is going on around here so that you understand my problems. Let's start with Brad. Swell architect, lousy businessman."

"He didn't want me for this commission, did he?"

"No, but that's immaterial. His opinion didn't count. Hobart had already made the decision. Brad had to put up with it. Though it didn't help his ulcer none." He pointed to the desk opposite. "Taken a look at my partner recently? Put on years in the past few months. Brad is a worrier. He grows ulcers like some guys cultivate tomatoes. He's cracking up on me, Merl. I mean it. The guy is right on the edge. And he's only one of my problems. Victor is another one."

"I was there when he found out about the Niedlander deal."

"Know why it hurt him so much?" said Westlake. "It was nothing to do with his pride. Vic borrowed money from the bank against that job. He was so convinced it was in his grasp that he raised the money to pay for an operation his wife needs to have. Cardiac surgery. That comes expensive. We had him weeping his eyes out in here because he won't be able to meet the repayments. On top of that—and I daren't even tell this to Brad—we got a jolt coming from Reed Cutler as well."

"Reed?"

"He's leaving us."

"He's said nothing to me."

"Nor to me yet, but I sense it coming. You thought that Victor was the jealous colleague, but Reed is the one to watch."

"He was so pleased for me when I got my break."

"And so pleased for Vic when the Niedlander deal seemed to fall into his lap. But deep down he hated the pair of you for it. Why should he be the one who was left out? No, Reed has been touting for a job elsewhere, and I reckon he's found one."

"Where?"

"Where else? Hengest and Munroe. I got to thinking, Merl. Why was it snatched away from us at the eleventh hour? Why was our bid turned down by Jerry Niedlander?" He nodded toward the outer office. "Answer? Reed Cutler. He fed Hengest and Munroe the dope they needed to outbid us and snaffle the contract."

"Can you prove that?"

"No, Merl. But ask yourself this. Was it really such an accident when he blurted out the truth to Victor? Or was it deliberate?"

"Reed did say that he'd heard it from a friend who worked as a draftsman with Hengest and Munroe."

"I rest my case. So tread lightly, eh? I'm playing nurse to Brad and to Victor and bracing myself for a desertion by Reed. That's not an excuse to evade your questions," he said, rallying slightly and managing a smile. "What I'm asking is this. Just put them quietly."

"Why did you pick me?"

"Because you had more than enough talent for the job."

"And?"

"You wouldn't cause any bother. How wrong I was!"

"How crooked is Hobart St. John?"

"Every businessman has to cut corners. He cuts more than most."

"Why is Donald Kruger watching my every move?"

"Haven't you figured that out yet? Maybe you turn him on."

"Be serious, Gus."

"Kruger is Hobart's lieutenant. He's sitting on your shoulder to make sure the house gets built exactly the way Alicia wants it. And—"

"Spit it out, Gus."

"To distract you so you won't ask how that prime site in Oak Park became available at such a convenient time. There was a house there before, you know. Quite a nice one. Hobart tried to buy it off the owners. But they wouldn't sell at any price."

"So how did he get his hands on that plot?"

Gus Westlake needed a long pause before parting with the truth.

"The house was burned to the ground."

Sally Fiske remembered the bear clearly. He was one of the acknowledged crowd-pleasers at the zoo, and she saw why. Bigger and browner than all of the other bears in the compound, he was yet the most childlike and appealing. The animals were kept in a huge pit. The surrounding trench was deep and wide, acting as a moat against the paying public and an impassable barrier against the bears. An old woman, ignoring the warning not to feed the animals, was dipping her hand into a paper bag and bringing out all manner of provender before tossing it across the divide. The big bear—Tiny, by name—stood on his hind feet and moved with the grace of a dancer, catching every morsel thrown to him and cheekily intercepting food destined for his companions.

A game quickly developed. The old woman tried to outthink him. One small cake went directly to Tiny, then a second immediately was hurled to one of the bears behind him. Tiny was equal to the ruse, rising to full height to catch the first cake in his mouth, then sticking out a massive paw to pluck the other from the air like an outfielder for the White Sox. The watching kids loved Tiny and cheered him on. He played to the audience shamelessly. When the old lady remonstrated with him, he looked hurt and indignant, curling into a ball and turning himself into such a picture of injured innocence that she felt sorry for him and threw him a consoling bun. Tiny was soon back at his piratical best.

Sally worked on the drawing for an hour in her apartment, trying to recapture Tiny's characteristic stance and the almost human expression on his face. Though the book she was illustrating was on wild animals, she took care that they would not frighten her young readers. Even the snarling lions and charging rhino would have an unthreatening look to them. Tiny was an ideal model. Strong enough to bite a man's face off and tear him to pieces, he yet performed at the zoo like an overgrown kid. That was the quality that Sally tried to put into her illustration. His cuddliness. His exuberance. His endearing naughtiness.

When she sat back to review the finished result, she was delighted with the way she had drawn the massive body and shaded in the coat. Sally had caught Tiny's movement perfectly. What caused her to blink was the bear's face. It had the wonder and mischievousness of a child, but it did not resemble the animal at the zoo. The big, friendly, wicked, smiling countenance bore an uncanny resemblance to that of Merlin Richards.

She made a coffee to revive herself and bought some thinking time. Her anger at Merlin had blotted out fond memories of the pleasure they had shared. When she noticed the packet of spaghetti on her kitchen shelf, she recalled a hilarious breakfast in bed with him, laughing over her culinary shortcomings, then finding a delightful way to combine eating with making love. Merlin Richards was a good man. Thoughtless at times, perhaps, and prone to lecture her on the joys of architecture, but those were minor faults. In their fleeting relationship, he had been good for her. Merlin was unlike almost all the other guys she dated. They had been cute beforehand. Merlin was nice to her afterward.

Why had she frozen him out? On her last night at the hotel, she was annoyed with him for not turning up to drive her home, and yet she had told him not to bother. Had his promise to be there withered in the heat of her rejection? She could hardly blame him for doing what she had, in fact, decreed. Merlin was no mind reader. He did not know that she might have second thoughts at the end of her last day as a hotel clerk. Then again, maybe he had a legitimate excuse for not turning up at the hotel. Some emergency might have held him up.

She remembered the item in the *Tribune*. Rescuing the paper from her trash can, she found the page and smoothed it out to read the item again.

The oddness had not struck her before. Why had someone hanged himself on a building site? And how? Reports of suicide were all too common in the newspapers, but they invariably told of distraught family members finding the dead body in the bedroom or the attic or some other part of the house. Only a week earlier a man had hanged himself in Brookfield in his garden shed, yet another despairing victim of financial ruin. Something else puzzled Sally. What was a transient doing in Oak Park in the first place? It was not an area where the waifs and strays tended to go. They drifted into Chicago itself and looked for pickings there. If they had the urge to kill themselves, they usually stepped in front of a train or drowned in Lake Michigan.

Was it conceivable that the discovery was made at the house that Merlin was designing? How many building sites were there in Oak Park? The body had been found on Saturday night. Merlin was very possessive about Saints' Rest. If a man hanged himself there, the architect would probably rush straight out there as soon as he heard. Could that be the reason he was not waiting outside the Beauregard Hotel? Or was there a simpler explanation? Sally left early, Merlin arrived late.

If nothing else, the item in the paper gave her an excuse to make contact. But would it be wise to do so? Wanting to see him again, Sally was hesitant about showing any eagerness to do so. She postponed the decision and went back to work, but even as she was removing Merlin's face from the paper with deft strokes of her india rubber, she felt him occupying her mind once more and touching her emotions.

It was time to emulate the old lady at the zoo.

Sally would toss her own bear a nourishing bun.

"THAT'S ABOUT ALL I can tell you, Mr. Richards, except that it was a shame."

"A shame?" echoed Merlin.

"Pretty house. Old-style clapboard. Have to tell you, I always prefer timber as a building material. I know you architects can work wonders with brick and steel and poured concrete, but give me a clapboard house with a picket fence any day. Trouble is," he conceded, "timber increases the fire risk. Insurance premiums are higher."

The fire chief in Oak Park was a stocky man with a gnarled face that had been toasted by a hundred conflagrations into a reddish hue. He was polite to his visitor but made it clear that he could not give him much time. Merlin pressed for the significant detail.

"Was it arson?"

"No, sir. We thought so at first, but we were mistaken."

"So what did cause the fire?"

"Faulty wiring."

"Wiring?"

"Electrician hadn't done his job properly," said the older man. "The fuse box was in the basement, and there were stacks of newspapers and magazines nearby. Something shorted, the sparks fell onto the paper, and that was that. Next thing I know, I had to send every appliance I got to the scene. The fire had got such a hold that I had to call the guys in Cicero to send one of their trucks as backup."

"And you couldn't save any of the house?"

"No, sir. Burned to a cinder. Some old newspapers cought fire and it spread to the books."

"Books?"

"Rare books," explained the fire chief. "Guy who owned the house was a rare-book dealer. Don't know much about the antiquarian scene myself, but I'm told there's a lot of dough in it. The owner had his own collection insured for thousands of dollars. Beats me why. All you can do with a book is read the damn thing and it's done for, but he sold his stock all over the country. And abroad in some cases. In fact, that's where he was when the fire broke out here."

"Abroad?"

"In England. Going to book fairs, he said. Trying to pick up first editions of Dickens. That was his favorite, Charles Dickens." He gave a harsh laugh. "I tell you this about Dickens, sir. Don't know what he puts into his books, but once they're on fire, they burn like merry hell!"

"Was nobody in the house when the fire broke out?"

"Thankfully, no."

"What time of day was it?"

"Late evening during last fall. It was quite dark."

"And you're sure the electrical fault was to blame?"

"Our findings were backed up by the fire investigator from

the insurance company. They were talking about suing the electrician."

"Did they?"

"Bit difficult. He died five years ago."

"Did he do the wiring on any other houses in Oak Park?"

"My only concern was the one in Chicago Avenue."

"I was just wondering if any other customers of his had reason to complain," said Merlin. "I work with electricians all the time. They know how lethal electricity can be, so they usually take great care. Did this man have a bad reputation in the trade?"

"Not so as you'd notice."

"So what went wrong?"

"All I can give you is the facts as I saw them, sir."

"An accidental fire that destroyed the whole property."

"But cost no lives," said the other. "That's the important thing. You can rebuild a house—as you're doing right now. But you can't replace skin and bone. No fatalities. That was the saving grace."

"How did you get in touch with the owner?"

"With difficulty, sir. He and his wife were moving around, and we had no address for him. But the cops finally tracked down his son in Connecticut and broke the news to him. He knew how to reach his parents."

"They must have been devastated."

"They were, sir. Mr. Perrott—that was his name, Cecil Perrott—was hurt bad. It wasn't so much the house as the rare books. A lifetime's collection wiped out in a couple of hours." He clicked his tongue in sympathy. "Mr. Perrott lost heart. Sold up and moved out of Oak Park. I heard they'd moved to Connecticut to be near their grandchildren. And that about sums it up, sir."

Merlin was grateful but faintly suspicious. He could not work out if the fire chief was telling the truth or repeating a well-rehearsed story. The man was highly plausible. He was also much more amenable to questioning than Sergeant Hogan had been. That suggested to Merlin that the fire chief had nothing to hide, but it did not remove the nagging doubts from his mind about the timing of the fire. After turning down successive offers for the house from Hobart St. John, the owners had found themselves burned out, and the plot of land became conveniently available. Merlin had already watched a murder on the property being transformed into a case of suicide. He wondered if an easy arson had been similarly disguised as defective wiring.

The bandaging had now been removed from his head, and he had combed his hair carefully over the scalp wound, but the stitches were still there, digging into him like needles. It was a painful reminder of the high personal cost of working on Saints' Rest, and it spurred him on to get to the bottom of the mystery surrounding the house.

"Thank you for your help," he said, rising to leave. "I don't suppose that you remember which insurance company was involved?"

"Not offhand, Mr. Richards."

"But the name would be in your files, presumably."

"They're confidential."

"Pity."

"Why? What's your interest? I'd have thought an architect would pay more attention to the house he's building than the one that was there before it. Ancient history now."

"You're right," agreed Merlin. "Won't bother you any further."

The fire chief opened the door of the office to let him out.

"Good-bye, sir."

"Good-bye. Oh, one thing—"

"What's that?"

"Does the name Donald Kruger mean anything to you?"

"Nope. Afraid that it doesn't."

The man's smile was impregnable. Merlin accepted his word. He nodded a farewell and went out into the corridor. The fire chief grew pensive. After a moment, he went back to his desk and took a pad from a drawer. He looked up a number and dialed.

"Hello," he said. "Could I speak to Mr. Kruger, please?"

WHEN MERLIN LEFT the fire station, he drove to the site and parked on Chicago Avenue. Sounds of activity came from the other side of the high fence. Letting himself in through the steel door, Merlin found the Ace Construction Company making up for lost time. Extra men had been drafted, and bodies seemed to be swarming over the site. Concrete mixers clanked away, and a small crane was hoisting some heavy precast slabs into place. A team of gardeners was laying turf and planting assiduously. Whatever reservations the men had about working in a place where a dead body was found, they were now swept away. There was an atmosphere of controlled urgency.

Jan Sarbiewski was in the middle of it all, consulting with his foreman, scolding an erratic bricklayer, helping three other men to shift a large window frame, then looking up at the darkening sky to assess the danger of rain. When he saw Merlin, he broke away from his employees and ambled across to greet him.

"How is it all going, Mr. Sarbiewski?"

"We're back on schedule now."

"So I see," said Merlin. "When I popped my head in yesterday, you were only just starting work on that bay. Your lads have made big strides since then. I'm relieved that Mrs. St. John decided to stick with my original design, or we'd really have been in a quagmire."

"Quagmire?"

"Case of back to the drawing board for me."

"Why, Mr. Richards?"

"To change the design of that bay window. It's the dominating feature at the front of the house. Alter that, and everything else has to be altered around it. We had a close shave, Mr. Sarbiewski."

"Did we? Didn't realize."

"But that was why they stood you down on Saturday."

"Oh, I see."

"Didn't they tell you?"

"No, Mr. Richards. No reason given."

"It seems that Mrs. St. John was having second thoughts. Actually, they're third, fourth, or fifth thoughts. We haggled for hours over the design of that bay. She had this obsession about an oval bedroom above an oval living room. Mrs. St. John wanted to vary the geometry of the house and break some of the straight lines."

"Straight walls are easier to build."

"Nobody is making this house easy for us."

Sarbiewski's face crinkled. "I know, Mr. Richards."

"Shall we take a look around?"

With the builder lumbering beside him, Merlin conducted a thorough survey, checking every detail and talking to all the trades on-site. No further work had been done in the wine cellar, though a door had now been fitted and locked. When Merlin asked to be let in, Sarbiewski was uneasy, but he got the key from the foreman and retrieved a battery torch from his car. Merlin could see his reluctance.

"You don't have to come in with me," he said.

"May help."

"Help what?"

"Settle the others. If I show I'm not afraid."

"Why—are they?"

"Some of them."

Merlin glanced around. Though the men continued to work, they were keeping one eye on the wine cellar. When the door was opened, Sarbiewski shone the beam of the torch and led the way in. The smell of disinfectant hit them. Evidently the cellar had been cleaned. It was the far bay that held interest for Merlin, and he borrowed the torch to shine it into every corner. The floor had been washed, but there were still splashes of blood on the walls and ceiling.

"This will all be whitewashed again," said Sarbiewski.

"Very appropriate."

"Appropriate?"

"Nothing," said Merlin, keeping the thought to himself.

He stood on tiptoe and attempted to touch the large hook embedded in the ceiling, but it was just out of reach. Sarbiewski pointed to the next bay.

"Use that crate in there. He did."

"He?"

"The man who committed suicide. He stood on that."

"Yes, yes. I suppose that he did," agreed Merlin.

But he knew that it was much more likely to have been used by the murderer. Nobody hanging from the hook could have kicked the crate that far away. It would have to be carried into the neighboring bay. Merlin tried to work out exactly how the murder had been committed. He stared at the hook.

"Mr. St. John insisted we put that in," explained Sarbiewski. "In case he wants to hang meat up down here. Might turn this bay into a walk-in refrigerator eventually."

"That's what he told me."

"Won't be short of meat."

"I know. He gave me the tour of his premises."

"We built one of those factories. Not a nice job."

"I can imagine."

"Seen enough?" said the other, anxious to leave.

"I think so."

"Good."

He took his torch and lit the route back up to ground level. As they came out into the fresh air again, they attracted a lot of curiosity from the men, but they ignored it. The Pole locked the door.

"Has Mrs. Sarbiewski forgiven me yet?" asked Merlin.

"For what?"

"Sunday."

"Ah."

"It was wrong of me to barge in on you like that, but I couldn't understand why none of your men didn't discover that dead body."

"We weren't here, Mr. Richards."

"I know that now. Sorry for ambushing you like that."

"We always go to mass on a Sunday."

"You've got three beautiful daughters."

"We bring them up in the Catholic Church. Like us."

Merlin was about to take his leave when a memory nudged him.

"Do you know someone called Father C.?" he asked.

"Who?"

"Father C.? I think he must be a Catholic priest."

"Not at St.Alban's. Our priest is Father O'Farrell."

"What about the other churches?" said Merlin. "I know that Chicago has a large Catholic population and a number of churches. Do you know of any of them who might have a Father C.?"

Sarbiewski shook his head, then a distant gleam came into his eye.

"Unless you mean St. Peter's."

"St. Peter's?"

"In Little Italy. They have a Father Calhoun there."

Merlin wondered if Father Calhoun's parishioners included a bald-headed man who broke into apartments and carried a gun. A look of mingled surprise and hope spread across the watermelon face.

"You wish to become a Roman Catholic?" he asked.

"Not exactly."

"Speak to Father O'Farrell. Wonderful man."

"I'm sure."

"He's quite young. Father Calhoun is very old."

"I think I'll call in at St. Peter's first, all the same."

Sarbiewski was moved. "Where were you converted?"

"On the floor of my apartment."

DONALD KRUGER COULD mask his feelings from most people, but he did not deceive her. She knew him too well. When he was icily pleasant, it meant that he was annoyed with himself. When he was excessively polite, he was brooding about something. When he kept on the move, he was sulking. Clare Brovik was worried. Kruger was overattentive to her. That meant that he was deeply aggrieved. She tried to ease the situation.

"Look, Donald," she said, "I'm very sorry about it."

"About what?"

"Not telling you that I was going to Oak Park on Saturday. It was wrong of me, I know that. I went on the spur of the moment."

"That's something I never do," he said coolly. "Act on the spur of the moment. I always look ahead. That way I never let anyone down."

"I've said I'm sorry."

"I was disappointed in you, Clare. And hurt."

"But you said I did the right thing. Calling you first."

"Yes, that's true."

"In a sense, it was a kind of blessing."

His upper lip curled. "That's not how I'd choose to describe it."

"Supposing that someone else had found that body first?" said Clare. "One of the construction crew. Would they have got in touch with you first? No, they'd have called the cops at once, maybe even tipped off the papers as well. The whole thing could have got out of hand. You should be glad that Merlin and I were the ones who made the discovery."

"There's something in that," he admitted.

"So stop punishing me."

"Is that what I'm doing?"

"You're oozing disapproval."

"Am I?"

He watched her in silence. They were in his office, dealing with some correspondence for St. John and working together with their customary efficiency. Kruger was very courteous and made a number of remarks that—from any other man—could be construed as flirtatious. But Clare knew what lay behind them. Now that she had drawn him out, he was curt and decisive.

"I need to speak with Merlin Richards," he announced.

"Why?"

"Set up a lunch date with him for tomorrow."

"Do you want me to be there, Donald?"

"No. Definitely not."

"Oh."

"In fact, I want you to steer well clear of him for a while," he said with a meaningful stare. "Before the relationship becomes unhealthy. I'll see him on my own. A private discussion is long overdue."

"As you wish. Where will you have lunch?"

"At one of the only three restaurants in Chicago I can bear to eat in," he said with disdain. "You know where they are. Choose one. Twelve thirty. Don't accept any excuses from him."

"No, Donald."

"I want Mr. Richards there at all costs."

"He will be, I'm sure."

"Remind him to wear a tie."

"He usually does."

"Properly, I mean," he said. "There are standards. I will not walk into a restaurant with a ragamuffin. Tell him that."

"I'll try."

"And make sure we have a table in a corner."

"I will."

"Somewhere private."

Clare nodded. She was ambivalent about Merlin Richards, but she was unhappy nonetheless about being excluded from the lunch and ordered to keep away from him. It jolted her. The limitations of her position had always been offset in the past by the substantial benefits of working for Hobart St. John, but she was now having doubts about that.

And she did have a definite urge to see Merlin again.

Having cleared the air, Kruger was now in a more relaxed mood.

"I managed to get those tickets, by the way."

"Tickets?"

"The opera. *Don Carlos*."

"Oh, yes. I'd forgotten."

"You are still going to come, aren't you?"

"Well, actually, I sort of planned to go somewhere else," she said. "When you didn't mention the tickets, I assumed that you couldn't get them. You said the opera was sold out."

"It is, Clare. I had to pull strings."

"You could always take someone else, Donald."

"I invited you," he reminded her. "I asked you to keep the evening free. You promised that you would."

"Something else came up."

"What is it?"

"It crossed my mind that I might go to the university."

"Whatever for?"

"Frank Lloyd Wright is giving a public lecture."

Kruger frowned. "You'd rather listen to him than see *Don Carlos*? A fading architect, down on his luck, long past his prime?"

"Merlin says he's still at the height of his powers."

"I'm not interested in Mr. Richards's opinion."

"Wright's work fascinates me."

"You can see it anytime," he pointed out. "It's all over Illinois. But you can only see *Don Carlos* on this one specific night. I was counting on you to be there with me, Clare. It will be a big social event."

"I know that, Donald."

"So you accept?" he said, forcing a decision.

"Can I think about it?"

"I need an answer now. Opera or architecture? Which will it be?"

There was no choice. His expression robbed her of any freedom.

"I'll be happy to come to *Don Carlos* with you," she whispered

"Good." He rose to leave, then paused. "Incidentally—"

"Yes?"

"That girl Richards was involved with when I did my first report on him. The one from the Beauregard Hotel. What was her name?"

"Sally Fiske."

"Is he still seeing her?"

"No," she said confidently.

"How do you know?"

"I just do, Donald. He has no attachments."

"Certain of that?"

"Absolutely."

"Good," he said. "That means he won't blab to anyone in bed. The Welsh are an extrovert nation. They wear their heart on their sleeves. If we're going to keep this quiet, Mr. Richards will have to learn to button his lip. Or suffer the consequences."

He went out swiftly and left Clare in turmoil.

AFTERNOON AT THE office was a species of ordeal for Merlin Richards. The tension was almost unbearable. It was very difficult to work effectively. Brad Davisson was very tetchy, Victor Goldblatt was swinging like a pendulum between vicious sniping and morose resignation, and Reed Cutler, relentlessly chatty, pretending to be the honest broker between his two colleagues, only made matters worse by exuding a complacence that made Merlin wonder if he really was about jump ship and swim to another practice. He wanted to challenge Cutler on the subject but feared doing so in front of Goldblatt, lest it send him off into an even worse state of paranoia. Office banter, so relaxed and enjoyable before, was now a minefield. Merlin was glad when Davisson interrupted them.

"Hey, Merl," he said, sticking his head around his door. "Call for you."

"Oh, thanks." He went into the inner office. "Who is it?"

"That broad who works for St. John."

"Clare Brovik?"

"Move it along, will you? I'm busy in here."

Merlin was keen to talk to Clare, but a private conversation was impossible. Davisson had company. He was talking with one of the junior draftsmen to whom he occasionally farmed out work. Merlin was only feet away. He turned him back on them and picked up the receiver.

"Clare?"

"Hello," she said briskly. "Mr. Kruger would like to invite you to lunch tomorrow. I've made a reservation at Luigi's in Adam Street. Twelve-thirty. Can you make that?"

"Well, yes. I suppose so. Er, will you be there?"

"No."

"Why not?"

"Mr. Kruger will meet you at the restaurant."

"When *can* I see you?"

"That won't be possible, I'm afraid."

"There are things to discuss."

"Take them up with Mr. Kruger tomorrow. And please make an effort to dress smartly. It's a high-class restaurant. Good-bye."

"Wait a moment!"

But she had gone. He tried to work out if Donald Kruger had been with her or if the brusque manner was evidence of her hostility. Though the stitches in his scalp continued to tingle, her slap across his face had more resonance. He felt as if the other cheek had just been slapped.

Merlin was still holding the receiver in his hand. "You're supposed to put it back down," said Davisson wryly.

"What? Oh, yes." He replaced it. "Sorry, Brad. See you."

He went back to his drafting table with two questions uppermost in his mind. Why did Donald Kruger wish to see him? And what were Clare Brovik's feelings toward him? He still had the marks of her teeth on his chest and her scratches on his back.

Merlin could still taste her. Had their time together in her apartment meant nothing to her?

The questions followed him all the way back home. When he left the office, he picked up some food at the delicatessen and took it back to his apartment. Mrs. Romario was balanced precariously on a chair as she replaced a lightbulb in the hallway. He helped her down, exchanged a few words, then went up the stairs. Reaching his door, he exercised caution, putting down the bag of food so that he had both hands free when he unlocked the door. Merlin was relieved to find that he had no unscheduled visitor with a loaded weapon this time, but someone had called at the apartment.

A piece of cartridge paper had been pushed under his door. He picked it up and saw that it bore a cartoon. The artist had drawn him with teasing accuracy. The tousled hair, the baggy suit, the wayward tie, and the gleam of idealism were all there. Pencil poised, Merlin was staring down at his drafting table, but there was no architectural design in front of him. Pasted onto his drawing board was an item that had been cut out of the *Chicago Tribune*. A large question mark hovered over it.

Sally Fiske was back in his life.

15

Father Calhoun was a holy midget. His diminutive frame seemed hardly strong enough to bear the weight of his vestments. Nearing retirement, he had the grateful look of someone who would soon escape responsibility for the souls of his parishioners. He was about to take confession when Merlin arrived in the vestry at St. Peter's Church, and was only able to spare him a few minutes.

Merlin's Welsh accent told the priest that he was not talking to a Roman Catholic. His visitor looked and sounded like an irretrievable Protestant. "What can I do for you, Mr. Richards?" asked Calhoun.

"I'm trying to trace a man who might attend your church."

"What's his name?"

"I'm hoping you can tell me that, Father Calhoun."

He described his nocturnal visitor in detail, tactfully omitting any mention of the fight and the loaded gun that brought it to such a painful end. The priest was impatient.

"Bald head. Black mustache. Middle-aged. Italian. You've

just described almost half the men in my congregation. I'll need much more to go on than that."

"He seemed—I don't know—troubled in his mind."

"Troubled?"

"Guilt ridden."

"Then he's unlikely to live around here."

"What do you mean?"

"Don't you read the papers, Mr. Richards?" said the other with a grimace. "This is Little Italy. A high-crime area. We have some appalling problems down here. When I first moved into this neighborhood, I loved the place. It was full of nice, God-fearing Catholic families. I spent most of my time marrying young couples and christening their children. Now it's funerals that dominate. And I'm not talking about natural deaths. Lots of the men I bury have had the lead removed from them first. If your friend is guilt-ridden, he's the odd one out. Most don't care. I only wish there was a lot more guilt and remorse around here, Mr. Richards, because it might stop the terrible crime."

"This man used to be criminal."

"Used to be?"

"Yes," said Merlin. "He told me he'd given it up. Repented."

"Well, that's one tiny victory for us, I suppose."

"And he had a brother called Benito."

"That's supposed to help identify him?" said the old man with a skeptical smile. "Walk down Halsted Street. Or Newberry, Sangamon, Miller. Call out the name 'Benito,' and you'll have all the brothers you want. I can think of three Benitos in Peoria Street alone."

"So I'm looking for a needle in a haystack."

"A field of haystacks."

Merlin gave up. His long shot was hopelessly wide of the mark.

"This was obviously a wasted journey, Father Calhoun," he admitted. "Thanks for your help. Sorry to have taken up your time."

"What put you onto me in the first place?"

"I thought he might have mentioned your name."

"Me?"

"Yes. Only he didn't call you Father Calhoun."

The priest sighed. "I get called lots of other things sometimes."

"He mentioned a Father C."

"Father C.?"

"I wondered if it might be C for Calhoun."

"I'm not the only Father C. around here," said the other. "There's Father Clarke at St. Elmo's and Father Costello at St. Mary the Virgin. No doubt they've both got their fair share of bald heads and mustaches among their parishioners." He tapped the air with a finger. "Of course, there is another possibility."

"What's that?"

"Do you ever listen to the radio?"

"Why?"

"I'm wondering if your friend was talking about *him*."

"Who?"

"Father Coughlin."

HOBART ST. JOHN came home early that evening. The meal was served in the dining room, washed down with a bottle of Chablis, part of an illegal consignment imported from France via Canada. He could see the specter of doubt in his wife's eyes.

"Don't worry about it, honey," he said reassuringly. "Everything will go fine. You'll knock 'em dead!"

"Will I, Hobart?"

"Of course. This part was written for Alicia Martinez."

"There may be others auditioning for it as well."

"Also-rans. You'll be first past the post."

"Do you think so?"

"They're not even in it."

"No," she said, recovering her confidence. "Why should I worry about them? The producers asked to see *me*. They wired me special to fly out there. That's got to be a good sign. They wouldn't make me go all that way in order to turn me down for the part."

"It's yours for the asking, hon."

"I hope so."

"And this will only be the start," he said, beaming at her. "What did I tell you? I'd bring you luck. When you became Mrs. St. John, it wasn't the end of Alicia Martinez, the movie star. Just a whole new beginning. Go to Hollywood. Wow the producers. Get this part."

"I will, Hobart!"

"I know you will!"

Since he had put money into the film in question, he was certain that she would be offered the part—it was a condition of his investment. But Alicia would never learn that. She would believe that she secured the role on her acting merit alone. Protecting her pride was essential. If he had to buy her screen success, he was more than happy to do so. In the long run, he reasoned, he stood to be the beneficiary.

"You spoil me," she said with a winsome smile.

"You deserve to be spoiled."

"A lot of men would be jealous of their wife's talent. I've seen it happen so often. They marry actresses and make them give up their careers. Not you, Hobart. You've encouraged me. Been my rock."

"I want movie audiences to know I married a star, Alicia."

"You can be so sweet."

"I'm proud of you, honey, is why. Get out there and show them. Tell you what, since you're flying all that way, why not take a small vacation? Palm Beach or somewhere."

"Would you come with me?"

"Not tomorrow, Alicia. I got a mountain of work to climb. But I might fly out at the weekend."

"That would be wonderful!"

"We could celebrate your success in landing this part."

"Yes!"

"Then you could stay on for a while, if you like. Lie in the sun. Catch up on old friends. Forget Chicago for a while. Take a week, two maybe. By the time you come back," he promised with a grin, "they'll have done much more work on the new house. I'll drive you out there."

"Not until it's finished. I hate building sites."

"Then I'll crack the whip and move them along."

"Thank you, Hobart."

"I'm here to please you."

"That cuts both ways."

She drank some wine, then ran her finger slowly around the rim of the glass. Alicia wore the blue silk dress he bought her during their honeymoon in Hawaii. He could almost feel its vibrant touch under his moist palms. His wife's trip to Hollywood would serve twin purposes. It would resuscitate a moribund movie career, and it would keep her out of the way while the problems at Saints' Rest were ironed out. The downside was that she would not be lying next to him in bed when he awoke in the mornings. That first reviving grope of the day would be denied him.

Alicia thought fondly about her new house.

"Oh, by the way," she said, "did I tell you that Merlin rang?"

"Merlin Richards?"

"Yes, I didn't know what he was talking about, to be honest."

"He shouldn't have bothered you at all, Alicia," said her husband with irritation. "That was the deal. He has worries, he contacts Clare Brovik or Donald Kruger. You were to be left alone."

"That's what I thought."

"So why call you?"

"He asked me why I was having doubts about the bay window. But I'm not. I told him. I'm happy with the decision we made. I want the house built exactly as we agreed."

"What did he say to that?"

"Nothing. He just apologized for bothering me and rang off."

"When was this, Alicia?"

"Earlier today."

A dark scowl settled on St. John's face. Alicia helped to remove it within seconds.

"Do you have to work this evening, sweetheart?"

"Not if you don't want me to, hon."

"I don't," she murmured.

He grinned lasciviously. "Then I'm all yours."

"I've been learning my lines. Could you take me through them?"

"Of course!"

"The truth is, I'm a bit nervous."

"Nervous? With your talent?"

"I've never been in a talkie before."

"You were in *Bride of Satan*."

"Yes," she agreed, "but I didn't get to *say* anything. They cut the scene where I rushed in to raise the alarm. I don't know why. I put everything I had into that scene. But all my other films were silents. That was where I shone. I knew how to seduce the camera."

"Not only the camera!"

"Anyway, I feel a bit nervous about this trip. So I want to be word-perfect by the time I take the screen test."

"We'll go over it as often as you like."

"Are you sure you won't get bored?"

"Dead sure."

"Can we start right now?"

"Why not?" he said with a chuckle. "Where shall we go?"

Alicia stood up slowly, then brushed against him so that he could feel that she was wearing nothing whatsoever under her dress.

"In the bath," she said.

WHEN MERLIN REACHED Sally Fiske's apartment, she was just leaving. He tooted the horn of the Ford, and she gave him a guarded smile. He felt that it was a promising start. Something to build on. He lowered the window.

"Can I give you a lift somewhere?"

"No, thanks. I was only going to call on a friend. She's a block away."

"I got your message."

"How did you know it was from me?"

"An educated guess."

Another guarded smile. He got out of the car and grinned at her.

"Well," he said. "Here we are again. At least I'm not sleeping in your doorway this time. And I'm stone cold sober. I suppose there's no chance of a chat over a cup of coffee or something?"

"I'm afraid not, Merlin."

"Just an idea."

"I'm not ready for it yet. Keep it on ice for a while."

"Why did you send that cutting from the *Tribune*?"

"I was curious. Does it have anything to do with your house?"

"*Everything* to do with it, Sally," he said with a mirthless laugh. "In fact, that's the reason I wasn't able to pick you up on Saturday night. I was trapped in the Oak Park Police Department."

"What happened?"

"Hop in the car, and I'll tell you."

She was uncertain. "Why the car?"

"More comfortable. Come on. I won't drive you off. I've got a lot to explain, and I'd rather do it with a small measure of privacy. Look upon the car as neutral territory. No commitments. You can walk away from it at any time. What can you lose, Sally?"

"Okay, five minutes."

"Start the clock."

He held the passenger door open for her to get in, then sat beside her. Without embellishment, he told her about the discovery of the body and his subsequent problems with the police and with his clients. Sally was full of sympathy, but it had a trace of jealousy in it.

"Who is this Clare Brovik?" she said.

"She works for Hobart St. John."

"Was it her idea to go to Oak Park that day?"

"Yes, it was, actually."

"And she bought your dinner by way of thanks?"

"That's right."

"Have you seen her since then?"

"Only once," he said defensively. "To compare notes with her."

"Notes?"

"About what we actually saw in that wine cellar."

"And?"

"Clare's going along with the official version. That's what she's paid to do, Sally. It was a suicide. Just like it said in the paper. She tried to persuade me to forget the whole thing."

"She picked the wrong man."

He chuckled. "You know me better than Clare does."

"Do I?"

It was a direct question, but he evaded it. He checked his watch.

"Five minutes, you said. I've already had fifteen."

"I asked you about Clare Brovik."

"She's a business contact, Sally. Nothing more. Not my type."

"Then why did you have that date with her in Oak Park?"

"It wasn't a date, believe me."

"Did you drive her home that night?"

"No," he said, glad of the chance to throw her off the scent. "She dumped me and went off with Donald Kruger instead. That's how much I excited her. She preferred to go back to Chicago with a homosexual."

"Is that what he is?"

"Apparently."

"I see."

"Thank heaven he didn't try to take *me* home!"

She gathered up her purse and reached for the door handle. Merlin put a gentle hand on her arm to detain her.

"You haven't told me how things are with you, Sally."

"Fine, thanks."

"Missing the hotel?"

"I pine for it!"

"Have you made a start on those illustrations?"

"Still playing around with ideas."

"We ought to go to the zoo sometime. Study the animals."

"I've already been, Merlin," she said pleasantly. "No offense, but it's the kind of thing I can do best on my own. Like you with your work."

She moved his hand aside and opened the car door halfway.

He was disappointed. "So is that it?"

"What else did you expect?"

"I thought that cartoon of yours was a flag of truce."

"Sort of. But it was no more than that."

"Are you telling me to buzz off, Sally?"

"Of course not," she said, turning back to him. "It's good to see you again, and I'm glad you told me about Saturday night. It explains a lot. I was unfair to you, Merlin. But that doesn't mean we fall back into each other's arms again. You've got a lot on your plate at the moment. Let's wait until you're through that stage. Until you get all these people out of your hair. Especially that Clare Brovik." She got out of the car. "Okay?"

"You're calling the shots, Sally."

"Take care. You're dealing with dangerous men."

"I noticed."

"See you around."

She closed the door. He spoke through the open window again.

"Before you leave—"

"Your five minutes was up ages ago."

"You might be able to help me. Who is Father Coughlin?"

"Do you mean *the* Father Coughlin?"

"How many are there?"

"Only one like him, Merlin."

"Who is he?"

"The radio priest."

"The what?"

"He has a program on the radio. With millions of listeners."

Merlin thought of the bald man who held a gun on him.

"I think I might have met one of them."

FATHER COUGHLIN STOOD beside the microphone with unimpeachable authority. His face was aglow, his eyes gleaming behind the rimless spectacles, his square jaw set above the clerical collar, his fist raised in defiance as he developed his argument. The zeal of the Lord burned inside him. He seemed to radiate spiritual truth.

"What are the grim facts, my friends?" he said. "I will tell you. The value of all listed stocks has dropped almost twenty-three million dollars. The profits of two hundred leading industrial corporations are down by nearly half. Railroad shares are down sixty-five points, industrials down a hundred and sixty-seven. Steel production and automobile production have plummeted. Banks are closing at the rate of sixty a month. It's a disaster. Everything is going down. Except the suicide rate."

The photograph had been cut out of a newspaper and pinned to the wall of his apartment. Seated beside his radio, the bald man with the pencil mustache watched his mentor and hung on his words. Father Coughlin had opened his eyes to economics, to politics, and most of all, to God. With its hint of Irish brogue, the voice had a mellow richness and passion that made it irresistible. Though he was addressing the listening millions, Father Coughlin, from the parish of Royal Oak, Michigan, seemed to be speaking directly to Benito's brother, and the latter thrilled to the sound of confiding intimacy. Father Coughlin was his personal salvation.

"You all know what I am against, my friends," said the voice with ingratiating charm. "I'm against social injustice, the power of bankers, and the evils of communism. But what do I stand *for*, people ask me. What is the standard under which Father Charles E. Coughlin fights? First and foremost, it is the standard of Christianity, for I am a humble parish priest, speaking to you with the permission and support of Bishop Michael Gallagher of Detroit. I also stand for equal rights and political honesty. Should a priest be allowed to meddle in politics? That is what my detractors ask. The answer is yes, my friends. Never forget that our Savior, Jesus Christ, was not afraid to get involved in politics—"

The man with the pencil mustache did not understand all that he heard, and much of the detail confused him, but the essential message came through. This was an inspired individual, a priest in whom he could have total faith, a politician brave enough to denounce the greedy men of power who brought economic ruin to America, a demagogue who could touch the hearts and minds of people across a vast social and ethnic spectrum. Here was the Revealed Word in a radio program.

"In conclusion, my friends," said the voice, softening to a whisper, "let me thank all those of you who have written to me and sent me a dollar for use by the Radio League of the Little Flower. Your money will be well spent in unraveling the economic web in which we are all so horribly entangled. I am your priest, and you are my congregation. I dedicate myself to your service. And I will continue to strive on your behalf against greedy politicians, ruthless bankers, and rabid Communists. God bless you all. Good-bye."

Caught up in the rhetoric, the man could not even reach out to turn off his radio for several minutes. Still staring at the photograph on the wall, he rose to his feet, reached for his gun, and slipped it into his holster. He was stricken with remorse at having to carry a dangerous weapon, but a brother's murder necessitated it.

"Sorry, Father Coughlin," he said. "It has to be done this way."

IT WAS DIFFICULT to be angry with Donald Kruger. His manner was so polite and his apologies so profuse that Merlin Richards was disarmed. A corner booth had been set aside for them in the exclusive restaurant, and Kruger already occupied it when Merlin arrived. He gave Merlin a warm welcome, guided him through the complex Italian menu, then got him talking about music. An accomplished harpist went into technicalities with a gifted pianist over the soup course. As they discussed their shared love of opera, Merlin realized he had not been given any of the information he was looking for.

"Is this deliberate?" he said bluntly. "Talking opera."

"Does it offend you?" asked Kruger solicitously.

"No, but it's not the reason you invited me here."

"That's true, Merlin. But it's not irrelevant. I wanted to show you how much common ground there is between us so that you'll stop viewing me as your sworn enemy."

"I don't see you as an enemy, Donald."

"Then what do you see me as?"

"A front man for Hobart St. John."

"My correct title is business consultant," said the other with amusement, "but it includes being a front man and an apologist. We all have to make a living in this harsh world, don't we? Even you are not immune from the lure of the salary check."

Merlin speared a tomato. "I have to eat."

"And in order to eat—and pay the rent—you work for Westlake and Davisson. In addition to your strictly architectural work, you also act as a front man and an apologist for the practice. In short, you do the same job as I do but not, perhaps, for the same remuneration."

"I'm not here to compare pay packets."

"I would never suggest anything quite so uncivilized. We meet as colleagues today, bonded by that beautiful house that you designed for Mr. and Mrs. St. John and which, unfortunately, has been tainted by the unfortunate discovery you made last Saturday."

"With Clare Brovik."

"With—as you remind me—Clare Brovik."

"Why did you insist on taking her home that night?"

"She was on the verge of hysteria. She needed to be talked down."

"I could have done that."

"You were still in a state of shock yourself, Merlin. In your place, I know that I would have been. What a hideous experience! To walk into a cellar and find a hanged man." He gave a shiver. "I would have fainted!"

"I don't think that anything could make you faint."

Kruger smiled. "You see? You're getting to know me. But let's stop walking around this, shall we? I invited you to lunch in order to put your mind at rest. That will not be easy, I know. You've had a rough ride and feel aggrieved. I'm sure you've brought some awkward questions to this table, Merlin." His palms opened. "Feel free to put them to me."

His charm was undeniable. He had a way of suffocating dissent. Donald Kruger's sophistication served as a kind of armor against any verbal assault. His immaculate suit and well-groomed hair gave Merlin pangs of inferiority, even though he had bought himself a new tie for the occasion and taken the trouble to wear it in closer proximity to the top button of his shirt than usual.

Kruger's sexual orientation was another disturbing factor. Merlin had been uncertain how to deal with that at first, but Kruger soon put him at ease. His companion was now ready for cross-examination.

Merlin accepted the invitation with alacrity. "Right," he said, leaning forward, "who started the fire in Oak Park that burned down the previous house on that site?"

"An incompetent electrician."

"That's what the fire chief told me."

"It's true," said the other smoothly. "I know it must seem like an extraordinary coincidence that a plot of land becomes available at a time when Mr. St. John wants it, but such things do tend to happen to him. Much to the chagrin of his rivals, Hobart St. John has the Midas touch."

"Mr. and Mrs. Perrott might not see it that way."

"They have my sympathy. I collect first editions myself, so I know what a blow it must have been to lose such a magnificent library. But there it is, Merlin. Now, let us be brutally frank. You think that we were personally involved in arson, don't you?"

"No, no," said Merlin, caught off guard.

"I think you should know that Mr. St. John was on honeymoon in Hawaii at the time. I was visiting my mother in Philadelphia, so you can absolve me of the crime as well." He gave a teasing smile. "Do you really think we're such monsters as to burn a decent old man and his wife out of their home? If you talked to the fire chief, he probably told you the insurance company reached the same conclusion that he did. The fire was caused by faulty wiring. Also, it might interest you to know that Mr. St. John had already put a deposit down on another plot of land in Oak Park, intending to build the house on that. He had no idea that this one would suddenly become available. Next question?"

"Why did you keep Sarbiewski off the site on Saturday?"

"So that we could sort out a contractual problem."

"With whom?"

"The lawyer acting for the Ace Construction Company."

"That's not what Clare told me."

"No," confessed the other. "I primed her with that excuse about Mrs. St. John having second thoughts about the bay window. I didn't want you or Sarbiewski to know there'd been a serious legal hitch until it'd been sorted out by our own lawyer. Which it now has been. If you want the details, you can double-check with our legal department." He gave a congratulatory nod. "In the way that you double-checked with Mrs. St. John about the bay window."

"I don't like being lied to, Donald."

"Unusual circumstances. I had no option."

"Now we come to the big question."

"Why the police are treating an apparent murder as suicide?"

"Yes."

"Because they don't want damaging publicity any more than we do. They don't want Oak Park crawling with reporters and cameramen, and Mr. St. John doesn't want his wife upset by the thought that a violent death occurred in the wine cellar of her new home. Yes," he said blithely, "I know that it could never happen in your country, but the police are a little more pragmatic here."

"Corrupt is the word I'd use."

"You're being too harsh on them, Merlin. It may have been reported as a suicide, but they haven't closed the file on this case. They're treating it as a murder investigation and are trying to find out who the man was and why he was killed on our property. But they're doing it away from the glare of publicity." His tone hardened. "We'll make sure they solve this crime, believe me. Don't forget that we were the victims."

"Victims?"

"That body was put there deliberately. Mr. St. John has a lot of enemies. This is in strictest confidence," he said, touching Merlin's arm. "There have been blackmail threats—I can't go into details—and Mr. St. John tried to ignore them. We believe that body in Oak Park was a warning from the blackmailer. We want him caught—and quickly!"

"But who was the dead man?"

"I wish we knew."

"Mr. St. John didn't mention any of this to me."

"He didn't want you to know about it, Merlin. He hoped that a gentle hint would be enough, but patently it wasn't. You kept on ferreting away."

"I want to get at the truth."

"The police will do that in their own way. They do not need you complicating matters. Discretion is vital here. Do you want the whole venture to collapse? Because that's what would have happened if Mrs. St. John had got wind of this. She would have refused to go anywhere near Oak Park. Face the facts. Westlake and Davisson can't afford to lose this commission. Neither can you."

"What do you mean?"

Kruger opened a briefcase and took out a folder.

"This is the report I prepared on you for Mr. St. John," he said, handing it over. "Full personal and professional details, including your financial problems. You'll even find Sally Fiske's name and address in there, though I understand that relationship has now expired."

Merlin opened the file and stared in horror at its contents. It was embarrassingly explicit. His period of unemployment was documented, along with a doomed attempt to raise a bank loan. He took no comfort from the eulogy on his capabilities as an architect. He felt invaded.

"Similar reports were prepared on Victor Goldblatt and Reed Cutler," continued Kruger. "We wanted to be sure that we picked the right man from the firm. Goldblatt was too erratic, and we felt that his domestic problems were preying on his mind. Cutler was too dull. His work is capable, but it has none of your flair." He showed perfect teeth in a confiding smile. "So now you know how Merlin Richards got lucky."

"Is that what it was?"

"Now, let's not have any ingratitude here," chided the other. "You must admit that I've been open with you. I've answered your questions as honestly as I can. As for that report, I didn't need to show it to you, but I felt that you were entitled to see it. I also wanted you to know just how meticulous we've been."

"Very meticulous!" said Merlin with an edge of sarcasm.

"We're one step ahead of you all the time."

"Don't bet on that!"

Merlin fought to contain the fury inside him. Much as he wanted to tear up the report and throw the pieces into Kruger's face, he knew that it would be folly. Only if he remained involved in the building of Saints' Rest could he hope to learn the full facts behind the crime that had taken place there. Donald Kruger was very plausible, but his urbane charm was irritating Merlin. The Welshman did not want to rely on him as his sole source of information.

"Well," said Kruger happily, "it's been a most productive lunch."

"Will you send in a report about exactly what I ate?"

His host laughed. "Not necessary. You're one of us now."

"Am I?"

"Of course. Accept that and enjoy the many benefits that go with it. Otherwise, you could hit an iceberg. Remember this, Merlin. Hobart St. John has enormous influence with your employers. One word from him, and you would disappear from Westlake and Davisson before you could say 'Frank Lloyd Wright.' "

"I was waiting for you to wave the big stick at me."

"It's not a big stick."

"Then what is it?"

"A simple fact," said Kruger quietly. "We *own* you."

Running was thinking time. As he pounded along the sidewalk on his morning circuit, Merlin Richards was able to go through it all once again in an attempt to sift truth from fabrication. How honest had Donald Kruger really been with him? It was difficult to guess. There had certainly been a show of honesty at the restaurant in Adams Street, but that might have been designed to placate Merlin rather than to take him wholly into the confidence of his clients. When the architect refused to be mollified by the suave assurances from Kruger, the latter had resorted to a gentle threat. They had bought him. Merlin was the property of Hobart St. John. His owner would reward obedience and punish any challenge to his authority. That was the unambiguous message. If he stepped out of line, Merlin would be treated as ruthlessly as the animals in the stockyards.

What hurt him most was the report that had been prepared about him. It was frighteningly comprehensive. Gus Westlake had clearly provided much of the information, and that was a cruel betrayal, but the personal detail had been acquired by other means. Merlin had been watched. They knew about his social life and his leisure interests. They knew what books he read, what rent he paid. Though it had been a short relationship, they even knew about Sally Fiske. Had she been spied on as well? He felt a pang of guilt that she had been dragged into it because of him. It made him even more determined to strike back somehow.

His decision was easier to make than to implement. Hobart St. John wielded immense power. He had influence with the police and control over the newspapers. He could manipulate the truth. Donald Kruger was an efficient henchman, smoothing out any problems that arose and making sure that his employer was protected from any unpleasantness. In their different ways, both men had issued a warning to Merlin. They would not do so again. He had now been given his last chance. But it was a third warning that echoed in his ears. It came from Clare Brovik, and it was couched in concern. She knew what her employers were capable of. Clare had put her affection for him before her loyalty to them. The one consolation he drew from his lunch with Donald Kruger was that—for all his boasted omniscience—the man did not know about his visit to the apartment in Kinzie Street.

Merlin needed to fight them with their own weapons. He had to compile his own report. Only when he looked behind the smoke screen created by his clients could he hope to find out what was really going on, and his one means of doing that was through Clare Brovik. She had taken a huge risk for him before, defying her boss, lowering her guard, and letting Merlin see—albeit briefly—what she felt about him. He now needed to persuade her to take some more risks on his behalf. That was the way forward. He would take it. The resolve put extra power into his legs, and he lengthened his stride.

When he turned the last corner, a familiar scene greeted him. A shopkeeper was cleaning his window, an old woman was mopping her porch, children were playing noisily, the mailman was delivering letters, people were setting off to work, a truck was rumbling along, a man was leaning against a car and reading a newspaper. Dogs were scavenging, a cat was snarling at a feline trespasser. At the far end of the street was the stall where a copy of the *Chicago Tribune* would be waiting for him. Merlin put on his usual spurt to reach it, but his finishing line came much earlier than anticipated. The man stepped casually away from his car, lowered his newspaper, and stood right in the middle of the sidewalk.

His bald head was covered by a cap, but Merlin recognized him at once and slowed to a halt. He could see the telltale bulge under the man's coat. The wound in his scalp tingled nostalgically.

"What are you doing here?" said Merlin, catching his breath.

"Waiting for you, friend."

"Last time you did that, I finished up in hospital."

"It hurt me to do that to you," said the man with a look of anguish. "How's your head? Did they put stitches in it for you?"

"Yes, they're taking them out today."

"Did you tell them how you got that crack on the skull?"

"I said that my girlfriend hit me with a flower vase."

The man grinned. "Some girlfriend!"

"It got me a lot of sympathy."

"One thing, anyway," said the other with approval, "you obviously didn't go to the cops. Or they'd have called Oak Park, linked me with Benito, and been around to pick me up."

"I gave you my word."

"That counts with me, friend."

"Good."

"So what else have you found out?"

"Only that my clients may not be the respectable people I took them for," said Merlin. "I was clubbed over the head by *them* yesterday, though they did it with a lunch in Adams Street. I didn't need stitches, but it hurt just as much as the blow from your gun."

"That figures. They're not nice people."

"How do you know?"

"I been checking Hobart St. John out."

"And?"

"Just that. I'm not trading here."

"Can you at least tell me one thing?" asked Merlin.

"Don't ask me my name."

"I just want to know why you picked on me. Of all people. How come you thought I was tied in with your brother in some way?"

"It was a guess. I had to start with someone."

"Why me?"

"You were the architect."

"I'm still none the wiser."

The man stroked his mustache while he appraised Merlin and tried to work out how far he could trust him. Then he looked up and down the street to make sure that they were not overheard.

"I'll tell you this much," he said, talking rapidly. "Benito told me he was going out to Oak Park on Friday night to collect some dough. A big score from some guy he did a job for. Something to do with a new house. That's all I knew. Until Benito doesn't show up or call next day. I mean, we're brothers. We're close. So I go out to Oak Park on Sunday, and the only house I can find being built is on Chicago Avenue."

"Saints' Rest."

"That what it's called?"

"Yes."

A wry smile. "Benito would've liked that. Saints' Rest, eh?"

"He went out there to collect some money, you say?"

"And ended up in the police morgue."

"So it seems."

"He was double-crossed."

"And you suspected *me*?" said Merlin in astonishment.

"Two names on the board outside the house."

"The builders and the architects."

"Yeah," said the man. "I looked at the Ace Construction Company first. They got an office down on Canal Street and lousy security. Took me two minutes to break in." He winced. "I felt so ashamed! Committing a crime on a Sunday. But it had to be done. Saw the accounts. Builders are doing okay, but they don't have the kind of money that my brother would have been paid. Benito was a high-class act. He came expensive."

"So what did you do?"

"Left everything as I found it and went to your office."

"You broke in there as well?"

"Yes—God forgive me!"

"But nobody mentioned a break-in to me."

"I went in and out without leaving a trace. Simply wanted the name of the architect who designed that house. Westlake and Davisson is all it said on that board. They could've employed a dozen architects, for all I knew. Your office gave me the guy I was after. Merlin Richards."

"You had a busy Sunday!"

"They had your address there but no number for your apartment. That's why I drove over next morning and talked to that ugly old broad."

"Mrs. Romario."

"By that time, of course, I seen the piece in the *Tribune* and made the connection. Benito and a building site in Oak Park. When I got over there, the cops gave me the shove-off treatment.

Wouldn't let me near the morgue. Said the dead man didn't match the description I gave of my brother. Had me out of there on my ass."

"What did you do?"

"Hung around. Watched, waited. Eventually you came."

"How did you know who I was?"

"Photo pinned on a board in your office," said the man. "You and two other guys horsing around. Someone had drawn little bubbles, you know, with words in them. The two guys were talking to 'Merl.' So I knew what you looked like. Unusual."

"I don't like the way you said that."

"Unusual," repeated the man, looking him up and down. "Easy to pick out in a crowd. I spotted you going in to see the cops. Figured you might've been involved in Benito's disappearance."

Merlin was amazed. "You said your brother came expensive. Do I look like the sort of person who has money?"

"No—but you look like a guy who needs it."

"So?"

"You could've been the one to double-cross him."

"Thanks for the character reference!"

"It was possible," reasoned the other. "Benito does the job. You're the bagman, sent to pay him. Only you bump him off instead, bribe the cops to say it was a suicide, and keep the rest of the dough yourself. That's why I broke into your apartment."

"To find the money."

"All I found was unpaid bills."

"Let's go back to your brother."

"No," said the man firmly. "I got to scram."

"What sort of job did he do for his client?"

"He didn't say. And I wouldn't tell you, anyway."

"Honor among thieves, eh?"

A fleeting embarrassment passed across the man's face.

"Benito was more than a thief." His eyes glazed over. "I was lucky. I met Father C. He changed my life. Made me want to put it all behind me. But not Benito. He used to laugh at me. Said I was stupid to pay any attention to some dumb priest on the radio. But that's only because he didn't let Father C. show him the road to redemption." He let out a long wheeze. "It's funny. As kids, *I* was the hoodlum. Benito never got into no trouble. He was the one who had a wife and family and an honest job. Then Maria and the kids were killed in an automobile accident, and Benito went crazy. We could do nothing with him. Turned his back on the Church there and then. Earned his living with a gun after that."

He folded the newspaper and handed it to Merlin before getting into the car. He was about to drive away when Merlin tapped hard on the window and spoke through the glass.

"You said that your brother used to have an honest job."

"That's right," confirmed the other.

"What as?"

"An electrician."

HOBART ST. JOHN kept up a steady stream of reassurances until the very last minute. Before she boarded the airplane, his wife was having an attack of nerves. She put a hand over her heart.

"Call it off!" she decided. "I can't go through with it."

"Of course you can, honey," he soothed.

"I'm not sure if this part is altogether right for me."

"You'll *make* it right. That's what movie stars do. They bend the character to suit them. The producers are buying Alicia Martinez, so they know you can deliver the goods."

"It's been such a long time since I was in front of a camera."

"You'll still make every bulb in the studio go pop."

"Will I, Hobart?"

"Yes, hon!"

His beaming smile instilled new confidence in her. She kissed him on the cheek in gratitude. Marriage to him had been a wise career move.

"If only you were coming with me!" she sighed.

"I'll be there in spirit if not in body."

"What happens if I don't get the part?"

"Impossible!"

"How can you be so sure?"

"Trust me, Alicia. It's yours."

"You have such wonderful faith in me."

"I know what you can do," he said with a grin. "On and off the screen. They should've had a camera in that bathroom last night!" He gave her a hug, then held her by the shoulders. "Go out there and slay 'em. I'll join you at the weekend, and we'll have dinner to celebrate. But I'll call you long distance before then."

"Promise?"

"Promise!"

"You're so good to me."

"I'm just crazy about my wife."

He kissed her on the cheek, then shepherded her to the door as the last call for passengers was heard over the public address system. Alicia Martinez was soon striding off on her way to a whole new career in movies. Her husband watched her fondly until she disappeared from sight, then stood at the window in the airport terminal. Only when he saw her airplane taxi toward the runway did he move off. The wistful expression vanished from his face at once.

The limousine was waiting for him. His chauffeur opened the door so that he could step into the rear and lower himself into the plush seating. When the engine started up, it was almost soundless.

"Back home, sir?" asked the chauffeur.

"Not right away, Michael."

"Where to, sir?"

"North State. There's a shop across from Holy Name Cathedral."

"The florist, sir?"

"Yes," said St. John. "I need to stop by and get some flowers."

STANDING ON THE platform with great dignity, Frank Lloyd Wright delivered his lecture to a packed hall at the University of Chicago. Young and old had come to hear him speak—students, professors, architects, friends, rivals, associates, former clients, and those who simply admired his work and came to view a living legend in the flesh. His topic was modern architecture, and there were a few cynics who suggested that his subject matter had already left him in its wake. Wright soon confounded them. His lecture was not a sentimental retrospective by a man taking his leave of his profession. Indeed, an elegiac note was singularly absent. What the audience was given was a stirring glimpse into the future of American architecture by a man who intended to be at the forefront of it. Instead of hearing the rambling reminiscences of an erratic genius, they were beguiled by the words of a true prophet.

Merlin Richards was fascinated. During his time with Wright he had heard many of the ideas discussed before, but they had acquired freshness and definition now. The lecture was structured as carefully as one of the master's own houses. Anecdotes were dovetailed with serious argument, piquant observations on the work of his rivals were supported like joists by a recital of architectural principles. The speech had light and shade, concentration and space. And it was delivered in a deep voice that lent it authority and with a theatricality that gave it luster. Merlin had heard Wright pontificate a hundred times, but he was still captivated from start to finish.

As applause thundered at the end of the lecture, he joined in enthusiastically and looked around the audience. Gus Westlake was there, seated near the front and clapping his hands like a seal in a circus act. Brad Davisson had also made the effort to come along, perched on the end of a row as if about to make a swift departure but sufficiently moved to pat his knee in acclamation. There was no sign of Victor Goldblatt, but Merlin knew that he would be visiting his wife at the hospital and that he did not, in any case, share the veneration of Frank Lloyd Wright. The contingent from Westlake and Davisson was completed by Reed Cutler, who sat near the back with his wife as if they were attending a movie.

Merlin had entertained the vague hope that Clare Brovik might be there, but she was nowhere in sight. It was a setback for him. A shared intoxication with heady architectural theories might have been a prelude to a closer acquaintance with her. He wanted to see her again, if only to convince himself that they had actually been lovers; it seemed so unlikely now, and he could hardly recruit her to his cause if she remained out of reach. If the magic of Frank Lloyd Wright could not entice her back to his side, he wondered what could.

But the evening had one rich reward—time alone with his icon.

"Great to see you again, Merlin! Thanks for coming."
"Do you think I'd miss an event like this, Mr. Wright?"
"I said nothing you hadn't heard before."
"That story about the monkey was new."

"Oh, that. Yes, I was glad I could work that in. A little humor always helps. That's what so many architects lack, Merlin. A sense of humor. It makes their work so dour and expressionless."

They were seated at a table in the corner of the refectory. Having sampled the refreshments and shaken the hand of their speaker, most of the audience had now departed, leaving only a handful of doting students and a clutch of university professors. Nobody dared to interrupt Merlin and Wright. They watched from a distance, noting the mutual respect between the two men.

"How is Mrs. Wright?" asked Merlin with affectionate curiosity.

"Olgivanna is fine. Sends her best wishes."

"Give her my love and tell her how much I miss her."

"I will."

"And the children?"

"The young scamps are in fine fettle. Svetlana has really taken to the harp since you introduced her to the instrument. You must come up to Taliesin and see us sometime."

"I'd like that, Mr. Wright."

"It would be nice to have you around again." He took a sip from a glass of water. "But how are things at Westlake and Davisson?"

"To be honest," said Merlin, "I've hit a rough patch."

"Oh? Gus gave me the impression that everything was going well."

"He would."

"When I talked to him earlier, he thanked me for putting in a good word for you. He said that my loss was his gain, and that you'd settled in without the slightest difficulty. What's this about a rough patch?"

"It's a long story, Mr. Wright."

"You just listened to me on that platform for the best part of an hour and a half," said the other with a tolerant grin. "I guess I owe you some time in return. Gus Westlake was excited about some new house you'd designed."

"That's right. A big break for me."

"Where is it?"

"Oak Park."

Frank Lloyd Wright gave a long sigh, and a faraway look came into his eye. A charismatic figure on stage, he appeared much taller than he really was. In reality he was relatively short and almost stocky, elegantly attired as usual in a loose-fitting coat, a pair of tweed trousers, one of his white shirts with a high detachable collar, and a tie that was like a miniature scarf. His cane was propped up against the table beside him, but it was more a part of a total image than a sign of infirmity. Now into his sixties, Frank Lloyd Wright had the vitality of a much younger man. But he also had the wisdom that can come only with age and an unparalleled experience dealing with troublesome clients.

Merlin gave a concise account of events at Saints' Rest, editing out both Clare Brovik and the bald-headed disciple of Father Coughlin and emphasizing the architectural implications throughout. Wright was a good listener, nodding soulfully and dropping in the occasional question. When the story was told, he ran a hand through his bardic white mane.

"You brought back a lot of memories for me," he confessed with a sigh. "Some good, some bad. No need to tell you how big a part Oak Park played in my early life and career. I had some happy times there until"—he searched for the best euphemism—"until that phase of my life ended. But I can't help feeling sorry for the folks who had the original house in Chicago Avenue."

"Mr. and Mrs. Perrott?"

"A fine old clapboard residence. I remember it well. I'm sorry to hear that it was destroyed by fire." A deeper sigh escaped him.

"I know only too well the horrors that fire can inflict. Taliesin was burned to the ground in 1914, killing seven people. Tragic incident! Soul-destroying!"

He went off into a reverie. Merlin waited. He knew that the victims included Mamah Borthwick Cheney, the client's wife with whom Wright had lived in Europe after abandoning his own family in Oak Park. A crazed employee had set fire to Taliesin, the house that Wright built in Spring Green, Wisconsin. Painful memories had been revived. Both of Mrs. Cheney's children had also died in the blaze. Frank Lloyd Wright had lost a house and a second family.

"We must be grateful that nobody was killed," resumed Wright.

"That's what the fire chief said."

"Those guys usually know their business. If he told you that fire was caused by defective wiring, I'd be inclined to believe him. It wouldn't be the first house that went up in smoke that way."

"No, I suppose not."

"As for this body you discovered, well, that's another matter."

"The man had been murdered. No question about it."

"But is it of any concern to you, Merlin? Except in the obvious sense that it's a bad omen for the house. What is your angle on all this?"

"I'm determined to find out the truth."

"You're an architect, not a private detective."

"I can't just turn my back."

"Why not?"

"Is that what you'd do?"

"Fortunately I've never been in this situation," said Wright, "but I've had some very ornery clients. Violent rows, wild accusations, threats of legal action—I've had them all. And I learned that you always have to remember that it's the client who pays the bill. The trick is to bring them slowly around to your point of view with a combination of flattery and persuasion. In your case, that may not be in the cards."

"Hobart St. John is used to giving orders and being obeyed."

"I've met the type."

"How do I stand up against a man like that?"

"You don't, Merlin."

"So what do I do? Just cave in?"

"No. You simply do the job that you were hired to do."

"But there was a murder victim in the wine cellar."

"That was a mistake," scolded Wright. "Designing a house with a cellar in the first place. What use are they? People only fill them with things they'll never use again, so why have them at all? Look at the Perrotts. They stored papers and magazines in their basement and turned it into a fire hazard. A house should be an organic whole. Every inch of space must earn its keep. You didn't need to put a wine cellar in that house at all."

"I did. Mr. and Mrs. St. John like their wine."

"Then you make allowance for that in the kitchen."

"They insisted on the cellar."

"Then you should have talked them out of it."

"Look," said Merlin with mild exasperation, "I didn't ask you for a critique. My design may not meet your exacting standards, but it's what the clients chose, and as you just pointed out, they foot the bill."

"They also live in the house when you walk away from it."

"Yes."

"So let *them* worry about a corpse in the cellar."

"But I was the one who found it."

"Found it, reported it to the police, and gave your statement. You were a model citizen, Merlin. You did the right thing. Now move on. It's not your problem anymore."

"But it is, Mr. Wright. I can't let it go."

"You must."

"I'm too far down the road for that."

"Turn back," urged the other, "turn back. I'd hate to see you come to grief over this because you antagonize a client."

"He's the one who is antagonizing me."

"Then let Gus Westlake handle him. That's what he's there for, Merlin. He's a wily old bird. Gus will know how to protect you from this Hobart St. John." He gave a chuckle. "I must say, I like the name of the house. Saints' Rest in dear old Saint's Rest. A nice symmetry there. Don't interfere with it. Let these saints rest in peace, Merlin."

"It's not that easy."

"It's part of what being an architect is all about."

"Turning a blind eye?"

"Using your common sense. You tangle with this client, you could do yourself a lot of damage. Take on the police at the same time, and you're asking for trouble. Be professional. Keep your eyes firmly on your work. Don't get involved."

Merlin retreated into a brooding silence. There was no point in burdening his friend with his problems any further. Frank Lloyd Wright had worries enough of his own with a family to support and a dearth of commissions. But he bore his sorrows lightly. Merlin wished that he could do the same. Wright turned to more personal matters.

"So you're not married yet?" he said with a twinkle in his eye.

"I can't afford to get married."

"A man can always afford what his heart impels him to, Merlin."

"In that case, I've never been impelled."

"Try it sometime. It helps."

"Helps?"

"This restlessness of yours. This tension. This getting too close to your clients and their mishaps. The love of a good woman would be a boon to a passionate man like you. Celts make lusty husbands."

"I'll bear that in mind."

"Bear my advice in mind as well."

"I will, Mr. Wright. And thanks."

"Forget that dead body. You're not a gravedigger."

It was sage counsel. But Merlin would ignore it.

UNDER ANY OTHER circumstances, Clare Brovik might have enjoyed the performance of *Don Carlos*. She liked Verdi's operas. His music had dramatic power, and some of his arias and duets could move her to tears. But the plight of Don Carlos and his stepmother, the erstwhile Elisabeth de Valois, had no impact on her, and Princess Eboli's haunting Song of the Veil went largely unheard. By the time the doomed lovers met at the tomb of Charles V in the last act, Clare had lost all interest. Her mind was on a tragedy much nearer to home.

Donald Kruger was well aware of her detachment. He was not just her escort, he was her guide to the world of opera. Until he began taking her with him, Clare had seen very little opera, and she was an eager convert. Kruger's patient tuition allowed her to appreciate the subtleties of each new work she encountered. He enjoyed his role, and he liked her company. Both of them usually relished their evenings with Verdi or Mozart or Wagner. Tonight it was markedly different.

He waited until they were driving home before confronting her.

"How much of it did you actually see?" he challenged.

"All of it, Donald."

"It never held your attention for a moment."

"Yes, it did."

"I'm not stupid, Clare."

"I was rather tired, that's all. I couldn't concentrate."

"That's never been a problem in the past. You've sat through much longer operas and cheered them to the final curtain. What's the point of getting all dressed up in your finery if you wear earplugs?"

"I was not wearing earplugs."

"You know what I mean. You were miles away."

Her head drooped. "I'm sorry."

"You're the loser. It was a superb performance."

"I just wasn't in the mood."

"Why not?"

"I don't know."

"I think you do," he said crisply. "While I was watching *Don Carlos*, you were drooling over a certain young architect."

"I was not drooling!" she said hotly.

"But he was on your mind?"

"Look, I've said that I'm sorry. I told you to take someone else, but you insisted that I go with you. You'd have been far better off with another friend, Donald. It was rotten of me to spoil it for you."

"You didn't spoil it."

"That's some consolation."

"I love opera," he said, glancing across at her. "I'd never let someone like Merlin Richards come between me and a night with Verdi. It was sublime. My real concern is for you. I'd hoped we were through all that nonsense."

"What nonsense?"

"Your interest in him."

"I don't have an interest."

"Forget him, Clare. He's off-limits. I don't wish to hurt your pride, but when we lunched together yesterday, he hardly mentioned you." He gave a snigger. "You should have seen the hideous tie he was wearing! It was so gaudy. I thought architects had an instinct for color."

Clare refused to be drawn further into the discussion. Her feelings about Merlin were far too uncertain to be brought out into the open, and she did not wish to subject him to Kruger's mockery. She let him do all the talking. His Packard eventually drew up outside her apartment block.

She made an effort to sound genuinely grateful.

"Thank you, Donald. I didn't mean to let you down."

"It was such a waste!"

"I know."

"You missed a real treat."

"At least you got something out of it."

"It was supposed to be a shared experience, Clare," he said. "But I daresay that you would have preferred to be at the university, listening to Frank Lloyd Wright drone on. I'll be glad when Saints' Rest is completed."

"So will I!" she said with feeling.

"Then we can all get back to our normal routine."

Clare hitched up her dress to get out of the car.

"It's late, Donald. I won't invite you in."

"No," he said with asperity. "Since you didn't actually see it, you're hardly qualified to discuss tonight's performance. It would be a trial for us both. I'll see you at the office tomorrow."

"Good night," she said, getting out of the car.

"Good night, Clare."

"This won't happen again. I promise."

She gave him a smile of appeasement, and he mellowed slightly.

"Well," he admitted, "perhaps you didn't miss all that much. It was not as wonderful as I made out. The king was disappointing, and Rodrigo was atrocious. He sounded as if he was gargling. The women carried it. Without them, it would have been unbearable."

She gave him a token kiss, then got out of the car, waving him off before going into the apartment block. It was only now that she had been forbidden to see Merlin that she realized how much she liked him, but her affection was tinged with fear. He was in danger. If she tried to see him again, she might endanger him even further and complicate her own situation—yet she was desperate to help Merlin in some way.

When she got to her apartment, she saw a light under the door, and her first thought was that he had somehow got in and was waiting for her. She opened the door with a rush of pleasure and surged in, but there was no sign of anyone. What confronted her was a huge bouquet of flowers, standing on the coffee table in the living room and giving off a fragrance that filled the room. Clare did not need to read the card in order to see who had brought the flowers.

She knew. It made her feel sick.

17

Victor Goldblatt was unexpectedly pleasant. When he arrived at work that morning, Merlin found him alone in the outer office, perched on his stool as he studied the drawings laid in front of him. Goldblatt looked up and even managed a cheery smile.

"Hi, Merl!" he said.

"Morning, Vic. First one here?"

"No, Reed got in long before me. He's in there with Brad." He got off his stool. "They tell me it went well last night."

"What did?"

"Frank Lloyd Wright's lecture."

"Yes," agreed Merlin. "It was mesmeric."

"His magic doesn't work for me anymore, I'm afraid. Believe it or not, I was a Wright fanatic when I was younger. Visited all his buildings like they were holy shrines. But I grew out of it. I mean, his stuff looks so horribly dated now. He's a dinosaur."

"Don't you believe it, Vic!"

"The game has moved on."

"Mr. Wright is still a major player in it."

Goldblatt glanced at the door of the inner office.

"Anyway," he said, walking across to Merlin, "I'm glad of a chance to have a private word with you, and that's not easy to get around here. I guess I owe you a big apology, Merl."

"For what?"

"Behaving like a prize asshole."

"I didn't notice," said Merlin tactfully.

"I'm surprised you didn't sock me. I asked for it."

"You've been under a lot of pressure lately, I know."

"That's no excuse," insisted the other. "When I come to work, I ought to leave my problems behind me. Not make everyone else suffer because of them. Simple fact is, I was eaten up with jealousy when you got the nod to design that house in Oak Park. And I let it get on top of me. Hell, we're colleagues here. That means we support each other, not go in for all that duel-at-dawn shit. I'm sorry, Merl." He offered a hand. "Friends?"

"Of course," Merlin said, accepting the shake.

"Small office. One of us whines, we all suffer."

"The atmosphere has been a bit fraught at times, Vic."

"That's behind us. I'll be all sweetness and light from now on."

"Don't overdo it."

They laughed, and Merlin patted him on the shoulder.

"By the way," he asked, "how's Rachel?"

Goldblatt's face clouded. "Much the same."

"I hear that she's going to have an operation."

"Yes. Pretty soon. It will only delay the inevitable, but at least it will give her more time. Of course, the kids don't know that. They think the surgery will solve everything and send their mom back home to them as good as new. It's tough, Merl. How do you tell your kids that their mother just won't be around one day? I daren't even think about it." He forced a smile. "There I go again!

Dumping my personal problems on you. We'll pull through somehow. So, tell me. How are things going out in Oak Park?"

"I've had easier jobs."

"Is the client treading on your toes?"

"That's putting it mildly!"

"I gathered that you were having a tough time out there."

"I am, Vic," said Merlin. "Be grateful that you didn't get mixed up in all this. I was thrilled to get that commission, but some of the glitter has definitely been knocked off it."

"Yes, Merl, but just imagine what it will be like when the house is finished. You'll forget about the hassles you had with the client. You'll be able to drive past and admire your work. It will give you a real bang." And so it should," he added seriously. "Never got around to telling you. You did a great job on that house."

"Thanks. I appreciate that."

"It was only anger that stopped me from admitting it. Should've been like Reed Cutler. He was big enough to feel pleased for you and to admire your design. I wasn't. Yes," he recalled, "and when I thought I'd got that commission from Jerry Niedlander, first person to congratulate me was Reed. That guy doesn't have an envious bone in his body."

"He's been a great help to me."

"And me. Blessed are the peacemakers!"

Merlin was delighted. Visits to the office would be far less troublesome from now on. The good-natured banter could return. He and Goldblatt worked happily alongside each other for a few minutes, chatting easily as if there had never been any tension between them. It felt good. Then the door of the inner office opened, and Reed Cutler came through it. After exchanging a greeting with Merlin, he moved to his drafting table as if about to start work.

Brad Davisson called from his office.

"Hey, Merl! Message from Gus!"

"What is it?"

"Come in here, and I'll tell you."

Merlin went into the other office and shut the door behind him. Davisson was seated at his desk with a look of profound discomfort on his face. He picked up a slip of paper and read from it.

"Gus called before you got in," he explained. "Said he'd have to cancel the meeting with you this morning. Something came up."

"But he promised to be here."

"He told me to say sorry."

"It's important that I see him, Brad!"

"Why? Anything I should know about?"

"Not really. It's personal."

"To do with Saints' Rest?"

"Indirectly," said Merlin. "When *will* he be here?"

"Who knows? Gus Westlake is a law unto himself."

"He's dodging me."

"I daresay he'll call again at some stage."

"Let me speak to him when he does," said Merlin.

"Take your turn in the queue. I'm at the head of it. Just had a long chat with Reed Cutler. I've got some bad news to break to Gus."

"What's that?"

"Reed has quit. Given us a month's notice."

"Does he have another job to go to?"

"Hengest and Munroe," said Davisson through gritted teeth. "I was shocked. It came right of the blue. Gus did tell me he thought Reed might have itchy feet, but I didn't believe him. Reed Cutler's been the most loyal and reliable guy we ever employed." He gave a shrug. "Yet he's been cozying up to Hengest and Munroe behind our backs."

"I'm sorry to see him go," said Merlin, recalling Westlake's earlier prediction, "but it won't be difficult to replace him. There are so many good people out of work, you'll be spoiled for choice."

"That's not the point. Reed was a pillar of strength to us. He lived for this practice. We can't buy that off the peg. It's a terrible loss. Then, of course, there's the other problem."

"What other problem?"

"It was Hengest and Munroe who took the Niedlander deal off us," Davisson reminded him. "Victor Goldblatt was counting on that. Just think how he'll react when he hears the news about Reed."

A howl of anguish came from the outer office.

"He just did," said Merlin.

PERSISTENCE EVENTUALLY PAID dividends. His fourth call was a revelation. The real estate office was on Lake Street, its windows looking out on the busy thoroughfare and across to the office of the realtor whom he had just left. He was wearing his best suit to suggest an air of prosperity and carrying a leather briefcase he had once stolen from a house in River West. The smart fedora had been doffed to reveal his bald head. He sat opposite the grinning executive and tried to sound businesslike.

"Well, that's about it," he explained. "Chicago is not a healthy city anymore. My wife and I would like to move somewhere where we don't have to step over dead gangsters on the sidewalk."

"Oak Park is the ideal place for you, sir."

"That's what we figured."

"You won't find many gangsters here," said the other with a daring snigger. "Dead or alive."

"So how much property is on the market?"

"Quite a lot, quite a lot. Though this is a wonderful town with all the facilities you could ask for, it's not, alas, immune to the financial problems that have hit the rest of America. We've had a spate of bankruptcies, and a number of people have been forced to sell. No getting away from it. The country is in deep crisis."

"Don't I know it!" said the other, hearing Father Coughlin's words.

"What it does mean is that some desirable properties have become available here, and we believe that we have the best selection of them. What exactly did you and your wife have in mind?"

"Something with real style."

"Yes, sir. But how many bedrooms?"

"Four, at least."

"What sort of price range?"

"The money is no problem."

"In that case," said the other, "what is your preferred location?" The executive, a rangy man in his forties with a wart to the side of his mouth, which he tried to hide with an incessant grin, smelled a sale. He pointed to a large street map of Oak Park pinned to the office wall. "Let me take you around it."

"No need. My wife and I have already had a stroll around."

"Good. Did you see anything you liked?"

"Yes," said the other. "A house being built on Chicago Avenue. That's exactly the kind of spot we had in mind. My wife loved it. In fact, she said we should consider buying a plot of land like that and building a new house ourselves. But we couldn't see any land available."

"There is none, I'm afraid, sir. That particular plot only became available when the house standing on it was destroyed by fire."

"Fire? When was this?"

"Last fall."

"What happened to the people who lived there?"

"They were so upset, they sold the plot and moved out. As a matter of fact," he said with a chuckle of pride, "I handled the sale myself. It was a rather complicated business, so I couldn't delegate it to a junior."

"What caused the fire?" asked the man casually.

"Faulty wiring in the basement."

"Faulty wiring?"

"Something blew, the sparks lit some paper, and the house was burned to the ground. The owners were heartbroken. They were looking to spend the rest of their days in Oak Park. Only something as terrible as this could have driven them out. Anyway," he continued, rubbing his palms, "the upshot was that a highly desirable plot of land suddenly became available."

"Did you hold an auction?"

"There was no need. A buyer stepped in at once and made an offer that was too generous to refuse. I persuaded Mr. and Mrs. Perrott to take it. They were reluctant at first, then they did."

"How much would a plot of land like that cost?"

"The details are confidential," said the other, "but I can tell you this, sir. When that house is built on Chicago Avenue, the total cost will have been well in excess of a million dollars."

"A million bucks!"

"He's a wealthy client. He wants the best."

"Count us out! We can't afford that kind of dough."

"You could always raise a loan from the bank."

"From a what?"

"A bank, sir."

The customer jumped to his feet with righteous indignation. "Bankers are all shitheads!" he roared. "They were the ones who got us into this mess in the first place. Greedy bankers, crooked politicians, and dirty Reds. Ruining this country. Don't you listen to Father C.?"

GUS WESTLAKE WAS annoyed to see the Ford drawing up in his drive. He regarded his home as sacrosanct and made that clear to his employees. They were not encouraged to pay random social calls. When he had shown Merlin Richards into his den, he rounded on him. "What are you doing here, Merl?"

"Looking for you."

"Couldn't it wait until tomorrow?"

"No. We had an appointment this morning, and you stood me up. I've been trying to track you down all day."

"I've been busy."

"Avoiding me."

"Talking to potential clients."

"Yes, they told me at the golf club that you'd been in today."

"You went *there*?" said Westlake in horror.

"I wanted to see you, Gus."

"Then you should have waited to be seen. I may be at the top of *your* agenda, Merl, but you're well down mine. What I do in the golf club is my own affair. As far as you're concerned, it's a no-go area. And so," he added with a sweeping gesture, "is my home. You're not wanted here."

"I wasn't asking for a ticker-tape reception."

"Get out, will you? See me in the morning."

"No, Gus. You'll have dreamed up a fresh crop of excuses by then."

"They weren't excuses."

"Stop hiding from me."

"I'm not. Now make tracks."

"Then why didn't you turn up this morning?" asked Merlin, holding his ground. "When I saw you at the university last night, you promised me faithfully you'd be there. You could see how important it was to me."

"I do not talk business in my own home, Merl!"

"You will now!"

Westlake glowered at him, but his visitor did not budge. Merlin was simmering with anger. He was determined to be heard. Westlake was forced to back down. Crossing to a cupboard, he took out two glasses and a bottle of bourbon. Afer pouring a measure into one glass, he looked inquiringly across at Merlin.

"Not for me, thanks, Gus. It's not a social call."

"I'm glad to hear it."

"This is what I came to talk about."

He tossed a folder onto the table that stood between them.

"What is it?" said Westlake.

"Can't you guess?"

Westlake took a long sip and flipped open the folder. When he had read a few lines of the typescript inside it, he turned guiltily away.

"Yes," said his visitor sardonically. "The Life and Times of Merlin Richards. Everything you want to know about him, down to his shoe size. Compiled by Donald Kruger. With additional material by Gus Westlake."

"All I did was answer a few questions."

"You gave them confidential information."

"They needed convincing."

"Did you have to show them my salary checks to do that?"

"They asked me."

"Did you have to tell them how I spent my evenings?"

"They asked me, they asked me," said the other irritably. "When a man like Hobart St. John asks you something, you give him an answer. I was so keen to land this commission, I told him all he wanted to know. I'm not ashamed of that, Merl. It worked, didn't it? I'd have told him the color of your eyes and the length of your dick if he'd asked me."

"Don't you have any feelings of loyalty toward your staff?"

"It was a means to an end."

"And that justifies it?"

"Yes," said Westlake. "Don't be so sensitive about it."

"I was spied on, Gus."

"They ran a routine check on you, that's all."

"I was spied on by them and let down by you. And you haven't even got the decency to be embarrassed about it." He snatched up the folder. "Donald Kruger gave me this just to humiliate me. I had lunch with him yesterday. Do you know why he wanted to see me?"

"A proposal of marriage?"

"This is no joke, Gus."

"You can never be sure with a guy like that."

"Kruger threatened me. In the nicest possible way, mind you. He'd never do anything as crude as wave his fist or yell at me. But he gave me a final warning. I had to be a good boy."

"I'd go along with that."

"The client is always right."

"Yes, Merl. He is. Because he signs the check."

"Don't you mind if the pen is dipped in someone's blood?"

"I don't care what it's dipped in so long as it writes."

Merlin was appalled. "And you call yourself an architect?"

"I'm a survivor! Frank Lloyd Wright is an architect. Probably the finest this country has ever seen. But where is he now? Giving lectures to students because nobody will employ him. Well, I'm not doing that, thank you. I want security for my wife and family. I want to play a round of golf when I choose. I want to change my car when it takes my fancy. So I hustle for work wherever I can find it. And I have one simple rule, Merl. A client is a client."

"Even when he's a crook?"

"It doesn't bother me if he's a child molester. I'm not here to run a moral tape measure over my fellow men. A client is a client. That means I build what he asks me to build, and I don't hand out any sermons on how to lead the good life."

"Have you got no ethical standards at all?"

"Good-bye, Merl. You had your conversation."

"All you've done is talk. You haven't listened to me, Gus. Well, you will now. First of all, Hobart St. John hauls me down to the stockyard to put the frighteners on me. Then I have a second warning from Donald Kruger over lunch. Doesn't that tell you anything?"

"Yes. You're plumb stupid, alienating them."

"What else?"

"Kruger has broken off your engagement."

"Be serious, Gus!" said Merlin vehemently. "It may look funny from where you stand, but I'm fed up with being pushed around. I'll tell you what those two warnings suggest to me. They're scared. Your client and his well-dressed hatchet man are scared that I'm going to dig up something that they want to keep buried. I'm getting closer all the time. I can feel it. And so can they. That's why they've resorted to intimidation. The problem is that I don't intimidate very easily. It's something you forgot to tell them about me, Gus. It's not in the report."

He opened the folder and flung the pages of the typescript

at Westlake's feet. The older man breathed deeply through his nose, then emptied his glass in one gulp. A cautious note came into his voice.

"We can't beat these guys, Merl," he said quietly.

"We?" Merlin was ironic. "You're back on my side now?"

"They got too much firepower. I've seen their arsenal."

"You provided one of their weapons against me. That report."

"All I did was to give them basic details."

"So where did the rest of that information come from?"

"Her, of course."

"Who?"

"That girl they tagged onto you. Clare Brovik."

Merlin was hurt. "Clare?"

"Hobart used her as his watchdog."

"How do you know?"

"Because I've seen him in action before," said Westlake. "He likes to control. You were obviously a ladies' man, and that ruled Donald Kruger out, so Clare Brovik was given the job instead. She's a smooth operator. I daresay that every word you ever exchanged with her found its way sooner or later back to Hobart St. John."

"No!" protested Merlin. "Clare wouldn't do that."

"She would."

"I don't believe that."

"That's because you don't know the setup."

"What setup?"

"With Clare Brovik."

"What are you on about?"

"Hobart's recreation," said Westlake. "Away from home. He bought her this fancy apartment somewhere. Clare tells him everything he wants to hear during their pillow talk. She's Hobart's mistress."

• • •

SHE DRESSED QUICKLY and went into the living room. Studying herself in the mirror, she wiped away the smudge of lipstick, then brushed her hair. She heard the shower being turned off in the bathroom. Clare Brovik sighed. It took a real effort of will for her to compose her features into a smile. When he came waddling out of the bathroom in a robe, she put a false brightness into her voice.

"Can I get you anything?"

"Coffee is all."

"There's more champagne on ice."

"Keep it for another time, Clare. I've got appointments."

"Oh," she said, concealing her relief. "That's a pity."

"Yes, it is. I'd have liked more time for us to get acquainted again. Been a long while." He raised a disapproving eyebrow. "It showed."

"I'm sorry, Hobart."

"We're out of practice."

"You always know where I am."

"I know where you live, Clare," he said pointedly, "but I'm not sure that I know where you *are*. That wasn't you in the bedroom. It was some anemic version of you. What's happened? You gone off me?"

"Of course not!"

"Is there someone else in the frame, then?"

"No!" she denied firmly.

"So what is it? Your conscience worrying you about Alicia?"

She forced herself to stop his questions with a long kiss on the lips. He ran his hands all over her and began to get aroused. He planted another kiss on her forehead, then stepped back.

"Real shame I got to go."

"Yes, it is."

"What are your plans for the evening?"

"Quiet night in."

"Donald tells me you went to the opera with him last night."

"That's right. *Don Carlos.*"

"Beats me why he doesn't take one of his boyfriends," said St. John. "Nobody would notice. Why does he need you as a cover girl?" He gave a harsh laugh. "Hey, that's not it, is it? You haven't seduced Donald Kruger and shown him what he's missing? You haven't brought him back to normality?"

"It's much too late for that, Hobart."

"Handsome guy. Alicia thinks he's dishy. Especially since she watched him play tennis on our lawn. She'd only seen him in a suit before. She hadn't realized what a fine sportsman he was."

"Donald is very proud of his fitness."

"Yeah," he said with a sigh. "Keeps himself in shape. Then wastes all that energy on those pretty boys of his. Still, at least they're human. Did I tell you they caught this guy at the stockyard trying to fuck one of the hogs? Jesus! How depraved can you get?"

"I'll put that coffee on."

She headed for the kitchen, but he intercepted her.

"Are you sure there's nothing wrong?"

"Nothing at all, Hobart."

"Donald is worried about you. Why?"

"I guess I'm still a bit jangled by what we found out in Oak Park."

"So am I," said the other grimly. "I'd sure as hell like to know who that poor guy was and who dumped him in my new house. But I'm trying not to let it depress me. Do the same."

"Yes, Hobart."

"Next time I call, I'd like to see her again."

"Who?"

"The real Clare Brovik. The one I picked out and raised up." She put a sincerity into her voice that she did not feel. "She'll be waiting for you."

THE BUTLER WAS alone in the house on Lake Shore Drive. Since the cook would not be required, she had been given the evening off, and the maid was employed on only a part-time basis. The butler was able to relax. A portly man of middle years, he had a kind of sculptural dignity that appealed to Hobart St. John, and he was totally discreet. That was the crucial factor. He could be trusted. The butler did not abuse that trust. Even when he was alone, he did not venture into the main rooms or help himself to some of his master's huge supply of illicit liquor. He simply retired to his pantry to put his feet up and listen to the Paul Whiteman Orchestra on the radio. That was Butler Heaven.

The music was so smooth and seductive that he was completely caught up in it. He did not even hear the click of the catch as the door was opened behind him. Without warning, the nose of a gun was pressed against the back of his head, and a voice shattered the spell of Paul Whiteman.

"Don't move! I've come to take a look around."

The intruder was glad that there was music on the radio.

A Catholic priest would have complicated matters.

MERLIN RICHARDS WAS in a frenzy. His visit to Gus Westlake had yielded a piece of information that could change everything. Clare Brovik was a spy. She had been attached to him so that she could keep him under surveillance and report back to Donald Kruger and Hobart St. John. If it was true, it eliminated any possibility of her cooperation. She was one of them. What disgusted him the most was the fact that she was her employer's mistress, occupying an apartment that he bought and maintained. It was Hobart St. John's tastes that the Kinzie Street apartment catered to, from the silk sheets on the bed to the ancient Egyptian pornography.

Torn between horror and disbelief, Merlin decided that there was only one way to learn the full truth. He had to confront Clare. Ignoring the danger and the risk of further shame, he drove to her apartment block, tipped the porter to gain access, and rode the elevator to the top floor. His thumb stayed hard on the electric bell until it finally produced a result.

The door came slightly ajar, and she peered through the crack.

"Merlin!" she exclaimed.

"At least you remember who I am."

"You can't come here again."

"We need to talk."

"But not here, not in this apartment."

"I can't think of a more appropriate venue," he said, pushing the door open and walking past her into the living room. "Thanks for inviting me in." He saw the bouquet of flowers. "I can guess who sent those. Or perhaps Mr. St. John delivered them himself."

Clare Brovik closed the door and came across to him. She was wearing a smart suit, but her hair was down. Her face was flushed.

"For your own good," she pleaded, "let's go somewhere else."

"I like it here."

"Merlin!"

He sat down. "I'm staying, whatever you say." He patted the sofa. "Come on. Over here. You'll be quite safe. I wouldn't touch you with a pair of gloves on now that I know."

"Know what?"

He looked meaningfully at the flowers, then back at her. Clare lowered her head in embarrassment. It was the confirmation he needed.

"Now I understand what he pays you for, Clare!"

"No, you don't."

"Services rendered."

"It's not like that."

"Then what is it like?"

"You wouldn't understand."

"Oh, I see," he said with heavy sarcasm. "This is a tale of true love, is it? The lowly employee and the mighty boss, drawn together in a touching romance. You and Hobart St. John. Beauty and the beast."

"Don't sneer!"

"What else am I supposed to do? I'm the victim here, Clare. I'm the one you spied on. I'm the one he ordered you to seduce in order to get complete control over me."

"That's a lie!"

"Hobart St. John was your pimp."

"No, Merlin!"

"Your boss set me up," he said, pointing to the bedroom, "then you took me in there to carry out his instructions." He stood up as she moved away. "And don't walk away from me, Clare. At least have the guts to face me. You had me. Hobart St. John rented out his whore."

Clare exploded, grabbing the vase that contained the flowers and throwing it to the ground with vicious force. The china was smashed to pieces, the flowers were strewn everywhere, and the water darkened the carpet as it spread in all directions. When she turned to look at him, there were tears in her eyes.

"He knows nothing about you coming here," she whispered.

"Do you expect me to believe that?"

"If he did, he'd probably kill me."

"Green-eyed jealousy, eh? Along with his other virtues."

"Mr. St. John does not share with anybody," she said. "He has intense pride, Merlin. What he owns, he regards as solely his. And he likes to think of me as one of his possessions."

"Isn't that what you are?"

"Some of the time," she murmured. "I admit it. Some of the time."

"Like the night that I came here?"

"No. That was different."

"An aberration on your part, you mean."

"It was a mistake."

"I agree with that."

"It should never have happened, Merlin."

"Then why the hell did it?"

"Because I wanted it to!"

She was shaking with emotion, her eyes brimming with tears. It took some of the bite out of his anger. He spread his arms in supplication. "Will someone tell me what's going on here?"

Clare used the back of her hand to stem further tears.

"We should never have gone to Oak Park that day," she said. "It was my fault, and I take all the blame. And before you jump down my throat again, I wasn't acting on instructions. I really did want to see the houses and the temple. I thought it would be a sort of bonus for me."

"Bonus!"

"Yes. I know it didn't work out that way. But how was I to know what we'd find at Saints' Rest? Donald was livid when I rang him. Why hadn't I told him that we were going to Oak Park?"

"Why hadn't you?"

"Because I didn't want him to know."

"So that's what I got, was it? An off-duty spy?"

"Call me what you like."

"I can't. I had a religious upbringing."

"Do you remember what happened when we left the cops that night?" she continued. "Donald insisted on taking me home in his car. That wasn't out of consideration. It was so that he could give free rein to his anger. Nice, quiet, polite, well-mannered Donald Kruger has a scathing tongue when he wants to use it. And he certainly used it on me."

"You didn't deliberately find that body, Clare."

"I was with you. And I had no permission."

"Was that the *real* reason behind his anger?"

"What else?"

"I'm beginning to wonder." He looked at the carnage on the floor. "Look, shall I give you a hand to clear this lot up? I'm partly responsible." He bent down and gathered up some china. "It was a nice vase."

"Leave it," she said, taking the pieces from him and tossing them back. "I'll do it later. When you've gone. I'd like you to finish first."

"Finish what?"

"Whatever you came to do. Accuse me. Hit me. Call me names. Unload the rest of that fury I can see swirling around inside you."

Merlin suppressed a reply and paced the room for a few moments, reflecting on what she had said, trying to master his temper. When he passed the bedroom, he glanced at it with a kind of wistful bitterness. He came to stand in front of her again and searched her eyes carefully.

Her composure was restored. She did not flinch.

"I mean what I said, Merlin. Because I wanted it."

"Only to regret it straight afterward."

"No, no," she confessed. "I loved it, I savored it. But I knew the position it would put you in, and I wanted you out of here fast. Mr. St. John wouldn't simply be jealous, Merlin. He's very vindictive."

"I gathered that."

"We'd both suffer."

His rage was slowly supplanted by concern for her safety. "Is this what you really want, Clare?" he said softly. "Living at his beck and call? Terrified to upset him? I thought you had more spirit in you than that. Don't you long for some sort of independence?"

"Of course."

"Then do something about it."

"I did, Merlin. With you."

He held her gaze for a long time. Having come to denounce her as an enemy, he saw once again the flickering possibility of friendship. When he held out his hand, she took it and allowed herself to be led to the sofa. They sat down together.

"Will you help me, please?" he said earnestly.

"Help you?"

"I can't do it on my own, Clare. I need you with me."

"What are you going to do?"

"Find out the truth." He held his thumb and forefinger an inch apart. "I'm that close. I've worked it all out, Clare. I'm certain I know what happened, but I need that last little bit of evidence."

"Evidence?"

"Do you know who that man in the wine cellar was?"

She shrunk from the memory. "No! I've tried to forget him."

"Well, his brother hasn't forgotten him. He paid me a visit and split my head open with his gun. He thought I was involved. I had a job convincing him that I wasn't."

"When was this?"

"Last Monday. At my apartment. He waited for me in the dark."

"He attacked you?" she said in alarm.

"We had quite a tussle till he stunned me with that gun."

"But why come after you?"

"He had to start somewhere, Clare, and he knew that I was the architect. He verified that fact by breaking into our offices. Then he read about that so-called suicide in the *Tribune* and drove out to Oak Park in the hopes of identifying the body. But the police wouldn't even let him see it. Donald had given them their orders."

"So who was the man we found?"

"All I can tell you is that his name is Benito. He went to Oak Park to collect a large amount of money for a job he did for someone, and he never came back. We both know why."

"Are you sure it's the same man?"

"No doubt about it. There was a clear likeness between the two brothers. In more ways than one. They both made a living on the other side of the law. Benito was wanted by the police for all kinds of things. I don't know what job he wanted payment for, but it certainly wasn't charitable work. Now, then," he said, "doesn't all this raise the question of why Hobart St. John wanted the whole matter covered up?"

"So that his wife would never find out."

"That was one reason."

"He didn't want bad publicity for the house."

"Think harder."

"Donald explained it to me. We had to play everything down." She gave a shudder. "To be honest, I was glad to go along with that. I just wanted to put the whole thing out of my mind."

"I'm afraid I can't let you do that, Clare."

"Why not?"

"Because I think I've finally cracked it."

"What do you mean?"

"I know why St. John made sure that murder was hushed up."

"Why?"

"He ordered it."

Clare Brovik listened with a mixture of interest and foreboding. Much of what she heard was difficult to believe at first, yet it had an inexorable logic to it. Merlin Richards had given the matter a great deal of thought. He developed his argument with quiet intensity. He had suffered. After being misled by Gus Westlake, deceived by Clare herself, pushed around by Hobart St. John, threatened by Donald Kruger, lied to by the Oak Park Police Department, and attacked by an armed man, he was fighting back hard. The one benefit of his multiple setbacks was that he had gleaned a whole array of crucial facts. Individually they were meaningless, but he now threaded them together to tell a frightening story. She tried hard to deny its implications.

"Hobart just wouldn't get involved in anything like that, Merlin."

"Wouldn't he?"

"I know him."

"You only know what he wants you to see, Clare."

"I still don't accept that there's any connection between him and the man we found in that cellar," she said. "You claim that

Benito—or whatever his name is—committed arson and that he went out to Oak Park on Friday to collect his payment. That's crazy."

"Why?"

"The house was burned down last fall. He wouldn't wait all this time to get his money. Surely he'd expect some money up front, with the rest paid immediately after the job was done?"

"That delay puzzled me," he admitted.

"Then how do you explain it?"

"Benito may have done another job for Mr. St. John."

"Then why kill him? Why not just pay him off?"

"Maybe there was some kind of argument."

"There are too many maybes here," she said. "The whole thing is elaborate guesswork. We know that the man went to Oak Park to collect some money, because his brother told you that. But you don't know what the money was for and who was actually paying it. According to Donald, the body was dumped there by someone who was trying to get back at Hobart. A kind of revenge."

"That's what he told me over lunch," recalled Merlin as a new thought dawned. "He said that Mr. St. John had been receiving blackmail threats." He snapped his fingers. "That's it, Clare! They came from Benito! That would account for the timing."

"What timing?"

"Look, this is the sequence. Hobart St. John wants that house, but the old couple there won't sell. So he arranges to have them burned out. Benito makes the arson attack look like an electrical defect. They pay him off. He probably didn't even know who he was working for. Mr. St. John would have been very careful to keep his own name out of it."

"That's true."

"Benito wonders why someone is ready to spend so much

money simply to get that plot of land. When a new house starts to go up on the site, he takes the trouble to find out who the owner is. Then he tries to put the squeeze on him."

"What squeeze?"

"Benito is greedy," reasoned Merlin. "Sees the chance of another big score here. He knows the truth about that fire. So he blackmails Mr. St. John. Pay up, or I'll spread the word about what really happened. Benito goes to get his money on Friday and is bumped off instead. It all fits, Clare," he said, getting up and pacing the room in excitement. "Don't you see? That's why nobody was allowed on-site the next day. Because the body would have been discovered. It was probably going to be disposed of that night under cover of darkness. No wonder Sarbiewski and his lads were kept away on Saturday."

"Donald explained that."

"No, he simply got you to pass on a downright lie."

"Mrs. St. John was having second throughts about the bay window."

"That's not what she said when I rang her. And Sarbiewski wasn't given that excuse either. When I challenged Donald, he came up with another story altogether."

"What was that?"

"Contractual problems."

"With whom?"

"The Ace Construction Company," said Merlin, still on the move. "There was a legal hitch. Until it was sorted out, work was suspended. It sounded plausible enough at the time, especially when Donald invited me to contact your legal department for confirmation. It was only afterward that I realized that he'd prime them to tell the latest lie—in the same way that he primed you, Clare."

"But how could Donald know there was a body on-site?"

"How else?"

Clare bit her lip as the full implications were borne in on her.

"Remember that drive home with him on Saturday?" continued Merlin. "Why was he so angry with you when he should have been grateful? After all, you called him first from Oak Park and allowed him to arrange that cover-up with the police. Yet he tore strips off you."

"Because I didn't tell him I was spending the day with you."

"Because you caused complications."

"Complications?"

"We found something we weren't supposed to find. Benito."

Clare pondered. Old loyalties hindered her powers of reasoning, deep fears held her back from recognizing the truth. The deepest fear of all was for Merlin himself, set on a course that he refused to alter and heading toward what she felt was certain disaster. She was still agonizing when Merlin came to crouch in front of her. He put soft hands either side of her face.

"I need you to help me, Clare."

"What can I do?"

"For a start, be honest with yourself."

"Honest?"

"Admit the truth about Mr. St. John. He has blood on his hands."

"No, Merlin!"

"You know how single-minded he is. And ruthless."

"He has to be. It's a dog-eat-dog world."

"When he wants something, he always gets it. Doesn't he?"

Clare moved his hands away and nodded. She rose to her feet and looked around the apartment. It was his. Hobart St. John had provided her with a home and advanced her career to a point that would have been impossible elsewhere. Clare had been grateful; she had a genuine affection for him. The price she paid was the loss of her freedom. He reserved the right to come whenever he chose.

Into her apartment. Into her life. Into her body.

She gave a shudder as she recalled how repulsive she now found his touch, how revolted she had been by the demands he made of her in the bedroom. His flowers lay scattered all over the carpet. There was a vivid symbolism in that. Clare stopped pretending.

Merlin stood close to apply the final bit of persuasion.

"Are you going to let him get away with it?" he asked. "Burning that house down, driving two harmless people out of their home, arranging a callous murder, getting the police to cover it up, gagging you, trying to gag me. Are you going to let him get away with all that, Clare?"

"What can I do to stop him?"

"Take me to the office."

"Why?"

"You have a key, don't you?"

HE WORKED QUICKLY and thoroughly. After tying up the butler, he went stealthily through the house to make sure that nobody else was there, then carried out a swift inventory. It left him excited but frustrated. The house was filled with valuable items, and his first instinct was to take his pick, but the disembodied voice of a Catholic priest held him back. If he succumbed to temptation, he would never be able to look Father Coughlin in the face again. He would forever be tormented by guilt.

The wall safe was in the living room, hidden behind a fake Caravaggio that swung out on hinges at a ninety-degree angle. He sensed that it would contain money and documents. There was a smaller safe in the dressing room off the master bedroom, cunningly concealed behind one of the mirrors and obviously containing the jewelry of the lady of the house. Spurning both, he found what he was after in the library. The filing cabinet was recessed into a wall behind one of the bookshelves. The shelves were hinged like a door, and he swung them back to reveal the oak cabinet. Its lock took seconds to unpick.

One glance told him that he had found something far more valuable to him than money or jewelry: files of personal correspondence. He slipped them into the bag that he had brought, closed the cabinet, swung the bookshelves back into place, and padded along to the butler's pantry. Bound and gagged, the man was watching the radio with pop-eyed stupor. His visitor reached forward to turn up the volume. The Paul Whiteman Orchestra had been replaced by the Clicquot Club Eskimos.

Banjos covered the sound of departure.

THEY WAITED UNTIL it was almost dark before they left Kinzie Street. At Clare's suggestion, they took her car so that it would arouse no suspicion when it was parked outside the offices. On the drive down Halsted Street, her doubts began to surface again.

"What if we don't find anything?" she asked.

"We're bound to, Clare."

"I mean, what if there's nothing to find?"

"Then I've got it all wrong," he conceded. "But I doubt it. There's a conspiracy of silence over that murder, and we've got to break through it somehow. Before he does."

"Who?"

"Benito's brother. He's on the trail as well."

"How do you know?"

"He's like me. He never gives up. Someone killed his

brother, and he wants to know why. Before he exacts revenge. In the biblical sense."

"Biblical?"

"An eye for an eye."

The office block was attached to one of the factories but insulated from its clamor by thick walls and reinforced glass. There were no lights on in the building, and an eerie silence hung over the stockyards. When they got out of the car, they could still smell the pungent aroma, but their ears were spared the railroad cacophony, the thunder of hooves, the protests of endless animals, the yelling of men, and the clanking of machines that filled the daylight hours.

Clare unlocked an outer gate, then led the way to the office block. When they were safely inside, she hustled Merlin along the corridor to the office she shared with Donald Kruger before she switched on any of the lights. The night watchman responded immediately. A retired policeman in a dark blue uniform, he was patrolling the yard when he saw the light go on. Taking his gun from its holster, he made his way to the office block and let himself in.

Clare Brovik was waiting for him with a labored smile.

"Hello, Joe," she said. "It's only me."

"Oh. Hi, Miss Brovik. What you doing here?"

"Put that gun away, and I'll tell you."

"What? Oh, sorry," he said, holstering his weapon. "Old habits die hard. When I was a cop, I held most conversations with a gun in my hand. Forgotten something?"

"Yes," she said. "And I need to do a little work while I'm here."

"Fine by me."

"I'll switch everything off before I leave."

"Give me a shout."

"I will."

She waved him off and went back to the office. Merlin had already done a preliminary survey. He was crouched in front of a large safe.

"What's in here?" he asked.

She hesitated again, caught between loyalty and curiosity.

"Do you know the combination, Clare?"

"Yes."

"Then what are we waiting for?"

IT WAS AN excellent meal, and the steaks were exceptional. Hobart St. John patronized only restaurants that bought his meat. He and Donald Kruger had much to discuss, and they did so over a leisurely dinner. The night at the opera with Clare Brovik did not look any better in retrospect, and it left Kruger feeling profoundly worried. He risked the other's anger.

"We need to talk about Clare," he said.

"Not now, Donald."

"I must insist. I'm very anxious about her."

"Why?"

"Small signs. Insignificant in themselves but, taken together, very worrying. We simply can't count on her in the way we could."

"Clare will be fine."

"I'm not sure that she will, Mr. St. John."

"Why not?"

"I believe that she's already gone astray."

"Astray?"

"Yes," said the other confidently. "The indications are there. I'm certain that she allowed herself to get close to Merlin Richards."

"Never!" denied the other hotly. "What has *he* got to offer her?"

"He's young, passably handsome."

"And struggling to pay off his debts. You read that report, Donald. When he came to Chicago, he didn't have a pot to piss in. Okay, he's a bright kid with a lot of talent, but Clare would want more than that."

"You must have noticed the change in her, Mr. St. John."

"Well, yes. Delayed shock, probably."

"Is that all it is?"

Hobart St. John thought about his disappointing visit to the apartment in Kinzie Street. Though he refused to accept Kruger's analysis, he knew that there was more than a grain of truth in it. Clare had changed. It had to be admitted.

"What do you suggest that we do, Donald?" he said.

Kruger was brutal. "I think it's time to let her go."

"No!"

"You asked me for my opinion."

"Let's drop the subject."

But it continued to peck away at his mind as St. John drove home. Donald Kruger spent a lot of time in Clare's company. He would pick up on the signals, and they would have to be fairly conclusive before he advocated such a drastic solution. There had never been the slightest trouble with her until Merlin Richards came on the scene. He recalled the way they danced together at his party. She had been acting on his instructions that night, but now she seemed to have gone beyond her remit. His jealousy began to surge. When he turned into the drive of his house, he was so preoccupied that he did not notice the car parked under the trees on the opposite side of the road.

Hobart St. John brought his own vehicle to a halt in front of the ornamental pond and got out. The sound of Harry Reser and the Clicquot Club Eskimos came wafting out to greet him. He frowned in annoyance. Letting himself into the house, he tracked the music to the pantry and flung the door open. Trussed up like a Thanksgiving turkey, his butler could do nothing more than roll his eyes in despair.

"Jesus!" exclaimed St. John. "What happened?"

THE STREETLAMP HELPED, but the battery torch was more use. Seated in a parked car on Lake Shore Drive, the man shone the beam on the files as he went methodically through them. The vast majority of what he found was irrelevant but revealing. Hobart St. John was a magpie. He stored pretty things. His personal correspondence consisted largely of love letters and photographs from past conquests, notches carved on his bedpost and retained for him to gloat over. One photo had clearly been sent to him in installments; it consisted of seven different pieces, each with a number on the back, sent in sequence to build up anticipation. When the man assembled them on his lap, he was looking at a naked woman in an alluring posture. It was Alicia Martinez, but he did not recognize her. The voice of Father Coughlin intervened.

The third file gave him what he wanted. It contained a dated letter from Alicia, gushing with gratitude that the plot of land in Oak Park was now theirs as a result of a fire that drove out the previous owners. A short note from Donald Kruger also emerged.

> He comes highly recommended. With your permission, I'll engage him at the price agreed for the assignment in Oak Park. We will get our money's worth from Mendoza.

There it was. Neatly typed on office stationery. Clear evidence. Three short lines that spelled out the death of a brother. Mendoza. The name for which the bald-headed man had been patiently searching.

"Benito!" he said.

He stared at the note until his attention was distracted by the approach of a vehicle. A Packard came hurtling along the road, slowed before it reached him, then turned into the drive of the house he had under surveillance. He heard it screeching to a halt in the distance.

Lou Mendoza pocketed the note and got out of the car.

DONALD KRUGER WAS horrified by the sight of the empty filing cabinet. He stood beside it with Hobart St. John and weighed up the possibilities.

"Nothing else was taken," said the latter. "There are rich pickings in the house, but nothing else was taken."

"This is what they were after, Mr. St. John."

"My personal correspondence?"

"Was there anything sensitive in there?"

"You bet!" roared the other. "It was full of highly confidential stuff. In the wrong hands, it could be very embarrassing for me. I mean, there are keepsakes. Letters. Photographs." He gulped hard. "Dear God! Those photographs. Alicia will never forgive me if she finds out."

"But was there anything else?" said Kruger.

"Isn't that bad enough? My home is broken into, my butler is held at gunpoint, and my private correspondence is stolen. Isn't that bad enough?" He moved to the telephone. "I'll call the cops."

"Don't do that!"

"We can't let them get away with it."

"This is something we can handle ourselves," insisted Kruger. "That's why I was glad when you called me straightaway. This is no random burglary, Mr. St. John. Whoever broke in was not here to steal. He was here to find evidence."

"Of what?" He looked back at the empty cabinet and got his answer. "You don't think it was *him*, do you? That damn architect, still poking around! Is he behind this, Donald?"

"It wouldn't surprise me."

"I'll slaughter him."

"What could he have found?"

"I'll take a meat cleaver to that thick skull of his!"

"What was in the files, Mr. St. John? Anything incriminating?"

"Not that I can think of," said the other. "I may have kept a note from you about the fire, but it would make no sense to anyone else. The real evidence is locked up at the office."

"Call the night watchman!"

"What?"

"Call him," urged Kruger. "If Richards has been hunting for evidence here, he may just as easily do the same at the stockyards. Give the night watchman a call. Put him on the alert."

"You're right."

St. John grabbed the receiver and dialed the number. There was a long wait, and he tapped his foot in irritation. When the night watchman came on the line, he got a snarl of disapproval in his ear.

"Where the hell were you, Joe!"

"That you, Mr. St. John?"

"Who do you think it is?"

"I was patrolling the factory when I heard the phone ring. Took me a while to get back down here, sir. What can I do for you, sir?"

"Keep your eyes peeled for an intruder."

"An intruder?"

"Somebody may try to get into the offices."

"Why?"

"Never mind why. Have you checked them recently?"

"Yes, sir. I went in there when Miss Brovik arrived."

"Clare? What's she doing there this late?"

"Said she'd forgotten something, sir."

"Is she alone, Joe?"

"I think so."

Hobart St. John had a hurried consultation with Kruger before speaking into the mouthpiece once more.

"Whatever happens," he ordered, "don't let her leave. Got it? We're on our way over there right now."

IT TOOK HER a long time to open the safe. As she knelt beside it, trembling with apprehension, Clare Brovik was conscious of the enormous risk she was taking and fearful of the consequences. In her confusion she had difficulty remembering the combination, and her moist fingers slipped on the tumblers more than once. Merlin Richards calmed her repeatedly and encouraged her to start again. They were both relieved when the tumblers finally clicked into place. Turning the handle, Merlin pulled hard, and the heavy door swung open. The first thing that caught his eye was a large metal box.

"What's in there?" he asked.

"Petty cash."

"Let's see."

He hauled it out, rested it on his knee, and opened the lid. Wads of hundred-dollar notes were neatly stacked inside. At the most modest estimate, he was holding at least fifty thousand dollars.

"*This* is petty cash?" he said in disbelief.

"That money wasn't there last time I looked."

"And when was that?"

"A week, ten days ago."

"Let's see what else we can find."

Letters and documents were stacked in the different compartments of the safe, but it was the ledger that claimed Merlin's attention. It was handwritten and clearly dealt with transactions that did not pass through the accounts department. He flicked through it with growing fascination. The amounts of money going out were substantial. Donald Kruger was evidently a licensed paymaster.

"What date was that fire?" asked Merlin.

"Last fall?"

"Can you be more specific?"

"November. It was definitely November."

Merlin found the relevant pages and went through them. His finger stopped opposite a payment of thirty thousand dollars.

"Who is B.M.?"

"B.M.?"

"There's a huge payment here to someone called B.M."

"Doesn't ring a bell, Merlin. Does it say what it's for?"

"I think I know what's it for," he said grimly, "and I bet I can guess what the first initial stands for—Benito. That was his payment for setting fire to the house in Oak Park. It's all here. In Kruger's handwriting."

He grinned in triumph, but his pleasure was short-lived.

"You still here, Miss Brovik?" called a voice.

"Yes, Joe!" she said, going down the corridor to head him off. "I'm almost done. You carry on with your patrol."

"Mr. St. John says you're to stay here until he comes."

Her blood froze. "Mr. St. John?"

"He just called. Said he's on his way over. He seemed to think there might be an intruder on the premises."

"An intruder?"

"Better check to be on the safe side," said the night watchman.

"There's nobody here but me, Joe."

"Mr. St. John sounded like he was in an ornery mood." He took out his gun. "I want to be able to tell him I checked every office. Personal. Out of my way, Miss Brovik."

Clare protested in vain. The night watchman went along the corridor and opened each door, putting the light on and peering into each room. When he came to her own office, she made a final attempt to divert him, but he moved her aside. Clare gritted her teeth, fearing that Merlin would be caught beside the open safe. The night watchman went in.

"Nobody in here," he grunted.

Clare blinked. The safe was shut. Merlin was gone.

IF IT HAD not been for the stoplights on Michigan Avenue, he might never have caught them up. When Hobart St. John and Donald Kruger came running out of the house, they leaped into the Packard and raced away. Lou Mendoza had to run down the drive to reclaim his own car. By the time he was mobile, they were out of sight, but he eventually spotted them. Keeping well back, he tailed them all the way to the Union Stock Yards. He parked nearby and followed them in.

Unaware of their escort, the two men bustled into the office to find Clare Brovik trying to persuade the night watchman to let her go. She blanched when she saw them arrive.

"What are you doing here?" demanded St. John.

"I forgot something."

"Yes," he said. "It's called loyalty."

Kruger was searching through his desk to see if anything had been taken. He then moved to the safe, only to discover it still unlocked. All that he had to do was turn the handle and pull. As soon as it swung open, he saw the empty compartment.

"My ledger! He's got my ledger!"

"There was nobody else here, Mr. Kruger," said the night watchman.

"Yes, there was, Joe. He gave you the slip."

"But I searched every office."

"Then he must be in the factory. Mustn't he, Clare?"

"Did you bring Merlin Richards here?" snapped St. John.

"No! I came on my own."

He struck her across the face, knocking her to the floor. Blood streamed from her nose. St. John stood menacingly over her.

"Is that bastard still here?"

"Yes," she whispered.

"Leave him to us," said Kruger, taking a gun from a drawer in his desk and grabbing a handful of bullets from the box. "Come on, Joe. There's an intruder on the premises. Shoot to kill."

"No!" pleaded Clare.

"Shut up!" yelled St. John.

While the others went out, he grabbed Clare, lifted her from the floor, and flung her down on a chair. She cowered and whimpered. He loomed over her with a bunched fist, ready to strike.

"After all I've done for you, Clare! Is this the reward I get? Teaming up with that baboon? Betraying me. Breaking into my home!"

"We didn't break into it, Hobart."

"You stole my personal correspondence."

"We didn't! I swear it!"

"Don't lie to me!"

He hit her again on the face, and she reeled from the blow.

"If it wasn't you, who the fuck was it?"

"Me, sir," said a voice behind him.

Hobart St. John swung around to see a gun pointing at him.

"Let me introduce myself," said the newcomer.

With a swift and merciless stroke, he smashed his weapon against the side of St. John's head and sent him crashing to the floor with blood spurting from the wound. Hobart St. John groaned in agony.

"I'm Lou Mendoza," said his attacker. "Benito's brother."

MERLIN RICHARDS WAS lost. Having fled into the factory to escape being discovered by the night watchman, he could not find his way out again. The place was hazardous in the darkness. As he picked his way past machines and conveyor belts, he kept banging against unseen protuberances. Clare Brovik was being kept there until her employer arrived. On her own, he hoped, she could talk her way out of the situation, but if she was caught with him, her plight was ominous. Merlin's aim was to slip away quietly into the night, but that was proving difficult. The factory was one huge obstacle course.

With the ledger under his arm, he groped his way slowly along and tried to suppress memories of his earlier visit, when Hobart St. John had shown him every stage of the meat-canning process. The stink told him that he was in the factory where hogs were chopped up. His guide had used the timeworn boast of the stockyards—"We use everything but the squeal." Merlin was certain that St. John would find a way to sell even that in due course. He came around the angle of a machine and walked straight into a huge stack of tinned pork, sending some of the cans flying.

The resulting clatter was his downfall.

"He's in here!" said a distant voice. "Switch on the lights!"

It was Donald Kruger. There was nobody he less wanted to see at that moment. Switches were heard clicking, and banks of lights came on in turn. Merlin ducked behind the tins to keep out of sight.

"Those were tins," said Kruger. "He must be in the loading bay."

"You go right," said the night watchman. "I'll go left."

"He stole something from my safe. Fire on sight."

Merlin heeded the warning. They had guns, he had a ledger. It was an uneven contest. It was time to get out. The lights at least gave him some idea of where the nearest door was. He stood up and sprinted toward it, diving to the floor as a first shot passed just over his head. Donald Kruger did not mean to take prisoners. Merlin wriggled along in the sawdust until he reached the cover of another machine, then rose to his feet and checked to see where they were. Both were hurrying in his direction. Throwing caution to the winds, he came back into view and charged toward the door in a snaking run to make himself a more elusive target. Three shots were fired this time, with deafening effect, but all missed him. He heard the bullets bouncing angrily off metal and spending their venom against the far wall.

When he got through the door, he was in another dark cavern. It was the part of the slaughterhouse where the carcasses of cattle were brought to be hacked and stored. He blundered about in search of cover and dived behind a conveyor belt. Seconds later the door opened behind him and more lights were switched on. Flight was too risky. He could not dodge the bullets forever. Diplomacy, too, was out of the question. Kruger was in no mood for peace negotiations. Merlin had seen the ledger. That was enough. He had to be silenced.

"Keep this door covered," said Kruger. "I'll work around to the far end. That's the only other way out. We'll have him trapped."

"Right, sir."

"Don't let him get past you, Joe."

"He won't. I promise."

It was a vast building, and it took Kruger some time to make his way to the far end, especially as he was searching every potential hiding place on the way. The night watchman did not want to miss out on the action. Keeping one eye on the door, he crept off along the wall to conduct his own search, listening for a telltale sound. When he saw a shadow in the distance, he moved up very slowly until he caught a glimpse of a leg. The intruder was lying behind a conveyor belt. There would be praise for the night watchman if he could hit the sitting target, perhaps even a bonus of some kind. It made him concentrate very hard.

He inched forward until almost the whole of Merlin's body was visible, then lifted his gun to take aim. Before he could pull the trigger, however, something struck him hard on the back of the skull, and he went down in a heap. Lou Mendoza kicked the man's gun away, took him by the collar, and dragged him across to the nearest walk-in refrigerator. The night watchman was shoved in, and the door slammed shut behind him.

"Is that you, Joe?" called Kruger. "Where are you?"

But there was no answer. The stalker was now the stalked.

Merlin took heart. One armed hunter was a very different matter from two. As he peeped over the top of the conveyor belt, he saw Kruger about thirty yards away, gun at the ready, thirsting for blood. Merlin needed a distraction, and his conducted tour of the premises came to his aid. His guide had shown him the buttons that controlled the conveyor belt and the overhead hooks that revolved around the building with the carcasses dangling from them. Merlin pressed every button he could see, and the slaughterhouse roared into life. Taken by surprise, Kruger spun around, firing indiscriminately and yelling at the top of his voice.

When Kruger had used all the bullets in his gun, Merlin went into action. Kruger thrust a hand into his pocket to grab more ammunition. He loaded it as quickly as he could, but he was far too slow. When he looked up, a large carcass was coming toward him on one of the overhead hooks, but it was no dead animal. It was Merlin Richards. He swung forward and kicked Kruger hard under the chin, sending him backward in a drunken stagger. Merlin was on him at once, grabbing the wrist of the hand that held the gun and beating it against an iron pillar until Kruger was forced to drop the weapon.

Kruger was surprisingly strong, and Merlin had to take a lot of punches in order to land his own. They grappled, fell to the floor, squirmed in the sawdust, and punched again. By the time Merlin finally overpowered him, they were both covered in blood. Sitting astride his adversary and panting stertorously, Merlin wanted a confession.

"Who killed that man in Oak Park?" he demanded.

When he got no reply, he pummeled hard again.

"Who was it?" he said. "Tell me, or you can have some more."

"It was me," gasped Kruger with a defiant pride. "I killed him."

"Why?"

"Because he deserved it."

"No man deserved to die like that."

"He tried to blackmail us. We paid him for the work he did, but he wanted more. So we pretended to agree. I met him at Saints' Rest and brought a bag with me. But there wasn't only money in it," he said with a boastful snigger. "There was a gun and some rope."

"So you clubbed him to death and hanged him?"

"No," said the other. "I tried to scare him off. I tied his hands, then strung him up by the neck to teach him a lesson. To let him know who he was dealing with. If he'd begged for mercy, I'd have let him go, but all he did was curse me. He refused to be frightened off. He cursed so loud that I had to shut him up."

"So you smashed his head in."

"Yes! It was disgusting. The blood ruined my suit."

Merlin had heard enough. His guesswork had paid off. The victim had been murdered by someone who intended to return the next night to dispose of the body. Donald Kruger was more concerned with the state of his suit than with the condition of a human being. There was no contrition in him. Getting to his feet, Merlin bent down to haul him up, but Kruger had been gathering his strength. With a sudden shove he sent Merlin sprawling onto the floor, then dived for the discarded gun. Before the Welshman could react, he found himself staring down the barrel of a gun once more.

When the shot was fired, its accuracy was deadly. But the bullet did not come from Kruger's gun, but from Lou Mendoza's. He shot his target between the eyes, then stood over the prone figure of Kruger and spat with disgust. The epitaph was short.

"I didn't like what he said about Benito."

"How did you get here?" said Merlin, scrambling up.

"You complaining?"

"No. You saved my life."

"There was two of them to one of you," said Mendoza. "So I evened things up. The night watchman is in one of the freezers. Someone better let him out before he turns into an iceberg."

"I found a ledger," explained Merlin. "I left it over there by the conveyor belt. It's got a record of a payment to someone called B.M."

"Benito Mendoza. My younger brother."

"Thirty thousand dollars."

"That would be him. I told you he came expensive."

The distant banshee wail of police cars was heard over the tumult of the slaughterhouse. Merlin was perplexed. Mendoza grinned.

"First time in my life I called the cops," he said.

"Why?"

"I knew there'd be a mess to mop up. I plugged St. John first, and now I got the guy who whacked Benito. I'm happy. You should go in there and calm that girl down. She's in hysterics."

"What about you?"

"I can't stay around after this," said the other soulfully. "I let myself down, and I let Father C. down. How can I call myself a good Catholic when I break into a man's house, then shoot him and his monkey here?" He offered his hand, and Merlin shook it. "Sorry I had to slug you that time. But it was all in a good cause. Don't think too bad of me."

"What do you mean?"

Lou Mendoza walked a few yards away, then turned to face him.

"I never knew guilt till I met Father C. Now I do."

He put the gun in his mouth and pulled the trigger.

ALICIA MARTINEZ WAS stretched languidly on the bed in her hotel room when the telephone rang. She was in a celebratory mood. The screen test had been a success, and she had been offered the part in the movie. The only thing that irritated her was that her huband had not yet rung to share in her triumph, but it sounded as if he was now rectifying that grave omission.

"Hello," she said into the mouthpiece.

"You have a long-distance call from Chicago," said the operator.

"Put him on." She heard a click. "Hobart? Is that you? Guess what?"

"I'm not your husband, lady," said a flat voice.

Alicia was peeved. "Who is this?"

"Lieutenant Greeney, Chicago Police Department."

"Police?"

"Homicide. I got some bad news for you."

MERLIN RICHARDS STOOD hand in hand with Sally Fiske and watched the boards being taken down. The names of Westlake and Davisson and of the Ace Construction Company were tossed indifferently into the back of a truck and driven away. In their place was a board advertising that the two-acre site was for sale. Merlin was both saddened and relieved.

"Another big opportunity bites the dust!"

"There'll be others," she reassured him.

"Not in Oak Park, I hope."

"I thought you liked it here."

"I did until I wandered into the wrong wine cellar."

"What will happen now?"

"Some nice, law-abiding, respectable people will build a house and move in. Oak Park had a narrow escape from Hobart St. John. He and his cohorts would have lowered the tone around here."

"Cohorts like Clare Brovik, you mean?" she said tartly.

"Now, I won't hear a word against Clare," he warned. "Without her, I'd never have found the evidence I knew must be there. She was a heroine."

"Does that mean you'll be seeing her again?"

"Not a chance. She's gone off to Ireland."

"Ireland?"

"Her mother has relatives there." He gave a quiet smile. "I wonder if any of them are called Coughlin."

"Who?"

"Private joke. The point is that Clare wanted to get as far away as possible from Chicago. She has a lot to forget."

"So do you, Merl."

"Yes," he said, kissing her on the nose. "I have a lot to remember as well. Thanks to Lou Mendoza. And you were top of the memory list."

"Liar!"

"You were, Sally!"

He gave her a hug, and they walked away from Saints' Rest.

"Do you know what Gus Westlake said to me?"

"What?

"That I was too honest to be an architect in Chicago."

"Something in that."

"It's not the only reason I have to move on."

"What's the other one?"

"This," he said, stopping to look back. "I must have been crazy. Thinking I could build something on the same street as Frank Lloyd Wright's home and studio. It's like trying to build a fence in the shadow of the Great Wall of China. Here in Oak Park, I'd always be in his shadow. That's the main reason I have to go, Sally."

"What is?"

"I have to find my own place in the sun."

She squeezed his arm tight as they strolled off toward the car.

"Fancy some burned spaghetti before you go?" she said.